Hot Lava

By Rob Rosen

FIERCE
PUBLISHING

Published in the United States by Fierce Publishing

ISBN-10: 0-9837678-8-2
ISBN-13: 978-0-9837678-8-6

For Kenny,
Mahalo for bringing Hawaii into my life and the
spirit of aloha into my heart.

PRAISE FOR *HOT LAVA*

"Rob Rosen knows his Hawaii better than any tour guide, and doesn't hesitate to mix the good, the bad and the steamy in this funny, sexy romp through the dark side of an island paradise."
-- Neil Plakcy, author of the *Mahu mystery series*

"Set in scenic Hawaii, *Hot Lava*, Rob Rosen's latest campy adventure, is true beach reading of the highest order, full of drinks, drag, daring adventure and dishy repartee."
-- Jim Provenzano, author of *PINS, Monkey Suits* and *Cyclizen*

"Rob Rosen has crafted a story that you just don't want to stop reading. There was "Thelma and Louise" for the girls and for us guys there is *Hot Lava*. So pour yourself a cocktail, make yourself comfortable and come along for the ride. You'll love it." -- Wayne Mansfield, author of *Highway Patrol*

"*Hot Lava*, a funny, sexy mystery novel with a tropical twist, is a who-done-it with a healthy dose of who-done-who. I laughed from beginning to end, and then looked for tickets to Oahu. Just to see if I could get into half as much mischief as Rosen's heroes." -- Michael Luongo, editor of *Looking for Love in Faraway Places*

"Make yourself a killer Mai Tai and settle in for another travel adventure from Rob Rosen. You can almost smell the plumeria blossoms and feel the trade winds in the air – a perfect book to take along on your summer vacation this year... or to read while you dream of taking one." -- Mark Abramson, author of the *Beach Reading* series

✸ Paradise Found ✸

Fear of Flying 101: don't board an aircraft that is about to travel five hours over nothing but open water. That's it. End of lesson. Class dismissed.

Sadly, I was never a very good student. I must've read through the syllabus too quickly (or not at all) this time around. In other words, I boarded Hawaiian Airlines flight 11 with nothing but a so-so book to read and a best friend who was more interested in joining the mile-high club than keeping my mind off more pressing matters, namely plunging forty thousand feet into the cold Pacific Ocean. Thankfully, said best friend also has a lifetime prescription of virtually every anti-anxiety drug on the market, hence the reason best friend is best friend. Go figure.

Two pretty, blue Xanax later, my fear had abated to mild hysteria with just a tinge of panic mixed in for good measure. And speaking of mixing, we were doing just that: pills and booze. Fuck the Surgeon General. What does he know, anyway? Besides, we were in first class, meaning drinks were free. Well, free minus the exorbitant price we paid for the tickets. But hey, isn't that what vacations are for?

Well, to be honest, not a vacation, mind you, so much as a severance package put to good use. Yippy for an ever-dwindling economy. Plus, Brandon was Rockefeller-rich. In other words, he was always on vacation. But that's all another story. And a long story. Real long. Well, to be honest, about as long as the one you're about to hear. In other words, if you have any booze and pills of your own, better go get them now—we're in for quite a bumpy ride.

In any case, I had ample spending money. Ample as is enough money for a trip to Waikiki, even without a job, of which I hadn't started hunting for yet on Craigslist. Though, to be fair, it is, um, hard to make it past that Men Seeking Men section—thank you, Craig, wherever you are.

Since my aforementioned best friend, Brandon, and I had never been to Hawaii before, not to mention that penchant for tropical drinks—and men—of ours, it seemed like a reasonable choice—five-hour plane trip excepted. In fact, it is the farthest distance from the nearest neighboring land in all directions than any other region on the friggin' planet. On a bright note, however, it's also the only state without a straight line in its boundary.

Anyway, several hours into the flight, and many more gin and tonics later, I had a wicked need to pee. Brandon had his eyes glued shut and was bobbing his head up and down to his iPod when I tapped him on his shoulder and informed, "Going to take a leak."

He pried a lid open, and replied, "Congratulations. Give it a shake for me." Then he just as quickly went back to ignoring me. Meaning, I downed the remainder of his drink and headed the three feet up to the first-class john. No waiting. No lines. Goody for me.

It was upon my exit, though, that I spotted him. Middle of the plane, his face bent down, engrossed in a magazine. My heart began to beat a furious samba in my chest as I raced back to my seat, breath catching in my throat.

"Oh shit," I whispered, my hands clenched to the armrest in a death-grip.

The iPod came off. "What? Your prick stopped working? Quit playing with it so much then."

"Fucker," I retorted. "My prick works just fine. How does yours still function, though? Hasn't the odometer rolled back around to zero yet?"

"Not to worry," he replied, his hand in the air, already ordering a new round. "I keep it well-oiled and take it in for a tune-up every thousand miles—or men—whichever or whomever comes first. In any case, why the look of impending doom? Did we run out of gas?"

The mere thought sent my stomach lurching to the floor. "No," I whispered in his ear. "I think there might be a terrorist behind us."

He looked out the window, his face craning to the right. "Nope. No one behind us. You bring some sort of radar in your backpack that I'm unaware of."

I punched his arm. "Not funny, shit for brains. I meant behind us, there's a guy chained to another guy, one with a dark complexion. Bet the first dude is one of those air marshals." I stopped, took a swig of my drink, naturally, and wiped the sweat off my brow. "What if there's a bomb on the plane somewhere?"

He turned his face back my way. "Dude, lay off the Xanax. It's one every six hours, not six every one."

I sighed and stared deep into his bloodshot eyes. "Brandon," I said, between gritted teeth, "There are two dudes chained together about ten rows behind us; what else could it be?"

He paused, slowly raised his head up, his blue peepers just above the top of the seat, and replied, "Only one dark dude, you moron, and he's Hawaiian, not Middle Eastern. Other guy is probably just bringing him back home for some legal bullshit that clearly doesn't concern us."

"Uh huh, uh huh," I coughed out, heart beating hummingbird-fast. "Or that air marshal caught someone trying to flush a bomb down the toilet." Seemed reasonable.

Brandon didn't respond. Instead, he sighed, stood up, and sidled past me. I too stood up and followed close behind. Maybe we'd just hide out in the…in the…well, fuck, where can you safely hide on a plane that's about to blow to bits? It wasn't until we made it mid-cabin that I realized where he was headed. He reached the marshal before I could protest. Or find a parachute to jump out of the plane with. Or, at the very least, make it to the amenities cart, to steal a mini-bottle, or three.

"Excuse me," Brandon said by way of greeting. "But are you an air marshal? And is the guy chained to you a terrorist? I'm just asking because I think I forgot to leave my cat enough kitty food before I left for the airport, and I'd like to call someone and let them know. I mean, a day or two is fine, but beyond that, she might start eating the furniture. And, let me tell you, that shit didn't come cheap."

The marshal, who we were soon to discover, wasn't one, sat there staring up at us, grinning widely, with a gleaming array of perfect pearly whites. My tummy, naturally, did a perfect somersault, which earned tens from all the judges. "Um," he umed, raising his left hand up, "I'm not an air marshal and this is not a terrorist. Your cat and your furniture should be just fine." One end of the handcuff was dangling from his wrist; the other was manacled to the man sitting next to him: Hawaiian, as Brandon had made note, and hot, mid-twenties at most, obviously no pretty white smile beaming up at us. Not the criminal looking type either. Whatever that means. Oh, and on a side note, not that it matters—okay, so it matters—but the marshal who wasn't a marshal was a total Stunner—and, yes, it deserves the capital S.

"Thanks," Brandon replied, a knowing grin aimed my way, in an I-told-you-so, dipshit, kind of way. "Okay then. Well, nice to meet you. Have fun with your, um, prisoner." And with that, we beat a hasty, albeit short, retreat.

We made it back just as another round of drinks was being served. Thank goodness. They were downed in a white-hot flash. Another batch was ordered, our livers no longer bothering to protest, falling on deaf and equally drunk ears.

"My bad, dude," I eventually thought to say.

Brandon turned to me. "Chase," he said, "you're as eloquent as ever."

"Thanks," I told him, sucking on an ice cube.

He placed the iPod back on his head. "I was being sarcastic," he said as he cranked up the sound.

"I know," I replied, willing my heart rate back down to

normal. "But I'll take what I can get."

And still I couldn't get my mind off the marshal who wasn't a marshal.

Something was setting my bells and whistles off. And, needless to say, those bells and whistles were playing a rather nice Barbra tune. Something about people needing other people. And the marshal who wasn't a marshal was definitely my kind of people.

***

Two hours later, Brandon pointed out his window. "Land," he uttered, much to my profound delight.

I leaned in, face to cold, hard glass. "Wow, look how beautiful." The coast of Oahu stretched out before us, with Diamond Head looming magnificently in the distance and Waikiki spread out below it, radiant beneath the brilliant overhead sun. Lush green palms swayed in the coastal breeze as the endless blue ocean at last gave way to, as Brandon so succinctly put it, land. Solid land. At last, I could breathe easy again.

The plane touched down, smooth as silk. Though that could've been the Xanax, cushioning my brain. Hard to tell.

"Aloha," announced the captain overhead. "Welcome to Hawaii."

"Alo-ha," came our reply, stretching the word out as we clinked our glasses together.

Soon thereafter, we gratefully deplaned. In fact, we skipped off. Well, trudged, really. Maybe mixing booze and pills wasn't such a swell idea after all. In any case, once through security, we were greeted by Liko, a six foot tall, almond colored, Hawaiian god replete with two massive leis and a warm, bright smile. Our names were written on the placard he held above his head, so we weren't merely flirting with him when we toddled over and eagerly shook his hand—lingering several seconds too long, naturally.

"You must be Chase and Brandon," he said to us, placing the fragrant flowers over our heads.

"And you must be the reason why we overthrew Queen Liliuokalani in 1893," Brandon replied, all googly-eyed. Don't be all that surprised, by the way; he read that little tidbit in the tourist guidebook during the flight over. Twenty more minutes and it would've been shaken clean from his memory, much like an Etch-a-Sketch drawing.

Liko grinned, but didn't comment. Instead, he told us, "I've been contracted by your hotel. Once we get your luggage, I'll be driving you back there."

"Shotgun!" we both yelled.

"Um, well," Liko interjected, now clearly flustered, "it's a limo; you'll both be in the back."

Deflated, we quickly acquiesced. I mean, who could be upset about a limo ride through paradise? "There's booze in the back, right?" I thought to ask, just to be on the safe side.

"Champagne okay?" he asked.

Our grins, obviously, made a rapid ascent.

Our driver—beau-hunk, really—walked us through the airport to claim our baggage. It took quite a while to gather it all up. "All this is yours?" he eventually asked, staring down at the rather large pile we'd amassed. "How long are you guys planning on staying?"

"Two weeks," I replied. "We come prepared." Or was it that we were prepared to come? The Boy Scouts, it seemed, had nothing on us.

Brandon bent down. "It's not as bad as it seems," he added, opening up one of the pieces. "See, this large one is empty. For whatever we buy while we're here."

"I see," Liko said, trudging along with what he could schlep. "You're right then; you guys packed lightly."

I laughed, grabbing two of the smaller items, and gaily followed the leader. Well, his ass at any rate. It was hard to take my eyes off it. Like two ripe melons, his cheeks were. Yum. Wait, wait. We were in Hawaii. Like two meaty coconuts, they were. Yum.

"Dibs," Brandon whispered in my ear.

"What's that supposed to mean?" I whispered back. "Hawaiian for take him, he's yours?"

"Playing stupid won't win you the prize."

"At least I'm only playing, fuckwad."

The verbal sparring abruptly stopped when we reached the jet-black stretch limo. That and the outside of the airport. The air was sweltering, so thick with water that it felt like we were wading through a pool—filled with Jell-O. And the heat, man, it hit you like an oven. In other words, we quickly hopped in and cranked up the air.

"First time to Oahu?" Liko asked through the overhead speakers.

"What gave it away?" Brandon replied. "The smell of our lungs melting?"

Our driver laughed, the sound like seashells gently tossed by the surf. I felt an instant stirring in my shorts. "Don't worry," he said. "You'll get used to it." Since I practically walked around with an ever-present boner, I was sure he was right. Except, I think he was talking about the weather, which I wasn't so certain about.

"And you?" I asked. "Were you born here?"

"Born, raised, and yet to travel beyond. Maybe someday. I just need a reason to get over my fear of flying, I guess." Which meant that, hah, it's wasn't just me!

His wistful tone plucked at the strings to my heart, the heavenly sound being drowned out by Brandon's window rolling down, and then by Brandon himself bellowing, much to my surprise, "Need a lift?"

I looked out and spotted the marshal who wasn't a marshal and his captive partner. He smiled at us and walked over. "Man, you guys really know how to travel in style, huh?" His eyes scanned the length of our transport before he added, "In any case, I was told to take a taxi to the Waikiki Police Substation and then to drop this guy off, safe and sound. This, suffice it to say, is no taxi."

Liko, upon hearing this, chimed in. "Your hotel is right next-door to the substation, guys. Up to you, but we can fit two more, if you want."

I leaned in to Brandon, and whispered, "A third wheel I can take, but a fourth one is pushing it. Especially one that's shackled."

To which he promptly replied, "Think of it as a new kink, my friend."

I pondered if I actually had any old kinks, but was too late in responding; Brandon was already opening the door. "Your chariot awaits, sir," he offered grandly.

Mister Stunning—capital S again—looked from his prisoner and then to us. The prisoner, of course, smiled and nodded. "Fine," he reluctantly agreed. "At least it saves Uncle Sam a buck or two. But if you guys tell anyone, I'll deny it. And then I'll have to kill you." We looked at him aghast. "Just joshing." He laughed and we exhaled. I know, old joke, but it takes on a whole new meaning when a guy with handcuffs and a bulge beneath his jacket is saying it to you. In any case, they both got in, the un-marshal's small suitcase flung to the floor.

Two was company, four was downright strange. "Champagne?" Brandon eventually asked.

The prisoner and I nodded; the captor said no for the both of them, thereby leaving more for me and Brandon. Woohoo! "So," I finally said, admitting that the elephant in the limo was stinking up the place, so to speak, "what did this guy do?"

"Nothing," the guy in question quickly replied.

"Drug trafficking," the detective amended, after he told us that he was a detective for—now get this—the F.B.I. As if he wasn't hot enough already. "From here to California and back again. Over a million dollar's worth of cocaine stashed up his…up his, um…rectum."

Brandon gave an appreciative whistle. "All at one time?" Difficult, but not impossible, I figured. At least not for the man who asked the question in the first place.

"No," came the reply. "Over a year, at least, we figure. The guy's a flight attendant. The money went to the mainland with him, the drugs came back."

I looked at the prisoner. A flight attendant, huh? That could mean only one thing: there were obviously three gay guys in our limo. Minimum.

"I didn't do it," the prisoner protested, once again.

"He was caught with eighty thousand dollars while leaving Waikiki three weeks ago. His rectum was torn and there were traces of cocaine detected." Brandon and I gave an involuntary wince at that one. "Three other flight attendants confirmed that they've noticed him spending vast amounts of cash as of late, and an island drug dealer testified that he was his carrier. He's being taken from California to Oahu to stand trial."

"I didn't do it," it was said, a third and final time, the prisoner not even facing us, but looking up instead.

Detective Stevenson—he'd flashed us his badge. Guy was a good flasher. Be still my heart—shook his head from side to side. "Be that as it may, I'm here to bring him to the station. Then he's the state of Hawaii's concern." And with a rectum that loose, he was sure to make a slew of friends in prison, if you know what I mean.

Minutes later, we pulled up to our hotel. "Welcome to the Moana Surfrider, gentlemen," Liko announced, running to the side of the limo to let us out. "The First Lady of Waikiki."

We all looked up, even the drug smuggler. "Holy fuck," I managed.

"Ditto," Brandon seconded.

"Check out the bathroom in the wing to the left," recommended the purported smuggler with the loose asshole.

And with that, the chained pair veered off, to walk the short distance to the substation, which we could actually see just down the street from us. Perhaps it wasn't such a swell thing to have a police station so close to Brandon and me, I thought. Better to keep the authorities at a safe distance. Though whose safety I was worried about was anybody's guess.

The two of us again looked up at our hotel. It was like a massive antebellum mansion, all in white, towering above us, its giant columns, arched windows, and chair-lined porch drawing us in like moths to a flame—which was kept at a reasonably low broil by the massive palms that shaded us from high overhead. Think Tara goes Hawaiian, and you wouldn't be far off the mark.

Liko led us in, with three porters gathering our belongings that would eventually make it up to our room. A fresh, cool glass of guava juice was offered, as was a damp towel to wipe our hands and sweat-drenched faces off with. Then two more fragrant leis were placed over our heads. In other words, we officially looked like tourists, albeit fancifully stinking ones.

"You look like a flower shop just vomited on you," said my supposed best buddy.

"Gee, thanks," I replied, smiling nonetheless. "Considering it's usually you who's usually throwing up on me, I think I'm one step ahead of the game."

At that point, and probably already sick of us, Liko bid his farewell. "Okay, guys, have a great stay at the Moana. I'm sure we'll bump into each other again over the next couple of weeks. And if you need a ride, here's my card; just give me a call."

Sadly, he was gone, but not forgotten, in a jiff, and the two of us were on our way up to our adjoining rooms. My recent money downpour assured, at least for this trip, that we wouldn't have to share a room. With Brandon's sexual proclivities, plus my desire for some, this was a good thing. When we saw our rooms, it became a grand one.

"Man, this day just keeps getting better and better," I proclaimed, plopping down on my king-sized bed and cushy down-cover. The room was old-school Hawaii, comfortable and elegant, with lots of polished wood and beautiful adornments. This being a Westin, it was, as they say, heavenly. Though it couldn't, of course, compare with the view.

I ran to the terrace just as the door that divided our suites opened. Brandon sauntered over and joined me, our arms atop the railing, our bodies leaning over, breathing in all that fresh ocean air.

"Gorgeous," I said.

"Thanks," he said.

"No, the view, asshole."

"Ah, that too, dickwit."

Though my initial comment was a gross understatement. The water, blue as sapphires and sparkling as such, broke gently along the sandy beach. Further out, the waves grew larger, attracting pods of surfers, intermixed with a few sailboats and outrigger canoes. The sky was dazzling and fairly cloudless, a soft, gentle breeze wafting languidly over us, rustling the palms that lined the edge of the hotel property. I smiled and sighed, as did Brandon.

"I'd say let's just lie out for the next two weeks and do nothing," I tried, looking his way, "but I think I know you better than that."

"Yes," he agreed, "you do." He turned and walked back inside. "But for now, let's wait for our luggage, get changed, and go jumping into that ocean down there. It's calling to me, like a…like a…"

"Drink?" I asked, holding up our complimentary bottle of wine.

"You read my mind," he replied, lifting up a glass.

"Short read," I told him as I popped the cork and the poured.

He smirked and clinked his glass against mine. "To a wonderful, relaxing vacation," he toasted.

"And to getting laid," I added. Not lei-ed, of which we had plenty of already.

"Here, here."

And amen to that.

***

Our luggage arrived, and we promptly got changed into our bathing suits and T-shirts.

"You're not wearing that, are you?" I asked Brandon, when he reemerged a short while later, clad in Speedos the size of a pocket swatch and a matching midriff-revealing, spaghetti-stringed, pink tank top. Not to mention flip-flops adorned with bright orange flowers.

"What's wrong with this?" he asked, admiring himself in the mirror.

I couldn't think of a response that wasn't homophobic, so instead I replied, "The other guests will be jealous." Sometimes it's better to go with the flow, especially when the current is so strong and dragging you under.

He smiled. "They can just eat their hearts out then."

Of course, when they saw his wardrobe choice, they'd be tossing the meal back up soon thereafter. "Yes, well, let's go," I said, instead, wisely changing the subject. "Time to bronze some of this ghastly pale."

Grabbing his sunglasses and heading for the door, he quipped, "Fine, we can just Botox the wrinkles away later."

Ah, that explains it.

And then we were off, heading down the elevator and back toward the open-air lobby, with its scattered, luxurious couches spread out atop large, gorgeous rugs. We headed to our right, out onto the veranda overlooking the courtyard, which had comfortable, cushioned wicker chairs that were lined up on either side of us. Then, to top this all off, as if the view wasn't exquisite enough, smack-dab in the middle of everything sat a majestic Banyan tree, its plaque informing us that it was planted all the way back in 1904. An outdoor café, with a perfect ocean view, hugged the tree on two sides, and off to the right of all this was the pool. The tree itself spread its grand, old branches high above everything, with a myriad of colorful chirping birds flitting about from limb to massive limb. Throw a snake and an apple into the mix, and you would've sworn you were in Eden.

In any case, we bypassed this area and headed straight—um,

gaily forward—toward the beach. Private beach, that is, roped off from the public, the riffraff, the common folk. There we were greeted by a lovely man who promptly set up two lounge chairs for us, just below a large umbrella. He blanketed the chairs in hotel towels and told us to have a nice day. This, I was certain, was a given, all things considered—ignorance, of course, being both blissful and blind. And, in our case, both deaf and dumb. And a tad tipsy.

We sank into our chairs, our feet digging beneath the warm sand, and let out a hearty sigh. "Ah," we both exhaled in relaxed unison.

"Let's move here," I suggested.

"Agreed," he agreed, once the cocktail waitress came over and we both ordered a Moana Sands, which consisted of Chambord and Peach Schnapps and everything tropical. "A superb place to retire," he added after his first cooling sip.

"Um, Brandon, in order to retire, I think you first have to have a job," I corrected him with.

"Yuck," he yucked. And I couldn't help but agree. Being without a job was stressful, but also quite wonderful. Being without health insurance was just the first, however, and certainly not the latter. Especially since hanging around with Brandon constantly put my health at risk.

And there we sat, sipping our fabulous concoctions, soaking in the rays, and watching the sun dapple off the ocean that lay spread out gloriously before us. It was both splendid and awe-inspiring. And, of course, we ogled the men as they walked by: dozens upon dozens of hot, shirtless, bare-legged men, also splendid and awe-inspiring; which, naturally, popped a new and twisted idea into my head. "Gotta take a pee break," I informed, hopping up. "Haven't gone since the plane."

Brandon gave me a cursory nod, enveloped as he was with his iPod and the ever-passing scenery. I re-shirted myself and re-flip-flopped my feet and was off, bypassing, of course, the outdoor lavatory as I headed for the indoor one, recalling what the smuggler had told us.

The bathroom was at the end of a long hall, situated on the first floor and on the wing adjacent to our own. It was quiet and deserted—in other words, ideal for clandestine trysts. Sadly, I was alone in the small bathroom upon arrival. I did have to pee, though, and headed for one of the two urinals.

And then, of course, I wasn't so alone anymore.

The door opened and someone joined me, standing to my right, suitcase placed between us. Out of the corner of my eye, I could tell he was tall and dark, the handsome part still yet to be determined. He coughed and tapped his feet, clear signage that he had more on his mind than taking a leak. I echoed his cough and moved an inch in reverse, allowing him viewing privileges to my privates. He followed suit, his privates more than a major eye-full. In fact, they were five-star general impressive.

My eyes roamed from his burgeoning prick, now arcing out, to his lean torso and wide chest. His stunning blue peepers met mine at the same instant. "Chase?" he practically hacked. Scratch that; it came spewing out in jagged shock.

"Detective Stevenson?" I nearly shouted, both of us instantly pushing our crotches forward into the porcelain, again out of dignified sight. "Um, Detective, what are you, uh, doing here?" I stuttered, finishing my stream before stuffing my shrinking prick back inside my bathing trunks.

"Bathroom break. I dropped the prisoner off and was headed back to my hotel."

Which wasn't at all what he was doing. "They didn't have a bathroom at the station?"

I looked over at him, his eyes once more locking onto mine, laser intense, burning a hole right on through me. He grinned, a red flush working its way across both cleanly-shaven cheeks. "You were paying attention back at the limo, too, huh?" he asked.

"Valuable information like that doesn't go, um, unrewarded, Detective."

"Will," he corrected. "I'm off duty now."

I upped the ante. "Wanna get off some more, Will?"

His grin widened, perfect white teeth glinting under the overhead lights. "You want to know something, Chase?" he said, his prick still hard and coming beautifully back into view. And wide angle lens view, at that.

"What's that, Will?" I asked, moving into the stall to my left, the turgid detective following close behind.

With the cubicle door locking us in, and with his arms wrapped tight around my waist, he told me, "Back on the plane, when you were worried about the…"

"Non-existent terrorist and equally non-existent bomb?"

"Yes, those. Well, to tell the truth, it was all I could do to not pull you into that bathroom with the non-existent bomb."

"Except that a bathroom on a plane wouldn't be the ideal place for that sort of thing," I commented, leaning up to place a warm, perfect kiss on his full, pink lips. "Plus, there was a bad guy chained to your arm at the time."

"Yeah, except for that. And because of that, I couldn't do this." He pulled me in and mashed his mouth into mine, his tongue darting forth, encircling my own in an oral tango. He smelled great, a heady mixture of both sweat and musk, and felt even better, with my lithe little body melding into his great big one. And speaking of big, his massive prick was insistently pushing up against my belly.

"Hey, Will," I rasped, breaking free from his lip-lock, "No pesky bombs to contend with in here."

"Nope, just a pesky bathing suit." He reached out and yanked them down, my prick springing out, pointing to his own like a flesh-seeking divining rod. "Yum," he groaned.

"Looks great, tastes even better," I informed.

He took the hint and sank to his knees, his magnificent blue eyes staring up at me as he downed my cock in one fell swoop, taking me to his throat's hilt as a happy, gagging tear streamed down his cheek. "Yep," he agreed, in between hungry sucks and slurps, "tastes great."

"Can two have a go at this buffet?"

He laughed and stood up. "Plenty to go around."

"Apparently," I noticed, staring down at the ample offering: meat and hefty potatoes for days. "But I'm more a rump roast kind of guy."

"Ah," he ahed, turning around, revealing a perfect little ass, two white mounds of muscled flesh and a hair-lined crack that begged to be spread apart. And then promptly were. "Dig in."

I crouched down, face to ass-level, taking a deep whiff of his hole as I parted his cheeks, taking a cursory lick before eagerly diving in, then reached between his hairy thighs, stroking his dick as I rimmed him. He moaned and ground his ass into my face. "Not going to last too long if you keep that up," he cautioned, his voice deep and hoarse.

Actually, with my free hand on my own prick, pumping steadily away, I knew what he meant. "Okay," I said, "then let's finish together."

I stood back up as he turned around, his lips once again finding mine. "You taste like my ass," he told me, with a chuckle.

"Lucky me," I said, once again grabbing his thick tool.

"Lucky me," he echoed, reaching for mine.

Our mouths crushed together, firm, insistent, as we picked up speed down below, our wrists working in overtime. "Close," I groaned.

"Closer," he moaned back.

And then we shot, both of us exploding in body-quaking spasms, our heavy loads hitting the tile floor below, splat, splat-splat, in one aromatic stream after the next, sending a million tingles up and down my spine before spreading out to all four limbs, releasing any shred of tension that still existed in my sweat-soaked body.

"Nice," I whispered, our eyes still open, locked.

He laughed. "That the best you can come up with?"

I grinned and thought it over. "Incredible, sublime, rousing. Take your pick."

He started to get dressed. "All three, Chase, and then some."

"Sweet talker," I said as I lifted up my trunks.

We quickly cleaned up our mess and vacated our makeshift love shack, his barely-there luggage in tow. "Well," he sighed, his smile briefly fading, "have a nice, um, vacation."

"Oh," I ohed, my own smile now faltering. "You, uh, leaving so quickly?"

"Just here for the night, Chase. Then back to D.C."

My smile returned in full force. "So, we still have the rest of the day then. And tonight. Why not join me and Brandon out on the beach?"

He looked down at his meager belongings. "Well, I did bring a bathing suit. You sure you won't mind the company?"

I reached into my trunks and removed my room card. "Here," I said, by way of an answer. "Go up to room 342 and get changed, then hurry back down. We're easy to spot. Just look for one guy wearing the biggest smile ever and another wearing the littlest speck of material possible; that'll be us."

He grinned, a smile so beautiful as to take your very breath away. Then he nodded as he ran down the hallway, ass majestically swaying like the palm trees out back. "Order me a drink," he hollered over his shoulder. "I'll be right down."

With a spring to my step, I hightailed it back to Brandon. A fresh drink awaited me upon my return.

"Took you long enough," he said, sniffing the air around us. "Ah, you went to the bathroom inside, huh?"

I shook my head from side to side. "Nothing gets passed you, does it?"

"Oh, God, no, nothing. Especially when it comes to cruisy bathrooms."

"Especially," I agreed. "But I do have a pleasant surprise for you."

"What, does your trick have a friend?"

"He's not exactly a trick," I replied.

"And what, pray tell, does that mean?"

"Wait," I said. "I know how you love surprises."

"I hate surprises, Chase."

"I know, but this one is a real doozie."

Before he could argue any further, the surprise can running over, his small suitcase slung over his wide shoulder. Brandon's jaw dropped. "No fucking way," he mouthed to me.

"I know," I mouthed back, a radiant smile stretched from one ear to the other.

"Fellows," said the new arrival, crouching down in front of us.

"Detective," Brandon said.

"Will," came the correction.

A chair was brought over and my so-called trick nestled in between us, his big feet digging into the sand as he winked over at me. "A guy could retire here," he said.

I laughed. "Yeah, we've already been there and done that conversation."

The three of us turned our attention back to the beautiful scenery set out before us. It was hard not to appreciate it: an extinct volcano looming to our left, the ocean sparkling in front, spectacular hotels on either side, and beautiful people scattered as far as the eye could see. Heaven on earth and a bar just off to our side. Utter perfection. Present company included.

"Anyone care for a dip?" Will soon asked, standing up and removing his T-shirt, revealing a densely-packed chest and taught ripped abs, all covered in a nice fuzzy down. Adonis, it should be noted, had nothing on this Fed. No sir, no how.

"I think you guys already had one," Brandon replied, gazing up at him.

Will didn't respond; instead, he ran headlong into the tranquil blue ocean. "Last one in is a rotten egg," he yelled back.

Brandon looked over to me with a smile. "Well, Chase, I have to say I taught you well."

I laughed. "Yep, Master. Grasshopper earned his black belt with that one."

He stood and started to saunter on ahead. "Pink belt, my friend," he corrected, pulling me with him. "Wear it proudly."

Brandon and I dove in, the water warm and wonderful, washing over us in a salty embrace. We stood up, the sandy bottom mashing beneath our feet, our heads bobbing above the water, the three of us staring down the Waikiki coast, Honolulu's glory. Our hotel towered high in front of us, its majestic Banyan tree spreading her protective limbs out and over the many guests. Will reached his hand for mine, just beneath the waves, holding on tightly, sending a volt of adrenalin coursing through my body that made my vision go blurry for just the briefest of seconds.

"Perfection," I sighed contentedly, breathing in the cool, salty air.

But perfection came with a hefty price—I know, icky foreshadowing. But there was no easy way to put it. If you have those pills and booze I was telling you about, now would be a good time to get them. There was less than five more minutes remaining before our bliss turned to bust.

We swam back in, eager to finish our drinks and soak in the sun. San Francisco, home base, is frequently sunny, but rarely warm. In other words, we had to take advantage of this now, while the getting was good.

Dripping wet, we returned to our starting point, sinking into our chairs like they were a second skin, the warm sand clinging to our bodies. "Alo-ha," I said, raising my glass up before taking a deep and satisfying swig.

"Alo-ha," my friends repeated, toasting the ocean that peacefully rolled in not thirty feet in front of us.

The peace, however, was suddenly shattered by the sound of a muffled phone.

"Your luggage is ringing," Brandon told Will.

He looked at it, confused. "Who'd be calling me now?" he wondered, aloud, opening said luggage and removing his cellphone. "Detective Stevenson," he said into it, and then nothing but, "Uh huh," over and over and over again, his face growing whiter and whiter, despite the sun that now baked him from high up above.

When he hung up, I asked, "What happened?"

He didn't answer at first, too stunned, it seemed, to speak.

"Fuck," he finally uttered.

"What fuck?" I asked.

"Me fucked. I mean, I'm fucked. Royally."

My stomach sank at the sound of his troubled muttering. "What is it?"

"The smuggler, the guy I just brought in, he escaped."

"So?" Brandon piped in. "He was no longer in your custody."

But Will wasn't looking any happier.

"How, exactly, did he escape?" I thought to ask.

"Two cops were taking him out to their squad car on their way to the Halawa Prison. He was in front of them, still apparently handcuffed. They were holding his arms on either side. Though, it seems, the handcuffs weren't locked anymore. The prisoner raised his hands and punched the officers in their kidneys, then swung wildly, smashing both of them in the face with the end of the cuffs. He was gone before either could get up and give pursuit."

"How did he get out of his cuffs?" I dreaded asking.

Will held his head in his hands. "They found the metal part of a champagne top in his holding cell." We all groaned audibly. "They don't know how he got it, but he picked the handcuff lock with it; that much they do know."

"And you can't tell them how he came by it, right?" Brandon asked.

"Not if I want to keep my job. I was supposed to take a taxi, not a limo. Taxis don't come with champagne. This is all my fault."

"Our fault," I corrected.

"Tangentially speaking," Brandon amended.

I knew why Will had gotten into the limo; he wanted to see me again, of that I was now fairly certain. In other words, it was my fault too, tangential or not. "We'll help you get him back, and then they can't blame you. Or at least fire you."

"We will?" Brandon piped in. "I thought we were on vacation."

"Come on," I said. "Three days with nothing to do but lie around, and you'll be begging to get into some sort of mischief. This way, now you'll have an excuse." As if he ever needed one of those before.

"I can't ask you to help me," Will chimed in with.

"You're not asking; we're telling. That way, if your superiors ever get wind of it, you can deny any wrongdoing."

"But it might be dangerous," he tried.

"Danger is my middle name," I countered with.

"No, it's not," Brandon counter countered. "It's Simon."

I reached out and held Will's hand. "Just let us know how we can help. There must be something we can do."

Will looked to the two of us, the smile briefly returning. "Well, I can't ask the police for their help, not without getting in trouble myself. After all, it's their case, not mine, as far as they're concerned." He paused and searched our faces. "Anyway, you know how the guy kept saying how he didn't do it?"

"Yeah," I said. "I remember. And?"

"And, you see, I sort of believed him. Maybe our looking for him will shed some light on that."

"You're looking," Brandon interrupted. "We're only helping, from a safe distance."

Will nodded, the smile now in full force. "Deal," he agreed. "Now, all I need to do is explain to my boss why I need to stay here a little bit longer."

Other than to fuck me silly, I thought. "Other than to fuck me silly," I said. Oops, sometimes these things just slip out.

"Um, yeah. Maybe I'll just tell him I need a vacation and leave it at that," he said, a blush adorably rising up his neck, the color fast returning to his cheeks.

"Trust me," I told him, "after a few days with the two of us, a vacation is exactly what you'll need."

"And a new liver," Brandon added.

"Well, yeah, that's a given," I said. "But these Moana Sands are well worth it."

Now, if we could keep our other vital organs up and running, maybe we'd survive the next two weeks.

Just maybe.

No promises, though.

✤ INNOCENCE LOST ✤

The next day, after an incredible night of sex—outside of a bathroom stall—Will was given a leave of absence. He hadn't had a vacation in quite some time, and his superiors agreed that he deserved one. Score one in the old plus-column for our little team. But then again, our little team wasn't really much of one to begin with. Will was out in the field, while Brandon and I were relegated to the hotel's measly computer, trying to find out all we could about our smuggler: Lenny Hallanah.

The scuttlebutt on Lenny was, as we quickly discovered, pretty much everything we already knew. He worked for Aloha Airlines for six years, flying mostly inter-island, with occasional trips to California and Nevada. When a raid on a local, penny-ante drug dealer turned up a larger than expected cache of cocaine, Lenny's name was offered up for a lighter sentence. Corroboration came with the testimony of several of his work associates and the subsequent finding of eighty thousand dollars on his person on a recent trip from Honolulu to Oakland. Lenny denied any wrongdoing, but a medical exam found, well, yuck, what Will had already told us. Rectum, remember?

Several additional items of note were: as we suspected, he was a gay man; he was from Oahu; his lover, apparently, vacated their house after the arrest, disappearing to points unknown; his family believed he was innocent—don't they always?; and, much to the relief of the great state of Hawaii, further drug arrests had been made since the capture of the man Lenny allegedly smuggled drugs for. All in all, a happy story, though not for Lenny. Or Will, of course. Or now us.

"Something doesn't sound right," Brandon said after the

initial read-through.

"Yeah, the whole butthole thing is really gross."

"No, not that. If guys can stick gerbils up their asses, why not pounds of coke? No, I mean, the dealer gave Lenny's name first in exchange for leniency. I always thought you gave your boss's name, not a subordinate's. Granted, smuggling is a no-no, but the chief of the whole operation holds the power and the wealth—not to mention, is usually wanted more by the cops. But then, soon after the arrest, that guy, the boss, was captured anyway, according to the articles we read."

"Makes sense," I said. "The investigators did their jobs properly."

He scratched his head. "I don't know; something's missing here. If Lenny is innocent, like he says he is, then he was just a scapegoat. And if he's guilty, then why, after supposedly smuggling for at least a year, does he all of a sudden start flashing money around like the other flight attendants said he did? If he was that stupid, he would've shown his cards a lot sooner, seems to me. Plus, why did the lover all of a sudden skip town?"

"Embarrassment? Fear of being implicated? Fear of retribution from the dealer or the dealer's boss?" I offered.

"Okay," he agreed. "Those all make sense, too."

"But?"

"But why does our new friend, Will, think he's innocent. And, for that matter, why do I?"

"Because Lenny's cute and gay? And cute gay guys don't smuggle drugs; they take them at clubs."

"An unfortunate stereotype, but okay, I'll give you that. Just one more question then: what was your first impression of Lenny?"

I paused and thought about it, eventually replying, "No way is this guy a criminal. Heart-breaker, sure. Drug smuggler, not a chance."

"And your first impression of me?"

No pause necessary. "An asshole. One hundred percent,

Grade-A, bona fide."

He nodded sagely. "See, always go with your gut instincts."

He had me with that one. In any case, Will had eight years on the force under his belt. I'd go with his gut instincts over our own, anytime. Still, Brandon was correct; I felt like Lenny was telling us the truth, despite what the evidence pointed to. And the evidence seemed shaky at best. For instance, whoever was selling the drugs to Lenny in California had yet to be captured. In fact, there were no clues as to who was doing just that. Only the dealer in Hawaii, who eventually received the drugs, was caught, and then, afterwards, his boss. Why didn't the dealer just turn over the name of the source for even greater leniency? Unless, of course, there really was no mainland source to implicate.

"Okay," I relented. "I agree. It's not an open and shut case. Still, what can we do?"

A Cheshire cat grin spread like wildfire across my friend's impossibly handsome face. "Well now, I think I know how we can kill two birds with one stone."

"Can we leave the word kill out of this for the time being, please?"

He nodded. "Fine, what I meant to say was, perhaps Lenny's lover can shed some light on all this, either about Lenny's current whereabouts or his guilt or innocence. Since that guy wasn't a suspect, and since no drugs turned up in their home, the police stopped their search for him. Perhaps, we can continue where they left off."

"I see," I said, knowing where he was going with all this. "In other words, we ask around at the gay beaches and bars, right? Your kind of stomping grounds."

He touched his finger to his nose. "Bingo."

"That's amazing how you did that?" I said, truly in awe.

"Did what?"

"Work all that out, and all to your own distinct advantage."

"Practice makes perfect, dear one. So, let's go shopping, to look our slutty best, then have dinner, then find ourselves a nice gay bar to camp out in?"

I grinned, still stunned at how detective work could be made to be such fun. "Agreed," I agreed. "Though, don't you already have enough slutty outfits?"

"How can anybody have enough slutty outfits, Chase?"

It was a rhetorical question, and one not meriting a reply. Again. Instead, I walked out of the hotel and back into the sun-kissed early afternoon. The sky was a beautiful azure blue, the Moana a brilliant white, the street an array of every color of the rainbow, with sidewalk-lined trees sprouting odd-shaped flowers and leaves, all tropical, all exotic. It was, of course, beautiful to behold, despite the heaping bucket of shit we now found ourselves knee-deep in.

I stopped to sniff a plumeria blossom, the fragrance pure Hawaiian, before we headed across the street, past the first of hundreds of ABC Stores⌐—Waikiki's version of 7-Eleven meets miniature Target, each one selling every kind of cheap island gift you can imagine: from macadamia nut pancake mix, to Kona coffee, to cigarette lighters in the shape of volcanoes with rims that light up red when you flick them on. Pure kitsch. Needless to say, in time, we bought one of everything. Sometimes two.

But our goal was just down the street and to our left: the International Marketplace, with well over a hundred shops and stands in an open-air setting. A strip-mall in paradise.

We entered beneath its massive wooden sign and came face to face with a (fake) waterfall containing (real) koi splashing about, all under a resplendent Banyan tree. On either side were tourist shops galore, and along the cement paths sat dozens of kiosks selling absolutely nothing we needed, but everything we wanted, just the same. After all, you can never have too many plastic ukuleles, synthetic leis, or, best of all, hula men car ornaments, complete with swaying hips. Not that either one of us owned a car, mind you, but still.

Amazingly, this craptopia went on and on, one booth of junk after the next, until we couldn't carry any more of it. Brandon and I, after all, truly are the ultimate demographic: half-drunk gay men with mucho disposable income—which we happily disposed of with wild abandon.

And those slutty outfits? Only Brandon can pull those off. I settled on a nice floral Hawaiian shirt, somewhat form-fitting surfer shorts, and a lovely pair of emerald green flip-flops. Slutty? Nope. Comfortable? Yep. And Brandon? Well now, within minutes, he was strolling about in a too-tight tank with Ride My Longboard stretched across his bulging chest, and a pair of shorts so snug that I could've sworn his voice went up two octaves after he tried them on.

"Lunch time," he eventually proclaimed.

I looked at his outfit, and replied, "Where will you put it. One extra calorie, and that ensemble of yours is gonna go boom."

It was then that our plan hit a fortuitous glitch. The food court, with over a dozen fast-food restaurants of every nationality, sat in the back of the marketplace. And in the corner of all this, his tiny ass resting along a metal railing, stood a tall, thin Hawaiian, very young, in flesh-hugging clothes that showed off his lean, hard body. He was a junior Brandon in Hawaiian bronze.

"Drug dealer or prostitute?" I asked.

"Why do you say that, Chase? He looks just fine to me."

I shook my head. I'd obviously asked the wrong person. In any case, the guy saw us staring and nodded our way. "We're being hailed," I whispered out of the corner of my mouth.

"What should we do?" he corner-mouthed back.

"Beats me. You're the expert."

He pinched my arm. "I neither pay for drugs nor sex, Chase."

I pinched him back. "I meant the, um, sexy side to all this, Brandon." Which is not what I meant, at all.

"Ah, okay. Then I say we go over and talk to him. He might be our in to finding Lenny's boyfriend. I mean, how big can this island be, anyway?"   It was five hundred and ninety-seven square miles and just under eight hundred thousand residents. I too read the guidebook on the plane. And you caught me just in time; another five minutes and I surely would've forgotten all that.

So, we headed over, the stranger's smile glowing like a lightening bug's ass. "Aloha," he said.

"Aloha," we also said.

"You here for lunch?" Groan, small-talk before business.

"Yep, what do you recommend?" I asked.

He smiled. "The Wendy's down the street. Food here is crap."

Brandon paused, clearly weighing his options. "And what's the alternative to food?" he asked.

The guy smiled even wider, glad, it seemed, that he didn't have to broach the subject first. "What alternatives are you looking for?"

Again, Brandon paused. Surprisingly, even for him, he was somewhat out of his element here. Apart from his pill popping, Brandon didn't do drugs. And if he ever did pay for sex, it wasn't out of necessity. "Um, how about we talk about that over lunch?"

"You buying, dude?" he asked.

"Lunch, yes," I chimed in with.

The stranger rubbed my head. "You're cute. What's your name?"

"Chase," I replied, grabbing a seat as far away from the masses as was possible.

"Mine's Anakoni." He also took a seat, as did Brandon. "Just call me Koni."

"And I'm Brandon," Brandon added. "Now that we've got that out of the way, you should know, we're not looking for sex or drugs."

"Not actively looking," I added.

"Yes, right," Brandon continued, shooting me a nasty-ass glare. "In any case, we do need help in finding something. Or, well, someone."

Koni tapped his fingers atop the metal table. "What makes you think I was selling either sex or drugs? Are you guys cops?"

Again, I laughed, seeing as that was the one profession no one would ever think we were associated with—despite the rather lovely fact that I'd just recently slept with a federal agent. "No," Brandon replied. "We're just looking for some information."

"That you're willing to pay for," Koni added.

"That we're willing to negotiate payment for, yes," Brandon told him.

Koni giggled, a boyish chuckle that only added to his overall cuteness. "You guys are in luck then. I was going to sell you baking powder that would've burned your noses something fierce. The sex, however, would've been primo, but the information will come cheaper. Provided that the lunch is all you can eat."

"Not a problem," Brandon told him. "Get whatever you like."

And get he did. One, it appeared, of everything. Mounds of it. And he ate it all with gusto. He'd either not eaten in ages or had a tapeworm the size of Cleveland. In any case, after a hundred- dollar tip, he was willing to talk.

"So, you guys are looking for someone. What makes you think I can help with that?" he asked, wiping the spaghetti, chow mein, burrito, and ice cream off his face.

"Do you know about the drug arrest of Lenny Hallanah?"

The smile at once left his face. He burped and shook his head. "Bad news, dudes. No can help."

"Can't or won't?" I asked.

"Little bit of both. You know that blow I was gonna sell you, the stuff you can clean your fridge with?" We nodded, and he continued. "See, a month ago, I would've been able to get you the real stuff. Crappy, but real."

"And now?" I asked.

He didn't answer, not until Brandon slipped him another twenty. "And now, my dealer's been busted. And his boss has been busted, too. And all I know is that it's got something to do with this Lenny Hallanah dude."

"So, you know Lenny? I asked, eagerly.

Again, no response. Not until another Andrew Jackson joined the first. "Never heard of him before he made the news. Then again, other than Makani, my ex-dealer, I didn't know anyone connected to the shit I sold. And Makani never mentioned anything but drugs and cash."

"So, you don't know if Lenny smuggled for Makani then, like it's being reported?"

He shook his head. "Don't know, don't care. Better to be ignorant than dead." If such was truly the case, Brandon was certain to live a long life.

"And do you know why Makani would turn Lenny in and not his boss? I mean, wouldn't the cops have been more lenient on him then, given him a lighter sentence?"

Koni snickered. "Small island, dudes. Nowhere to run to. You turn in your boss around here, you're one dead motherfucker. Better to serve your sentence, whatever they give you."

That, at least, made some sense. And still, we couldn't help but wonder how the big boss got found out anyway if Makani didn't turn him in. We also weren't any closer to locating Lenny or his boyfriend.

"Last question, last twenty," Brandon informed, sliding the bill forward. "We hear Lenny had a boyfriend. Any knowledge of him?"

"All I know is the word on the streets, dudes. Guy's name is Jed. White dude. Disappeared. This other dude, Lenny, you're asking about, no one's ever heard of him before. But this guy Jed, he's got a rep."

"A good rep or a bad one?" I asked.

"Only one kind trickles down my pipeline, dude. All bad. Like hot lava, stay clear or get burned. In other words, if it's Jed you're searching for, turn around and go back to the mainland. Shit's gonna find you in the long run; don't go looking for it."

He stopped his sage advice and looked down at the wad he'd accumulated. Easy money. Easier than he was obviously accustomed to. "Freebie, dudes," he concluded with. "Guy's a pimp. Trades the locals to the Japanese tourists. Big money in that."

"Big money you're not looking for?"

"Nah, small dicks, no English. Not worth the hassle. Besides, they don't tip. Like I said, not worth it. Worth it for Jed, maybe, I suppose."

"Only, he's disappeared," Brandon added.

"So they say, dude. So they say."

"And what do you say?" I asked.

"What's it matter what I say, cute dude?" He grinned and winked at me. Give the kid five years and ten pounds, and I might've winked back. "Okay, I say the guy skipped to take any possible heat off him. But he'll be back. The Japanese swarm this island. Big money." He pocketed the cash. "We through, dudes?"

I looked at Brandon, and got a nod in return. "All through," we said.

"Then mahalo, dudes. Thanks for the bread."

"Mahalo," we thanked him with, and quickly departed, virtually none the wiser and a hundred and sixty dollars poorer.

We started back along the sidewalk, toward our hotel and a good stiff drink. We'd only made it fifty feet or so, when we heard, "Dudes, wait up." Koni was jogging towards us, his flip-flops shuffling along the ground, the grin still spread from cheek to smooth cheek.

"I'm out of money, Koni," Brandon informed.

"ATMs everywhere, dude," he informed back.

"Why, did you neglect to tell us something?" I asked.

"Nope. Picked my brain clean, cute dude." Truth be told, the nickname was warming up to me. "But I know a guy that works for Jed; maybe, he can add something."

"For a price," I added.

"Oh, everything has a price, dude. But this guy owes me.

Maybe, it'll come cheap."

Brandon looked to me, his face tilted to the side. Perhaps, we were getting in over our heads here. Two prostitutes, an escaped prisoner, and a missing pimp, and we'd only been on vacation a short twenty-four hours. "Can a friend of ours join us?" Brandon asked.

"Cute as you two? Not a cop?"

Brandon coughed, then stretched the truth a bit. "Cute as us. Not a cop. More invested in the search than us, though."

Koni nodded, the rat-tail dangling from the back of his head shaking as he did so. "No problemo."

But there's always a problemo. "And what's in it for you?" I asked.

The grin faded for the briefest of moments, a certain world-weariness creeping in around his eyes, wrinkling his brow. His seemingly usual bravado temporarily faded away like the San Francisco fog at midday. "I'll tell you, but first I want to show you something, okay?"

I looked warily at our new friend. "Something safe? And legal?" I thought to ask.

His grin returned. "Sure, cute dude. Just follow. You'll be safe and sound." The sound part was a matter of opinion, I supposed, and up for debate.

We nodded and trailed behind him, his little ass leading the way. He cut up a side street that ran parallel with the marketplace. Waikiki's beauty was only skin deep, the plush and tropical oceanfront quickly giving way to cheap hotels and rundown apartments the further we moved away from the water. San Francisco is no different; downtown tourist traps meld into the Tenderloin in mere minutes, with its crack dealers and street hustlers and seedy bars obliterating all the historic beauty.

A short walk later, we found ourselves at the rear of a small grocery store, boxes of questionable fruits and vegetables stacked all around. "Home sweet home," Koni told us with a noticeable grimace. In shock, we moved in behind him as he walked between some empty crates. A ratty, dirty mattress sat between these and a dilapidated fence. "My summer palace," he informed, the sadness evident, despite the forced smile.

"And when it rains?" I asked.

He unfurled a sleeping bag. "At least the zipper works. Keeps out most of the elements, anyhow." The melancholy returned to his face. "But hey, it could be worse. The cops don't know I'm here, and Mister Chen doesn't mind either, so long as I help him clean up, from time to time."

"Where do you shower and stuff?" Brandon asked, looking around.

"Public beach. Outdoor shower, indoor toilet. Scenic as shit, dude."

Brandon looked at him, confused. As did I. "And why are you showing this to us?" he asked.

"I scratch your back, you scratch mine," he replied cryptically, pointing to his meager belongings.

"Ah," I ahed, the proverbial light bulb going off over my not-so-proverbial noggin. "You want to trade information for a place to crash."

"Just for one night, cute dude. I want to sleep in a real bed and take a bath, and not wake up to the sound of garbage trucks and the smell of, well, this shithole."

The point was well taken. To say we were eager to help him, however, was pushing it. After all, taking in drug dealing prostitutes, albeit adorable ones, was not what we signed up for when we booked this trip. Still, our hearts were not that small. Well, mine wasn't, at any rate. Brandon had relinquished his years ago to make room for certain other alcohol processing organs.

"Fine," I agreed for the both of us. "One night only. Provided you take us to this friend of yours. And you keep us out of trouble."

"And," Brandon interrupted, "you show us some identification. If you're underage, the deal is off."

For once, Brandon was thinking clearly, prison jumpsuits not being his wardrobe of choice. Koni grimaced, but soon agreed, removing a state I.D. from inside his shorts. He covered his name and address with his fingers, but the birth date was clearly visible. He was younger looking than his actual age, but still barely legal at nineteen. At least, we figured, we wouldn't be arrested for harboring an underage runaway prostitute. My mom would've been so proud of that little accomplishment.

"Come on then," Brandon said. "I need a drink. This vacation really isn't turning out as planned."

And so, we left the dismal surroundings and walked briskly back to Kalakaua Avenue and to our hotel.

"Jackpot," Koni soon said with a low whistle when he realized where he'd ended up.

"Don't get too comfortable," Brandon warned. "This back-scratching thing will only be in effect for twenty-four hours, tops."

"Fine by me," Koni agreed, following us into the elevator and up to our rooms, where the whistle was repeated, loudly. "Did I say jackpot already?"

"Yes, you did," I said, retrieving my valuables and placing them in Brandon's room—plus the remnants of the wine, the TV remote control, and the cords to both telephones.

"What about the mini-bar?" Koni asked, a sly grin cocked upwards.

Brandon ran over, unhooked it, and slid it into his room. "We'll be needing this, too, I would think."

I followed him inside and turned to our new guest from between the adjoining doors. "Make yourself at home, Koni. We'll be down at the beach if you need us."

"How about a bathing suit?" he asked.

I grabbed one of Brandon's less skimpy ones— the only one, really—and tossed it to Koni, then shut the door behind us. "Well, Lucy," I whispered, "this is a dilly of a pickle we're in."

"Yes, Ethel. And won't Ricky be surprised when he comes home and finds out what we've got stashed in your room."

We didn't have too long to wait for that one.

We found Will sitting by the pool, looking yummy as ever. He greeted me with a luxuriant bear hug.

"What about me?" Brandon asked.

"Get your own," I replied.

"Selfish," he said, arms folded over insanely defined chest.

Will laughed and offered us a seat on either side of him. "So, guys, what've you been up to today?"

I smiled, nervously, and answered his question with one of my own, "Other than taking in a teenage, drug dealing prostitute?"

Will's grin slipped downward like a landslide. "Please, tell me you're joking."

I shook my head. "On the bright side, we're hot on the trail of Lenny's boyfriend. And I bought you a frog that croaks when you rub a stick across its back." OK, I really bought it for me, but I figured it couldn't hurt to temper the situation, stressful as it was.

We then filled him in on the details as he eagerly downed his drink. "Well, you discovered more than I did," he eventually said. "But I can't go with you tonight, as you had planned. Legally, I'd have to tell this friend of a friend who I was and who I worked for if he started to give us pertinent information. That, I think, would put a hasty end to everything. In any case, it doesn't sound too risky, so instead I'll just follow and keep a close eye on the three of you."

"My hero," I sighed.

"I hope it won't come to that," he sighed back. "I'll have to keep myself as much on the down-low as possible, so as not to alert the local police to all of this. Hopefully, you'll get some info on this Jed character, and then I can go searching for him. Maybe, we'll even find Lenny at the end of the trail. Better still, we'll find him and nobody will want to know why I was looking or how we did it."

Unlikely as all that sounded, I squeezed his hand and agreed. It was, after all, one thing to find Lenny; it was quite another getting him back to the authorities without their finding out that it was Will's fault that he escaped in the first place. Oh, what a tangled web we weave, right?

Our trio moved from the pool and back to our sandy oceanfront view, the chairs and umbrella instantly appearing. Will's leg rubbed against mine, followed soon thereafter by his pinky finger hooking into my pinky finger. Paradise, again, was still paradise, if not slightly tainted by the day's events. "I did find out one thing," Will eventually blurted out.

"Which is?" I asked, turning to lock eyes with him, sending a jolt of adrenalin up and down my back and a boing inside my board shorts.

"I have minimal access to the F.B.I. computers from my cellphone, but at least I could get both Lenny's address as well as his parent's."

This, I figured, was a good thing. Though, strangely, he wasn't smiling. "What's wrong?" I asked. "I know we won't find Lenny at either place, not unless he's doesn't think the police are watching, which I'm sure they are, but at least we might find some clues as to where he might be hiding."

"Yep," he said. "Problem is that he might've told his parents about me already. Or his parents will warn him that I'm looking for him, because I will have to identify myself. Also, I don't want him to know that you two are looking for him, and getting you into even more hot water than we're already in. After all, he is potentially a drug smuggler with any number of criminal ties."

"Uh oh," Brandon uh-ohed.

"Uh oh, what?" I asked, my typical clueless self.

"Uh oh, he wants us to go undercover, so no one recognizes us and tries to find us later. And this face and body was not meant to be hidden."

I shook my head from side to side at my new bed-mate. He nodded his up and down. "It's for your own safety," he explained. "If you two are going to help me, you'll need disguises. It's fine if someone figures out that I'm looking for Lenny and Jed; that at least makes some sense. It's not fine if they think you guys are. It's questionably legal and definitely unsafe."

"Well fuck me," I said.

"He already did," Brandon said.

"I meant that figuratively." Though the literal version was quite enjoyable, too.

Will piped in, already knowing how our verbal escapades could go on and on—and on. "I'm not asking for full-on body suites or anything; just simple disguises.

"Drag!" Brandon shouted, his disarming smile suddenly returning.

"Not drag!" I shouted back.

"Drag!" my friend repeated. "With gorgeous, frilly numbers."

Will just sighed and looked from me to Brandon and then back again. "You can go as men, if you like. Though female camouflage would ensure that neither of them knows that any of us are looking for them."

I smiled. "So, you'll be dressing like a girl as well?" The thought was comical, at best. Will was six-two and built like a linebacker. All man.

"Um," he hemmed, and then hawed, "that might cause unneeded attention to us. I said disguises, not Halloween costumes."

I squeezed his hand. "I was only joking. And fine, we can go undercover. But as boys, for the time being."

Brandon's smile turned upside down. "Damn," he groaned. "We could've done a lot more shopping as girls."

I threw the lime from my drink at him. "That's because you always end up being the pretty one."

"Don't blame me," he said, catching it and tossing it back. "That's just good genetics."

I tossed it back again, with Will promptly blocking it and then burying it in the sand. "What?" I yelled at Brandon. "Your drag DNA ensures that you look good in a dress?"

He ran his fingers up and down his cheek. "Bone structure, dude. It's all about the bone structure."

Will sighed, yet again. "I can't believe we're having this

conversation," he said.

"Welcome to our world," I told him. "Welcome to our fucking world."

***

A half hour or so later, our trio became a foursome, with Koni sashaying down in nothing but Brandon's shorts. His tan, ripped body glistened in the brilliant afternoon sun, smooth as silk, rich as milk chocolate. My jaw hit the sand in a dull thud.

"Aloha, dudes," he said, waiting patiently for the chair that was quick to arrive for him.

"Aloha," we said, introducing him to Will, but neglecting to inform him of his connection to the U.S. government. Deceitful but wise, all things considered.

"Yikes," the lad said, taking in my new beau. "The thermometer just shot up to hot."

"Down boy," I cautioned. "Better yet, go cool off in the ocean."

"Better still," Will said, pointing to the yellow catamaran with the red and yellow striped sails, the Na Hoku II, which was roped in just to our right, "let's all go in. On that."

Brandon yelled to the man with a clipboard who was standing where the rope ended. "Is there booze on that there boat?"

The man nodded, hollering back, "One low price, all you can drink margaritas."

If the guy only knew how much we two could drink, he might've not made that offer. In any case, we were up in a flash, jumping over the barrier between our private lot of sand and the, blech, public one. The guy took our names and our money, a paltry twenty dollars each, and told us to watch our steps going up and on. For twenty bucks, all you could drink, it wasn't the going up he should've been cautioning us about. In fact, I couldn't imagine how we'd ever make it back down. Or even want to.

It was our first catamaran ride. None of the four of us had ever been on one. For Brandon and I, though we live a mere five miles from the water, our particular stretch of ocean is always cold, always choppy, and usually fogged in. In other words, the closest we ever get to boats were the ones that float by us with sushi on top of them—and sake nearby, of course. Needless to say, we were all excited, and showed it by graciously accepting the first margarita. None for our underage friend, though, try as he might to lay his grubby little mitts on one.

Minutes later, with the catamaran full of grinning tourists, the rope was untied and we were off, the engine pulling us quickly out to sea as a crewman—one of three, plus a waddling dachshund—blew a conch shell, warning the swimmers and surfers in front of us to move the hell out of the way. We four watched on, mesmerized, as our beautiful hotel and banyan tree grew smaller and smaller, our line of vision growing wider and wider, taking in the whole of the stunning Waikiki coastline. It was long, narrow, and lush. Which, ironically, could also be used to describe Brandon. The ocean was calm—enough—and a deep, cool blue. Diamond Head, off to our far right, towered high above, loomed ever-present. It was all picture-postcard perfect!

"Beautiful," I yelled into Will's ear, over the sound of the whipping breeze and engine roar.

He locked eyes with me and grinned. "Yes," he said lustfully, sending a ripple through my bathing trunks and a pounding to my heart.

We stood up and leaned over the railing, our body's rising and falling and swaying with the waves. My eyes scanned the shore, moving from hotel to hotel, from palm tree to palm tree, to the mountains that rose up just beyond Waikiki, dotted with endless houses nestled among impossibly steep slopes. The clouds, white and billowing, moved in and around them. Breathtaking. As was the company. Will's hand covered my own as he leaned in tight to me. Snug as a bug in a, um, boat.

And then he was pointing excitedly and hollering. "Whale!"

he shouted, his voice full of excitement.

The entirety of the boat ran to our side, all of them pointing, all of them shouting. A whale had breached the surface not a hundred feet from the right of the bow, massive in size, dark and knobby, its humongous frame lunging sideways, with a fin seemingly waving to us before it crashed back down. My smile was so wide that it hurt, and my breath was caught in my throat. A whale! A fucking whale!

"A whale! A fucking whale!" Brandon yelled. Yes, I know, scary that our minds are in sync like that.

All those around us watched in silent awe, until the peace was shattered by the dog barking behind us. We all ran to the other side, thinking that the whale had swam around us and breached, yet again. Sadly, it wasn't the whale that had breached; it was a body, upside down and floating, lifeless and blue as the water.

Most of the boat averted their eyes, save for Will and the crewmen. The captain steered us closer, and two of the men pulled the body out. Again, there was silence, except for a few of the women, who were now sobbing. The body was dragged up front and flipped over.

It was Will who spoke first. "Lenny," he whispered, making the sign of the cross over his chest.

Brandon and I couldn't help but look. The man was naked, blue, as I've said, and bloated. Still, it seemed he'd not been dead all that long. It was clearly the man we'd been searching for, his neck slashed, the wound gaping, jagged. We wretched and quickly turned away.

Koni walked over and had a look, then came back over to our group. "That the guy you were looking for, dudes?" he asked.

"Was looking for, yes," I replied with a whimper.

"Hmm," he hummed, pulling on the small goatee that managed to sprout from his chin.

"Why hmm?" Brandon asked.

"He's the drug smuggler? I mean, was the drug smuggler?"

Koni asked.

"Supposed drug smuggler," I replied. "Again, why?"

"Dude was dumber than dirt. I mean, I don't know how smart you have to be to be a drug smuggler, but I'd think it takes a bit of, I don't know, common sense."

"But you told us that you didn't know Lenny," I reminded him.

"I don't. Didn't. Not by name, anyway. Used to see the guy at the bars. Hard to miss. He was cute. And stupid. Ditzy. Nellie as the day is long. Flight attendant I can believe. Drug smuggler, nah, no way. But that's just my opinion. Guess anyone can smuggle drugs up their ass, even idiots. I suppose it made for a good cover."

Brandon and I looked at each other, clearly thinking the same thing. You had to be stupid to smuggle drugs, but to get away for it for a year, at least, you couldn't be that big of an idiot and not get caught. Maybe we were seeing things as we wanted to see them, but still, it was proving our hunch correct. Then again, seeing as the dead told no tales, we weren't going to find that out from Lenny.

I leaned in to Will and held my hand over his ear. "I know you're not going to want to hear this, and I know it's inappropriate to say," I whispered, "but you're off the hook now. The authorities can't tie his escape to you or us, anymore."

He frowned, and whispered back, "True, but his death is my fault. He'd still be alive if I didn't get into the limo with you two. But at least now I can offer my services to the local police, under the pretense that I brought him in, and the murder of an interstate drug smuggler falls under the F.B.I.'s umbrella."

"Supposed interstate drug smuggler," I corrected with.

"Maybe," Will said. "Still, he knew something about something, or he wouldn't be wearing that new neckline of his. And the kid was right about one thing: a stupid flight attendant does make for a good cover. In any case, you two are out of this now. Too dangerous."

I looked back out to Waikiki, our hotel growing closer and

closer, beautiful, majestic, tainted forever by what lay behind us on the boat. He was wrong, though; we'd still help. Had to help. It was our fault, too. Inadvertently, but still our fault. I could see it in the crease in Brandon's forehead that he was thinking the same thing. Or maybe he was thinking that he needed a drink, his cup now empty. Yep, the latter did seem the more likely of the two.

"Okay," I lied to Will, and then leaned in to Brandon's ear. "You thinking what I'm thinking?"

"What? That I need a drink? Or three?" See! "Or that we need to do some Judy and Liza shopping when we get back? Our drag alter-egos are about to make a comeback, I take it." Too bad our minds were in sync on that one. I liked the drink option a whole lot better.

"Well," I said, forcing a smile, "at least we get to do some clothes shopping."

"Way to go, Chase. Always look on the bright side."

We both turned and stared at the corpse not twenty feet from us. "Let's hope there is a bright side, Brandon. 'Cause right now, things are looking kinda dark."

And they were going to get a hell of a lot darker.

Cue the ominous music.

❀ Information Gained ❀

The body was taken away. Brandon and I, along with Koni, returned to our beach chairs. Will, not wanting to let on to Koni about who he really was, said he was going back to his hotel, when, in reality, he was following poor Lenny. Or his remains, at any rate.

"That was fucked up," our newly-acquired friend said, thereby stating the obvious.

"But you're still gonna help us find Jed, right?" I asked.

"You still want to find him? What's the point? His boyfriend is dead. Case closed."

Brandon looked my way and shrugged, replying, "Humor us, kid."

"Fine," he agreed, "just so long as I still get the room for the night. And board."

We both turned to look at him. "Who said anything about board?" I asked.

"My price went up when the dead dude floated by," he informed, his arm raised, motioning for a cocktail waitress to come over. "You guys want anything?"

"Drinks!" we both hollered in unison. See, there goes that scary mind-meld again. Sometimes, I guess, it does come in handy.

***

Exhausted by the day's events, we soon lumbered back to our rooms for a much-needed nap. Brandon and I went to his room, Koni to mine. Strangely, I didn't mind the company, all things considered. I mean, there's safety in numbers, you know.

"I have to say, I agree with the kid," Brandon said, behind closed doors. "That was fucked up."

"Truly," I concurred. "And let me guess, you're feeling a tad guilty about poor Lenny, right?"

"One needs a conscience, dear friend, in order to feel guilty."

I shook my head and hopped into bed. He followed close behind. "Please," I said, "I know you better than that."

"And I know you, too. You're in this to help Will; Lenny is more of an afterthought."

He did know me, all too well. I dropped the subject and moved on. "And what about Koni?"

"What about him?" he asked, his hands behind his head, staring up at the ceiling.

"He's not spending just one night, is he? I mean, we're not letting him go back to that nasty grocery store, are we?"

He didn't answer, not immediately. "We're in danger now, Chase. What with Lenny and Jed, and all. Is it safe to keep the kid around?"

"Is it safe for him to be alone on the streets?"

He sighed. "I'm in bed with Mother Fucking Teresa." And then he paused, eventually replying, "Fine. Besides, we'll need a guide. Might as well be a cute one."

The cute one in question knocked on the door a short while later. We opened it up and let him in. He had a cellphone in his hand and a beguiling smile on his face. "I called my friend. He's meeting us at Hula's at ten. I'd advise bringing some cash along; he's going to strike a hard bargain."

"I thought you said he owed you one," I politely reminded him.

"He does, which is why he's willing to meet. Information is extra, kind of like fries and pickles. Which, by the way, we're getting beforehand. There's a restaurant, Cheeseburger in Paradise, near the bar."

"Do they have drinks there?" Brandon asked, beating me to the punch.

"Big ones, and very potent," came the glorious response.

"Good choice then," said Brandon. "Now, let the adults get some rest. I fear it's gonna be a long and painful night." I know, I know. There's that foreshadowing again. Sorry. I like to make sure you're prepared.

***

The burger joint was just up the street, past the substation and down a beautiful stretch of sidewalk, with the ocean to our right and hotels and shops and restaurants to our left. Dusk was fast approaching, and brightly lit tiki torches appeared on all sides of us. As we strolled along, we passed endless varieties of trees, none of which I'd ever seen before, each with its own signature flower and bouquet. The sun, descending rapidly now, cast a brilliant orange and pink tinge across the sky, which was stunningly reflected in the ocean below. It was hard not to get swept up in the moment.

Within minutes, we reached a statue of Duke Kahanamoku, the Father of International Surfing, his arms outstretched, dozens upon dozens of purple and white leis festooned over them, draping beautifully downward. Koni pulled us over, onto the public—yuck, again—beach, already lined with hundreds of people waiting for the inevitable brilliant Hawaiian sunset.

We plopped down on the warm sand, Brandon and I sandwiching our new friend, temporarily forgetting the awful circumstances that had brought us together. Cruise ships amassed along the horizon, each trying to get an optimal view of the sun as it made its expected plunge. We watched from our own vantage point, stunned by the natural beauty, awed by the grandeur of it all.

"Not like back home," I commented.

"Back home, the buildings are too tall or the fog too thick," Brandon responded.

Koni coughed and looked wistfully forward, not saying a word. Perhaps, the mention of home was too depressing. I instinctively put my arm around him. He turned my way and smiled. "Pretty, ain't it?" he asked. "The free things in life always are."

I nodded and again stared ahead. The sun met the ocean in a blaze of red, turning the coast a golden hue. "Beautiful," I finally answered with a heavy sigh.

The sky just as quickly changed to a darkening purple as the temperature comfortably dropped. We stood back up and continued on to our destination, a mere few short blocks away. It hit me how all the beauty, the spectacle, was oceanside, while a mere few blocks away, life, dirty and sometimes cruel, reigned supreme. A strange dichotomy. Easy to turn a blind eye to. Unless your eyes were suddenly pried opened, as ours had been merely by our chance encounter with Koni. I ached to know his circumstances; sadly, we had other fish to fry. The timing just wasn't quite right, not yet. But soon. It was as unavoidable as the sunset we'd just witnessed.

"Busy restaurant," Brandon mentioned upon our approach.

"Tourist trap," Koni explained. "Big burgers, big fries, big drinks. Cheaper than hotel food. Sometimes, they give me leftovers out the back door. Nice to be entering through the front for a change."

Brandon and I frowned. "I need a drink," I proclaimed.

"Oh, God, yes," Brandon agreed.

Koni laughed. "Sorry, dudes. I forget how depressing my life is. I'll try to perk things up for the rest of the night, promise."

Trust me, perking up is just what we needed. Or at least soon would. Luckily, we got the last remaining table. Then again, with Brandon flirting with the host, I wasn't all that surprised. Sometimes it pays to have an easy lay for a best friend. Drinks and dinner were then quickly ordered, the drinks being downed lickety-split and just as quickly re-ordered.

"You guys have a serious problem," Koni said.

"Not a problem so much as a mild addiction. We could stop if we wanted to," I said.

To which Brandon promptly added, "We just don't want to."

"No," Koni told us, his face scrunched up. "I mean, you guys have a problem." He was pointing outside the window. A cop car was across the street, its lights whirling red. Two officers were shoving a man inside. "That's my friend, Buck. The one we were meeting in a couple of hours. Were, as in not any more, obviously."

"Fuck," I cursed with a well-merited groan.

Koni grinned. "Maybe not. This could be a blessing in disguise."

"How so?" Brandon asked.

"Buck works for Jed. Well, worked, anyway. With Jed gone missing, Buck is pimpless."

"Ah," Brandon ahed. "Meaning, no one to bail him out."

"You catch on fast," Koni said.

"Not normally," I said. "The booze must've lubricated his brain. In any case, what you're saying is, we're not done scratching backs just yet, are we?"

"Correct," came the reply. "Besides, he's probably pissed off that Jed flew the coup. Your bailing him out might be just the thing to get his tongue to wagging."

"So, let me get this, for lack of a better word, straight: we're not leaving here and going to a gay bar; we're leaving here and going to a police station?" Brandon asked, with a scowl.

Koni nodded and took a giant bight of the burger that had arrived.

"Goody," I said, shoving a fistful of fries inside my mouth.

"I hate police stations," Brandon made note.

"Trust me, I know," Koni agreed, in between chews and swallows. "But it's for the greater good. Plus, he'll owe me one, too. A win-win all the way around."

I raised my hand up for the waiter. "Speaking of rounds, how about a drink-drink," I said. "I think we'll be needing them-them."

***

We finished our meals and took the short walk back to the substation. Needless to say, the reverse stroll was not as pleasant. There was, however, a silver lining: my itsy-bitsy bladder proving beneficial, for a change.

Brandon and Koni went up to the front desk to see what they could do about bailing Buck out. I veered to my right, inside the john. I caught sight of him immediately, a smile spreading mischievously across my face. "We have to stop meeting like this," I announced as I zipped down my fly and walked over to the urinal next to him.

Will looked over and grinned. "Not smart to pick up men in police bathrooms," he cautioned.

"Safer than a bar, I'd imagine," I replied.

"Good point. Mind if I ask what you're doing here? I mean, you're not really here to pick up men, are you?"

I grinned. "Jealous much?"

He grinned back, shaking his burgeoning prick at me, the head already slick with copious amounts of precome. "Not jealous so much as curious." He started a slow even stroke on it.

"Well, in fact, we are here to pick a man up; only, not how you meant it."

I explained the sordid details as I led him into the lone stall. My lips were on him in two seconds flat, my hands yanking down his shorts. "Interesting story," he replied, in between hungry sucks and slurps on my neck. "And after I get you off, I'll see what I can do about doing the same for Buck out there. Getting him off, I mean. Or out."

"Sounds hot," I groaned. "Now bend over, and let's see that asshole of yours."

"Right to the point, huh?" he said, turning around before bending over.

"I give us three minutes before Brandon comes looking for me. He can smell sex from fifty feet away. Like a homo-homing pigeon."

"Then suck away," he offered, spreading his cheeks apart and winking his hole at me. I took a whiff and a suck, wetting him up before sliding one, then two, spit-slit digits up and in and back. He groaned and pushed his ass down, stroking his massive schlong as I released my own from within my trunks, matching his rhythm, pump for pump. His prostate grew hard in less than a minute flat. "Almost," he rasped.

"Wait," I told him, stroking faster, feeling the come rise from my balls. "Now."

With my fingers ramming up against granite, I watched from between his thighs as he shot and shot and shot, the come splattering up against the wall before sliding down the tile. My own cock quivered and erupted, white-hot spunk coating the floor beneath us. We muffled our moans as best we could, our bodies shaking in delight.

He turned around as I stood up, to get eye-to-eye with him. "Nice," he purred, his lips soft and tender on mine.

"Ditto," said I with a sly grin. "Now let's go rescue this Buck guy before the cops throw Brandon and Koni in with him. By now, my friend out there has probably aggravated half the police department."

We hurried out, Will to a side door for personnel use only, me back to my friends, who hadn't made the least bit of headway. Brandon gave me a strange look and a sniff of his nose. "Again?" he whispered in my ear. "What's with you and bathrooms lately?"

I held my finger to my lips, hushing him up. "I've got it covered, go sit down."

"I wouldn't get that finger any closer to your mouth. Smells funky."

I laughed and pulled the two of them to a sitting area. Twenty minutes later, Buck emerged. He looked at us in confusion. Par for the course, right?

"Dude," he said to Koni. "How did you know I was here? Did you bail me out? And who are these two geezers." Yes, I took an instant and obvious disliking to him.

Koni chuckled at the comment. "We saw the cops take you in, and thought we'd help. These are my friends, Chase and

Brandon." He paused, obviously contemplating his next move, and then lied like a rug, much to our pride and delight. "And yes, they bailed you out." So much for going undercover, as planned. Then again, the rules seemed to have changed all of a sudden.

Buck was short and runty, baby-faced with a scraggly goatee. What he lacked in stature, he clearly made up for in attitude. He didn't so much as thank us, but merely nodded and pushed on by, out the door and onto the sidewalk. "Let's go to Hula's; I need a drink," he proclaimed, not waiting for our response. Though, clearly, we agreed wholeheartedly with him on that one.

We arrived at a hotel, the Waikiki Grand. Sadly, by the looks of it, there was nothing grand about it. The club was on the second floor, through the dated lobby and up a flight of dirtied stairs. Brandon and I looked at each other, but kept our mouths shut. The only difference between this place and any other strip-mall bar was the open-air windows and spectacular, though somewhat blocked, view of the ocean and Diamond Head. The place was sparsely populated, mostly occupied by tired looking tourists. The dance floor was small, the pool table dimly lit, the music lamentable. In other words, not our scene, not by a long shot. Luckily, the drinks were strong if not super pricey. Buck chugged two shots of vodka right off the bat. Koni had a coke and a smile. Brandon and I, naturally, went tropical: lots of fruit and booze. Then we got down to business.

"Thanks for bailing me out," Buck managed, barely looking at us. "Fucking cops have been all over my ass lately."

"No problem," Brandon and I said.

"Must be tough," Koni interjected. "Being without Jed, and all."

"Yeah," he agreed, starting in on his third drink, slower this time. "Sucks. Jed used to set everything up for me. I don't know how you do it on your own, dealing with all the scum."

My stomach sank at hearing him say this. I'd temporarily forgotten about Koni's awful circumstances, his choice of employment. If choice is even the right word.

"And turning a hundred percent of the profits," Koni replied. "Guess it's a tradeoff."

The two "men" nodded. And that was our chance to get some much-needed info. "What happened to this Jed guy?" Brandon asked, already sliding Buck's fourth drink his way.

Buck grimaced. "Fuck if I know. His boyfriend gets busted for smuggling, and he up and vanishes. Only thing is, Jed ain't no drug dealer, and he's got some sleazy lawyers for any time the cops start nosing around. So, why he vanished is a mystery. Plus, when he's gone, he ain't making no money. And Jed loves his money. A lot."

"Maybe he's just lying low, until the cops finish their investigation of his boyfriend. Makes sense," I suggested, omitting the fact that said boyfriend was now quite dead.

"Not really," Buck said. "If anything, it makes him look guilty of something. Only reason to run is if you're guilty."

Brandon moved the subject in a new direction. "Did you know the boyfriend?"

Buck snickered. "Met him once. Some stewardess. Cute and stupid." Seems to have been an agreed upon opinion.

Koni asked the next question. "Too stupid to be a drug smuggler?"

Buck paused before answering. "Maybe. I mean, I don't know how smart you have to be to do it, except, if he was doing it for as long as they're saying, I'd guess you couldn't be that much of a moron. Still, if you met the guy, you'd never in a million years believe it." Also, an agreed upon opinion.

"There was some damning evidence, though," Brandon said. "The traces of coke up his ass, the excess of money for a lowly flight attendant."

Buck snickered. "Dude, coke up your ass doesn't mean you're a smuggler, necessarily."

Koni explained, "Nope. Some guys put coke on their dicks, to numb 'em up, keep 'em harder, longer. Also, it numbs the bottom's hole, so they can get fucked longer. And, in terms of the money, you don't need to be dealing drugs to come into a lot of cash. Trust me, sometimes it just falls into your lap." He looked at us knowingly, causing a hot blush to creep up my neck.

"Meaning," Brandon said, "he could've just as easily been set up, and the evidence was circumstantial?" The two of them nodded at the two of us. "Which would mean," Brandon continued, "the dealer, Makani, turned in someone who was innocent in order to get a lighter sentence, and not get in any deeper shit with the bad guys. But why Lenny?"

"And more bad guys seem to have been caught anyway," I quickly added.

"Happens all the time," Buck said. "Not a long-term career, drug dealing. Most dealers get caught, sooner or later. Turned in by each other or their customers."

I shook my head and downed my drink. The whole thing was giving me a migraine, and not getting us any closer to the truth. "So," I eventually thought to ask, "if you were Jed, where would you be hiding?"

Buck held up his palm, asking us to grease it. "This ain't no idle questioning, is it, dudes?" The guy was obviously smarter than we gave him credit for.

Brandon discreetly slipped him a twenty. When no further information was forthcoming, he added another to the pot. "Well?" he asked.

"Jed has a house at the North Shore. Only reason I know about it is because I overheard him talking about it this one time. Meaning, if you find him up there, better not tell him how it is you came by this little piece of knowledge. And if I was you, I wouldn't go looking anyway. Jed don't like to be found if he doesn't want to be."

In any case, and after another fifty bucks, Buck wrote the address down on a Hula's napkin. It was then that I thought of Lenny and his fate. Did he find Jed when Jed didn't want to be found? A pang tore at my heart at the thought of it. Then again, we had found his body in Waikiki, the opposite end of the island to the North Shore. If that's where Jed was in hiding, it seemed unlikely that Lenny would turn up where he did.

We left Buck at Hula's, heading back to our hotel with at least a modicum of information—well, more than what we started out with, anyway. Half-way back, my cellphone rang. I read the screen. It was Will. I'd given him my number the night before.

"Howdy," I said, mighty glad to hear from him.

"Don't turn around," he said. "I'm twenty feet behind you."

I laughed. "Dude, you've got a big dick, but it'll never reach." My companions looked at me quizzically, but I ignored them.

"Wanna bet," he said. "Anyway, I've been watching you guys, just to be on the safe side. Learn anything?"

"Uh huh," I replied. "You?"

"A little. After we dropped Lenny off at the morgue, I went back to the substation, as you're now well aware. The locals were glad that I decided to stay around a bit longer. Seems the press isn't reporting everything. See, the cops know that Lenny's boyfriend is a pimp, and a successful one at that. They figured that he has some connection with all this, hence his disappearance. Could be he set Lenny up and then killed him. Only problem is, he was never in the drug trade, just the flesh one, so the tie is tenuous at best. Plus, until Makani turned Lenny in, Lenny was never even on their radar. Not even a blip. They think he was too stupid to be a smuggler."

"Them and everyone else," I lamented. "I'll see you in the you-know-where and we can compare notes."

He laughed. "Ah, the bathroom, yet again. See you in ten."

"Roger. Over and out."

We continued walking in silence, until Brandon said, "Well, that was cryptic."

"Yeah," Koni chimed in. "Who's this big-dicked Roger dude, and when can we meet him?"

I turned the invisible key in front of my lips just as we reached our hotel. Will, I was sure, ducked into the other entrance. The three of us then hunkered down on the outdoor veranda, rocking quietly on the comfortable wooden chairs as we watched the tourists stroll by. Soon after, I excused myself to go to the restroom. Brandon looked up, but didn't blow my cover; he merely winked and stared back ahead.

I walked inside the hotel and down the corridor. As planned, Will was waiting for me with a kiss and a single red rose. My heart beat a pitter-patter at the sight of him. I quickly filled him in, and then got him off. Bathrooms were, for better or worse, becoming Pavlovian for me: the mere sight of them sending all the blood flowing to my cock.

He then followed me back to the boys. "Hi," he said, taking a rocking chair.

"Um, look who I bumped into," I announced sheepishly.

Brandon crinkled his nose and shook his head back and forth, while Koni said, "Oh, so this is Mister Big Dick. Good to know."

I sat in between them, and told him, "No, it's not. Promptly forget about it."

And then Will changed the subject. "So," he said. "Who's up for a trip to the North Shore tomorrow? I'd like to see these boss waves everyone talks about."

We all raised our hands. But then Koni slowly lowered his, and his chair stopped rocking. "I guess count me out. My back scratching twenty-four hours will be up by then."

I looked at Brandon and grinned. "It's been extended. We'll need a guide."

"Just so happens," Koni said, returning to his grinning and rocking, "I know this island like the back of my hand."

"So now, one more question," Brandon thought to ask. "Anybody have a car?"

For a change, I actually had an answer to that one. "Will a limo do?" I asked, already dialing the number on my cell. It looked like that card Liko gave me was going to come in handy. Luckily, Liko was wide open, and our hunky limo driver was only too happy to drive us anywhere we wanted to go. We arranged for him to pick us up the next morning, bright and early at ten. For Brandon, that was about as bright and early as he could muster. Then we sat there and again watched the happy masses go by.

"Strange," I said. "There are as many Japanese tourists as there are Americans."

"Yep," Koni commented, "they count for something like thirty percent of the tourist trade around here. And all those ABC stores you see everywhere, they all take the Japanese Yen. And all the restaurants have their menus in English and Japanese. Heck, they get married here at this very hotel practically all day long."

I hesitated, but then added, "And the Japanese men appreciate the Hawaiian girls and boys for, um, other less wholesome activities as well?"

He paused. "Yes, which they pay for in Yen, too."

"Which you don't take," I added.

"I'm not the fucking bank of Tokyo," he replied, almost in a whisper.

"Sorry," I said. "Not my business."

He sighed. "Nah. It's okay, cute dude. You've been dying to ask me all day about this shit."

I laughed, and asked, "How could you tell?"

And he also laughed. "Because you never brought it up, which is a sure sign that you were thinking about it." Smart kid. Smarter than us by a long shot.

"And the reason you don't use a pimp, like your friend, Buck, does?" Brandon asked. "It's not only because you get to keep all the money, is it?"

He turned to us and smiled. "Partly. But mainly it's so I can pick and choose who I...who I, um, do. Buck has to take whatever Jed gives him. Like it or not."

"And he can't quit if he wants to, can he?" Brandon added.

The smile dropped for the briefest of seconds. "No, he can't. Remember what I said: this is a small island; no were to run to, nowhere to hide. Maybe that's what happened to Lenny. Maybe he tried to quit smuggling. Who knows?"

"So, no pimp means you can quit whenever you want to, right?" I asked.

He turned his head to stare at the street, gleaming as it was in the silvery bright moonlight. "Look at all these tourists," he said, by way of an answer. "Funny how they see the same things I see. The same sunsets. The same hotel lobbies. The same crappy gift stores. Except, those things make them happy. Me? They just remind me of what I don't have. And all I do have is the freedom to do something different someday. If I lose that, what's left?"

I stifled back a tear. Even Brandon had to look away for a second. "Hey, kid," he said.

"What is it, Brandon?"

"You've got one more thing," my friend said.

"Yeah? What's that?"

Brandon reached out and put his hand over Koni's. "You've got us, kid."

Koni smiled, though it now looked somewhat forced. "Yeah, Brandon. But for you, this is a vacation. Two weeks, and then back to reality. For me, this is my reality. Fifty-two weeks a year."

For that we had no answer.

At least not yet.

***

The next day, as planned, the limo pulled up just as we trotted down the hotel steps and over to the sidewalk. Liko hopped out, dressed in a pair of smart shorts and a tight, short sleeve, Hawaiian shirt. The gods had clearly smiled on him. And us. His own smile faltered only briefly when he saw that Brandon and I were now a foursome, one of whom was the F.B.I. agent he'd driven upon our arrival, the other a teenager, and one he most probably recognized as the street trash everyone thought him to be. In truth, we did make an odd menagerie. Liko, the professional that he was, however, merely wished us a good morning and escorted us into the limo, where a chilled carafe of mimosas gratefully awaited us.

Liko then ran around to the driver's side and jumped back in. His voice greeted us over the speaker. "Aloha, gentlemen," he said, his voice as smooth and silky as the drinks Brandon and I now had grasped in our greedy, little hands. "A good day to you all."

"Aloha," we shouted back.

"Where to this fine morning?" he asked, the engine revving and the limo pulling away.

"The North Shore," we all said in unison.

"Any place in particular?"

To which I replied, "the most beautiful beach you can think to take us to."

He laughed. "You're on Oahu, sirs. They're all beautiful. But I think I know the perfect spot."

And then Will added what I'd been dreading since we'd discussed it the night before. "Afterward, Liko," he said, "we'd appreciate it if you could drive us to two other places; they should be near to one other, and we hopefully won't be at them for very long."

"Whatever you like," he told us. "You've paid for the whole day."

Waikiki being long as opposed to wide, we were on the H-1 Highway in just minutes, driving west, the Koolau mountain range to our right, sprawling suburbs on either side of us, the ocean now far to our left, mostly out of sight. We cranked up the radio. Journey was blaring, taking us back to a time we could just barely remember.

"Who's Journey?" Koni asked.

We groaned and ignored the question. "How far to the other end of the island?" I asked instead.

"About fifty miles, close to an hour's drive," Liko replied over the intercom.

Brandon looked at the carafe and then back over to me. "Just enough time," he noted.

"Just enough mimosas," I amended with.

Will turned off the intercom. "Hey guys, remember, this is only partly a joy ride."

Brandon grimaced. "Then I'll only get partly drunk."

I clinked my glass to his, adding, "And I'll take the other part."

Journey turned to Blondie, while we sat back, rolled down the window, and stared out at the passing scenery. The tune hummed in my already addled brain. One way or another, I'm gonna find ya, I'm gonna getcha, getcha, getcha, getcha.

"Who's Blondie?" Koni asked.

"Shut up, kid," Brandon admonished. "Just please shut the fuck up."

***

We turned north, heading up H-2 toward our destination. The city gave way to rolling countryside, small communities, middle-class houses and middle-class lives. Koni looked out the window glumly. I patted his hand, but didn't ask any more questions; I'd found that the answers weren't to my liking.

Minutes later, we approached a Hawaiian landmark. "Look," I said, pointing. "The Dole Plantation and Pineapple Garden Maze." I read in our guidebook that over a million tourists visited every year to experience Hawaii's premier pineapple experience. Which begs the question: what's an inferior pineapple experience like?

Brandon shook his head. "Tourist hell. Besides, you're lost half the time as it is. Put you in a maze, and we might never see you again." He hesitated. "Then again…"

"Hardy har," I said. "I get your point. They also have a massive gift shop."

His face noticeably brightened. "Maybe on the way back then."

We soon reached the town of Haleiwa, the surfing capital of the world, though similar looking to the ones that dotted the

California coast, with its myriad of tourist shops, quaint eateries, and galleries. Which was great, because we were almost out of finely decorated conch shells. In any case, a pleasant breeze wafted through the open window, smelling of the ocean that lay just barely out of sight. We eagerly stared, watching, waiting.

And then there it was, the Pacific, much different looking on this end of the island than our own. The waves were massive, breaking in a torrent of white. The surfers, in their black wetsuits, rode high above or just within, appearing and then disappearing as the water enveloped them. It was just like the surfer movies I'd seen on television, only real and breathtaking.

The limo pulled into a lot. We hopped out as Liko retrieved the items I'd ordered the night before: two blankets and a picnic basket for four. It felt strange leaving the driver behind, but stranger still to invite him to join us. What did Britney and Paris do? I wondered. Probably slept with their drivers. Not an unpleasant thought, all things considered.

We walked onto the beach, which was small, almost private, perhaps fifty other spectators, most of whom were surfers. We set up shop off to the side, just below a wide tree that covered our pristine swatch of sand. The sun was super strong, broiling at midday. Tanning was one thing, cooking something else entirely. The shade was nicer, smarter, less wrinkle-inducing.

We spread the blankets out and arranged the food and iced beers, soda for the minor. Then we settled in. The surfers gave us a show as we chowed down. Athletes on the water, majestic as ballet dancers, agile as gymnasts. And so, we sat there, staring, mesmerized.

"Well," Koni said, midway through our meal. "What's the plan?"

We did indeed have one, but hadn't filled him in just yet. After all, he was still in the dark about Will, who he thought was simply a friend of ours, albeit a helpful one with a purported— and confirmed—big dick. We therefore thought it best to dish out information on an as needed basis. "First, we're going to see Lenny's parents. Will managed to get us the address through, um, some contacts of his. Then we're going to check out the place that Buck told us about." Afterward, we'd tell the local police only if we found out anything. I mean, the word of a street hustler wasn't exactly golden, especially one such as Buck, and the cops might not be so willing to act on what he'd said.

"I think I've lost my appetite," Koni lamented.

"Yeah," I concurred. "It's not going to be pleasant. But the police, from what we know, have already come and gone, and concluded that Lenny's parents were oblivious to their son's dealings." Again, we neglected to tell him that what we knew all came from Will.

"Suspected dealings," Brandon corrected with.

"Uh huh, exactly. In any case, if we find out anything, it can only help now," I explained, and hoped I was right. We were, in fact, treading on shaky ground here. But, since Will had told us that the police were indeed through with Lenny's parents, they were now fair game for us. He, of course, being on the case now, could use any information we successfully gathered. And perhaps our not being the police would enable us to find out something they had not. After all, the cops hadn't been on Lenny's side up until this point, which his parents certainly were well aware of, thanks to all the press coverage.

I know, I know. The whole thing was iffy at best. We were sticking our noses in where they didn't belong. But please remember, we each felt responsible for Lenny's death. Had he not escaped, he'd still be alive, perhaps even found innocent by the police and then subsequently released. As things stood, the authorities weren't convinced either way about his guilt or innocence. At least our snooping might shed some light on that, maybe even help solve the case. We couldn't, after all, bring Lenny back, but at least we might clear his name. And with Will by our side, we were, we figured, safe. Well safer and, um, you know, well-fucked.

So, we ate our meals, enjoyed the surroundings and the company, and tried, as hard as it was to do so, to push the near future to the back of our much-worried brains, for the time being. When I looked over at Koni and noticed him grinning, I asked, "What's the big smile for?"

"Wanna see something cool?" he replied, obviously brimming with excitement.

"Cooler than that?" I asked, pointing to the surfing spectacle.

He nodded and jumped up. The three of us followed, our feet digging into the hot sand as we plodded ahead. A small crowd had gathered off to the far-right side of the beach. Obviously, this is where we were headed. A jolt of adrenalin pumped through me. What new display did this magical place hold in store for us? I could see through the throng that a large greenish-gray lump lay sprawled out. "Is that what I think it is?" I asked as we approached.

"Uh huh," Koni said. "Cool, huh?"

"A turtle?" Brandon asked, the four of us crowding around, though no too close, giving it ample breathing room.

"Honu," Koni informed. "The green sea turtle. She's come here to lay her eggs. See how her back flippers are pushing the sand behind her? She's burying them. Keeping them warm before they hatch. She'll lay about a hundred leathery eggs; then she'll swim back to sea and forget about them." In an instant, he looked sad, dejected. "Some parents do that," he added, the frown evident. "Give birth and then beat it, letting their children fend for themselves."

I put my arm around him. "Thanks for showing us. It is cool. Way cool. And then when they're hatched, they won't be alone; they'll have each other."

He looked over at me and smiled. "We're not talking about the honu any more, are we, cute dude?"

I grinned. "Too smart for your own good, kid," I said.

"Gotta be, cute dude. Gotta be."

***

We finished our meals, packed up, and left. Liko was waiting for us back at the limo. Will handed him Lenny's parent's

62

address, which he looked at, questioningly. "Residential neighborhood," he informed. "Nothing worth seeing out there. Ugly homes. No beach. No shopping. You sure you wouldn't like the Dole Plantation better?"

"You're right, we would like that better," Will said. "But this visit is more business than pleasure."

He took the paper and didn't say another word. We all then piled back inside the limo, my heart pumping madly in my chest. This was not, after all, the business I liked being in. No way, no how.

"What do we say to them once we get there?" Koni asked.

"Let me do the talking," Will suggested, and we all readily agreed. I, for one, was all in favor of staying in the limo. Or, better yet, being dropped off at the Dole gift store. Better still, a local bar. Heck, let the fucking honu bury me in the sand, for all I cared.

We pulled up to their home not fifteen minutes later. It was fairly ramshackle. A small patch of brown grass surrounded the place. A few chickens clucked and pecked off to the side, with a tiny vegetable garden sprouting from the rear. Lenny obviously came from meager beginnings—and ignoble endings.

We trudged up to the front door. Liko and the limo pulled out of sight, perhaps not wanting to frighten them too much. As if four complete strangers wouldn't do exactly just that. We caught our breaths and knocked. A short woman answered, fifty at most, and looking every day of it. Her graying hair lay piled atop her head, slightly disheveled. Her eyes were red-rimmed, chestnut brown, tired looking.

"Can I help you?" she asked timidly.

Will, as planned, spoke up first. "Sorry to disturb you, ma'am. We wanted to pay our respects. We were, um, well, we knew your son." Which wasn't a lie. As an agent, Will wouldn't or couldn't do that. In fact, his very being there and not identifying himself was a no-no. Then again, these people weren't suspects and we'd probably never see them again after today.

Her face brightened for just an instant. "Friends of Lenny? How nice. Please, come in."

We didn't correct her, just followed her inside instead. The place was small but charming. "You have a beautiful home," I complemented, my voice slightly trembling, innards rumbling.

"Thank you," she said, looking around, the smile again evident, if not weak. "I'm afraid my husband isn't here to say hello. He's down at the store. Busy season. Can't afford to close for a day. You understand."

We did, and nodded so. She offered us some iced tea, which we gladly accepted. My throat, by then, was dry and tight. "Lenny was born here?" Will asked.

"Born and raised. His only real home. His room is still in the back." Her eyes watered just slightly as she stared off into the distance. "He didn't do it, you know. He was a good boy." She was staring at a picture of him, high school graduation, not that many years prior. A good-looking kid.

"Honestly, ma'am," Will said, "we don't think so either."

She looked back at us, the smile returning in full force. "I know how this sounds, you know. A mother claiming her son's innocence. But I knew my boy. He never did drugs. He came home often; I would've known. As for the smuggling, I spoke to him from the jail in Oakland. He swore he didn't know anything about it."

"He told us the same thing, ma'am. We believed him, too," I said, and meant it.

She took a seat, as did we, filling up the small room with our presence. "And his, his boyfriend, ma'am, the one that's gone missing?" It was an open-ended question, one we weren't sure there'd be any answers to.

Strangely, the smile remained. "A nice boy," she replied. "Don't know why he ran away. Maybe he was scared they'd blame him, too."

Brandon piped in, clearly surprised as we all were. "You...you knew Lenny's boyfriend?"

She nodded. "Only met him the one time. They were passing

through on their way to the beach and stopped in for a bite. Handsome boy. A local."

We looked at her unsurely. "How long ago was that, Mrs. Hallanah?" Will asked.

"Oh, maybe a few weeks ago at most. Didn't you know him, you being friends with Lenny, and all?"

We all looked at each other, unsure of how to answer her. "No ma'am," Brandon finally said. "We only heard about him. Didn't know he was a local, though. You mean Hawaiian, right?"

"Oh yes. Hawaiian. Very handsome," she replied, dumbfounding us.

"And his name?" Will asked as nonchalantly as possible.

She looked at him, scratching her chin. "Oh," she said, "I don't rightly remember off the top of my head." She paused and thought on it. "No, sorry. But it's been a trying week. You understand."

We nodded and stood. "Thank you for the iced tea and hospitality, ma'am," Will said. "We were just passing through and wanted to pay our respects, as we said."

Again, she smiled, thereby melting my heart. "No problem, boys. Any friends of Lenny are always welcome here."

We smiled and started to leave, when Koni surprised us all. "Um, Mrs. Hallanah, would you mind if I asked you a personal question?"

She tilted her head, but the smile remained. "Sure, son, anything."

He stopped, obviously thinking of how to phrase whatever it was that was on his mind. We all waited, staring at him. "Well, it's, um, it's just that I was wondering, a lot of Hawaiians they're, they're very religious people."

She cut him short. "You want to know if I was okay with him being gay? If I was okay that he had a boyfriend and that he brought him around?" Koni merely nodded, clearly stunned at her being so open about it. "We loved our son, young man. It was who he was. It was what he'd always been. If he was happy, we were happy."

"That's…that's the way it should be," he said, obviously trying hard not to choke up. "Thanks."

Again, she surprised us by walking over and hugging him. Koni hugged her back, hard and with feeling. We turned, giving them a moment. And then we left, waving at her as she hollered, "Come back any time, boys. Any time."

We walked down the cracked sidewalk, spotting the limo at the end of the street. It was Brandon who broke the silence. "Your parents, Koni, they weren't like that, huh?"

Our young friend hung his head low and didn't immediately reply. "No," he eventually said, ten feet from the limo. "They kicked me out; never wanted to see me again."

My heart broke, yet again. My parents were more like Lenny's. Brandon's the same. I never even knew parents could be so cold, so unforgiving. We got back inside the limo, the silence nearly deafening.

"Well," I said as the limo pulled off.

"Yeah, well," Brandon echoed. "What do we make of that?"

"You mean that Lenny brought a boyfriend home recently that couldn't have been Jed, Jed being white, and all?" Will asked.

Koni joined in, happy to be off the topic of himself. "Plenty of guys have more than one boyfriend."

"But the press is only reporting on the one that disappeared, namely Jed. Who is this second one?" I asked. "Will, have you heard if the police are looking for anyone else?" To which I quickly amended with, "On the news, I mean."

He shook his head. "I was as surprised as you guys. Guess we have to find both of them now. Would've helped if Mrs. Hallanah had remembered a name." He then turned on the speaker and gave Liko the second address. The limo came to a surprisingly screeching halt.

"You sure about that?" our driver asked. "Bad neighborhood. Probably not a good idea to visit."

We all looked at each other, trepidation evident on all our

faces. "If you could just drive by, we won't be going in." Will told him. The limo sat idling. Liko didn't reply. "Just for a couple of minutes," Will added, then we can go to the Dole Plantation."

The limo revved up and pulled away. Turns out, the address Buck had given us was barely twenty minutes away, down badly paved roads, lined with houses that made Lenny's look like a mansion. Heartbreaking.

Our destination was the last house on the block, fenced in, security cameras mounted to two posts. Strange, we thought. What could be worth stealing out here? Then again, if it was Jed's hideout, it wasn't to catch people breaking in; it was to monitor anyone snooping. Like us. Needless to say, we didn't stop. Not along that block anyway.

"Pull around the corner, Liko. Out of sight of the cameras. I'm just going to take a quick look. No more than a few minutes. Keep the engine running," Will told him.

He did as was asked, not saying a word to us. More than likely, he was probably just as eager to get the hell out of there as we were.

"Be careful," I told Will as he hopped out.

He turned and smiled at me. "Don't worry, I will be."

He was only gone for five minutes. Which is all it took to rile the hornet's nest. He came running back, slamming the door behind him and yelling for Liko to take off. Fast.

"What happened?" I shouted. "Did you see Jed?"

Not Jed, no. But five big Hawaiian guys seemed to be expecting me. As soon as I neared the back fence, they came running out, big-ass guns aimed my way."

"Fuck," I cursed.

"Fuck is right," he agreed. "And they sure as hell looked like bodyguards to me."

We all sat there, our heads turned, looking behind us. Gratefully, we weren't being followed.

"I don't get it," Koni eventually said.

"What?" I asked.

"Well," he continued, "if Lenny was as innocent as we think he was, then why was he dating a pimp with a posse like that? Trust me, only guilty people hang out with men like Jed."

"Good point," I said.

"Unless he was as stupid as everyone seems to think," Brandon added.

"He'd have to be," I concurred. "Unless love really is that blind."

"Or he wasn't dating Jed, as everyone says he was. After all, the mom only knew about this mystery Hawaiian guy," Will suggested.

"Which also doesn't make any sense," I said, and then added, "In any case, I say we start looking for boyfriend number two, because number one is apparently way too dangerous. Maybe this unknown guy can shed some light on this darkening mess."

"And where do we look?" Brandon asked.

"Ah, now that one may be the easiest question yet," I replied. "Coworkers. Gay coworkers. Gay coworkers who like booze and cheap attractive men."

"Ah," Brandon repeated. "Which is where I step into the picture."

"Swish in, but yes," I told him. "If anyone can pry information out of flight attendant, it's definitely you, my dear."

He smiled, clearly pleased with this bit of semi-flattery. "And I won't need to be in drag for that."

"Not for that, no," I said with a frown.

"What does that mean?" he asked, echoing my frown with one of his own.

"Wait," I said. "I'll tell you in a few minutes."

"While we're in the gift store?" he asked.

"Safer than that," I replied. "The middle of the maze."

***

The Pineapple Garden Maze: the Guinness Book record holder that covers an area of three acres, was set off to the right side of the plantation. To say it was huge, not to mention daunting, was putting it mildly—and trying to get Brandon to agree to run through it was doubly so. Quadruply. Wait, is that even a word? Fuck it, it is now.

"There's a bar in the center," I tried. "With fruity libations for the weary maze runner."

"Weary lab rat is more like it," he corrected, arms akimbo. "Plus, you're lying. I can tell."

"How's that?" I asked.

"Because, if such was the case, you'd already be in there, guzzling."

Which was true. "Fine," I relented. "How about, your life will be in danger if we don't get some privacy in about five friggin' minutes, asshole."

He was off and running in no time flat.

The point of the maze was to find small phone-booth type stands that you ticked off on a maze card when you found them. Seeing as that wasn't really our goal, we blatantly ignored the rules of the game and headed for dead, gulp, center. In other words, we cheated. Thankfully, the shrubs weren't all that thick. Or prickly.

"Was all this really necessary?" Brandon whined, the others echoing his sentiment. "It's a hundred fucking degrees out here, no shade, no bar, no fruity libations, not even a cute guy in a chest-revealing tank top. In other words, not my idea of fun."

I shrugged. "Suit yourself. But don't say I didn't warn you."

I started to go back, um, forward, um, well, in reverse. Hell, it was a fucking maze, and it was a hundred fucking degrees, so, needless to say, I was all turned around. In any case, I was summarily stopped. "Just tell us why we're here, Chase," said Will, the lone voice of reason.

"The limo, it's not safe," I replied.

"Bad tires? Leaky transmission? What?" Brandon fired out.

"Bad driver, leaky brained best friend, that's what," I told him.

"It's too hot for this, Chase. Stop with the word play and get on with it. Or no gift shop for you," said my so-called best friend threateningly.

I nodded, afraid that he was serious. "Four things aren't sitting right with me," I began. "One, how did those guards back there know you were about to walk up to the house, Will?"

"Cameras?" he guessed.

"Maybe," I said. "Or perhaps they were tipped off."

"Fuck," Brandon swore. "By Liko?"

I nodded. "Who also didn't want to take us to either the Hallanah abode or that awful other house. That's number two."

"Which he had good reasons for," Koni piped in with.

"True, but there's number three, which has been sitting in my craw for the last two days now," I said, three fingers now waiving in the air.

"What's a craw?" Koni asked. "That like popcorn getting stuck in your teeth?"

I ignored him. "Three," I continued. "Didn't you think it strange that Liko stopped to pick up a man with another man chained to his wrist? If it was me, I'd have locked the doors and rolled the windows up." We'd told Koni this part of the story, still leaving Will out of the equation.

"Meaning?" Will asked.

"Meaning, maybe he knew Lenny already. Maybe he wanted to make sure Lenny wasn't telling us anything of importance."

"Which he didn't," Brandon reminded us.

"Maybe, maybe not," I amended. "He kept proclaiming his innocence. But perhaps that wasn't directed toward us. The intercom was on, after all. Maybe Lenny wanted Liko to know that he was innocent. He did, in fact, repeat the statement enough times."

"And four?" Brandon asked, his head hung low, resigned to the fate of my long-windedness. And the absence of a nearby bar.

"Four, and the worst of them all: when Lenny escaped from the police, where exactly did he run to? He couldn't hide on the beach."

"Fuck," Brandon reiterated. "Our hotel is right next to the substation. Liko probably went back inside after he dropped us off. He'd be easy enough to find, if you knew where to look."

"And if Lenny knew him already," I added, "he'd have found him right quick."

"Uh oh," Koni uh-ohed, figuring out where I was going with all this.

"Uh oh is right," I said. "And then Lenny turns up just off our beach. Maybe he ran to Liko for shelter and ended up as fish food."

"Or," Brandon said, sinking to the ground, "maybe that last brain cell of yours is finally flickering off and you're simply a raving lunatic."

"I'm explaining, not raving," I informed.

"Fine," he informed back. "An explaining lunatic then."

"But it does all make sense, right?" I asked, a smug grin forming on my sweat-soaked face.

The three of them ruefully nodded, finally accepting my utter genius. And all accomplished, as Brandon so eloquently put it, with just one remaining brain cell. Ta da!

Will spoke up first. "I, um, have a friend on the force out here. College buddy. I'll see if there's anything he can find on Liko when we get back. And then tell him to check out that house back there, where the police will hopefully find Jed." If Koni suspected anything, he didn't let on. Still, we'd have to tell him about Will soon enough, and pray he didn't get scared and run off.

"And if nothing turns up on our limo driver back there?" I asked, tilting my head to the right. Then to the left. Then to the right again. See, I told you I was all turned the hell around.

"Oh no," Brandon lamented, not waiting for a reply, but sensing where I was going with the question.

"Do you have a better idea?" I asked.

"Plenty. And they all start and end with a good stiff drink."

"Um," Koni interrupted, unaccustomed to our good-natured bickering, "would you two let us two in on this conversation.

Or would you like a nice Hawaiian punch instead?"

"What this idiot is getting at, or not getting at quickly enough for everybody's liking, is that he intends for the two of us to go undercover," Brandon explained, now lying down on the grass, clearly exhausted.

"As what?" Koni asked. "Japanese tourists that need a limo ride?"

"Oh, to be so lucky," came Brandon's response. "Koni," he said, "you're about to meet Judy and Liza."

"Who are they?" he asked.

"They are us," I replied, smiling at my ingenuity.

"Fuck," Will interjected, stealing Brandon's usual line.

"If we're lucky," Brandon said. "Which doesn't seem the case right about now."

I sat on the ground and stroked his hair. "May I remind you, we didn't pack for Judy and Liza, dear Brandon."

He bolted straight up. "Oh," he fairly moaned. "Shopping. Lots of shopping." A trickle of drool formed at the corner of his upturned mouth.

"Lots and lots," I agreed, helping him to his feet.

"But that's too dangerous," Will told us.

"Not if we warn the stores that we're coming," I replied, trying to figure out which way to go to get the fuck out of there. Maybe the maze wasn't such a good idea after all. I mean, if they found our dead bodies in there, then my plan wouldn't have done us very much good.

"No," Will said, clearly exasperated. "I mean, too dangerous to go undercover like that. Especially, if you're correct about all this."

"Oh, come on now, what can go wrong?" I said, moving in circles and generally not getting anywhere.

The three of them groaned and started to walk through the bushes and out to safety.

Yes, a lot could go wrong.

And, naturally, a lot did.

Again, go figure.

✹ Sarongs Bought (Yes, Seriously) ✹

So, we had a plan. Well, plans. Plural. Were they good plans, well thought out plans, safe plans? Oh, hell no. Did we get to go shopping, get laid, get drunk, get laid again? Well, of course. As I said, we had a plan, and, generally speaking, our plans always include these things. Like, duh. More importantly, though, did we accomplish anything?

Ah, now therein lies the crux. Strange word crux. Synonym: nitty-gritty, core, bottom. Bottom is better. But I digress. Again. In any case, yes, we accomplished certain things, garnered new bits of information. Did anyone get hurt in the process? Injured, maimed, murdered? Come on now, look who we're talking about here.

Yes, murder and mayhem ensured. It bears repeating: like, duh.

So, let's backtrack. Here's what went down. Or who went down, as was the case.

Will, as promised, upon our return, searched the police records for anything he could find on Liko. Not surprisingly, as life is never that easy, our driver came up squeaky clean. To make matters worse, when the cops went back to the house that was purportedly Jed's, it was quite empty. Not even a lowly fingerprint remained. Nor was it in his name, and the owner couldn't readily be tracked down.

So, back to square one.

Since we no longer had a fix on Jed, we needed to find this supposed other boyfriend. Plus, we needed to figure out limo-driving Liko's connection to Lenny. Perhaps, any and all information we uncovered would point to Lenny's killer, or maybe even to his innocence.

"Let's start with the flight attendants," Brandon suggested the next morning when we awoke, again, in the same bed. No, Koni didn't go back to his mattress. Nor did he ask to stay on. For the time being, he was just our live-in guide, no questions asked. Gratefully. After all, we had enough questions to go around—and around—without having to worry about any more.

"Agreed," I said. "Start with the point of least resistance."

"And," he added, "the most likely place to get laid."

"Goes without saying."

"But let's not go without saying it."

So, he donned his tightest, skimpiest ensemble, plus a dandy cap and wrap-around shades, in order to remain as incognito as possible—I stuck with a baseball cap and cheap sunglasses—and we headed back to the airport. Will stayed with Koni on the beach, keeping both of them, hopefully, out of trouble.

Aloha Airlines, before it went out of business, and at the time all this took place, was a large carrier, with flights in and out of Honolulu all day long. We simply plopped our asses down outside their security gate and waited. Every so often, large pods of flight attendants filed past. The women didn't give us the time of day; the men, naturally, did double-takes. At Brandon, of course. Yes, my best friend is that gorgeous, much to my constant irritation.

"Like taking candy from a baby," he whispered in my ear.

"Have you ever done that?" I whispered back. "Take candy from a baby, I mean?"

"It's an expression, Chase."

"I'll take that as a yes. Anyway, let's get this over with. I miss the beach. And the bar. And my man."

He smiled and yawned, stretching his arms to the ceiling, revealing a taught belly and a trimmed love trail. Needless to say, several of the male flight attendants passing by nearly fell over from craning their necks around so damned fast.

"Too easy," he whispered in between clenched teeth.

He nodded their way. The gaggle paused, stopping dead in their tracks. Brandon gave them his best come hither look. Naturally, they came hither.

"Aloha," they said, all three of them, all surfer-dude Hawaiians, only nellier.

"Aloha," we said, and introduced ourselves. They did the same.

Two of them were making connections. The third, David—thank goodness we didn't have to learn yet another Hawaiian name—was in for two days before he had to turn back around and head for the mainland. It was with him that Brandon hooked up with, quick as a wink.

The others dejectedly said their goodbyes, while the three of us made our way to a nearby lounge. "You guys just getting in?" he asked, slipping into a booth across from me and snug up against Brandon.

"Oh, um, yeah," we lied.

"Cool," he said. "Beautiful here. You'll love it."

Brandon ran his hand across our new friend's cheek. "Already do," he practically purred.

David probably blushed; it was hard to tell, what with his natural skin color and added tan. "Um, do you have any plans while you're here?" he asked us.

Brandon leaned in and cupped his hand over David's ear. David whispered something I couldn't hear in response. Something filthy, no doubt, because the blush managed its way through just the same, molten red and quickly spreading. Brandon sat back and gave me a conspiratorial wink. I replied by kicking him under the table, then I excused myself, three being more than a crowd in this particular instance.

I walked back outside, a warm breeze sending goosebumps up my arm, then sat down on a bench, watching the tourists stroll by: the new ones eager and pale, the ones returning home tan and glum. I felt a tap on my shoulder and jumped. It was one of the other flight attendants we'd just met, Peter, which was short for something long and tongue-twistery.

"This seat taken?" he asked.

"It is now," I replied, patting the area next to me.

"I've got an hour until my connection. I like sitting out here, watching the tourists, trying to guess where they're from."

"What about me then?" I asked.

He looked me up and down and side to side—not a little bit disconcerting, but still enjoyable, just the same. "Bay area, for sure." He scanned me again. "Within ten miles of the Castro."

"Wow," I said, duly impressed. "Do I really look that gay?"

"Well, it's more how you and your friend carry yourselves. Very cock-sure."

"Nice description," said I with a wink. He nudged in closer, his smooth, tan arm rubbing against my own.

My shorts began to tent. I hid my arousal with my hands and got down to business instead. I pointed to his lapel. "Aloha Airlines," I read. "I seem to recall hearing something about you guys in the news recently."

He grimaced. "One of our flight attendants. Caught smuggling drugs. Reportedly."

"Up his ass, if I'm not mistaken. Not a bad job, if you can get it. Did you know him?"

His smile returned. "We flew together on occasion. Lenny. Nice guy. Dumb as a brick, though." Poor Lenny. Not the most shining epithet.

"You'd have to be, to smuggle drugs, right?" I asked, locking eyes with him, brown on brown, the goosebumps returning to my arms before they traveled to other various body parts.

"Maybe. Though he didn't seem the type. We were at a party this one time. Lenny and his boyfriend show up. Lots of booze and pot and coke available. But I remember that they stayed clear."

The word boyfriend zoomed around my brain. "I remember reading that the boyfriend went missing after the arrest," I commented.

"Probably lying low. Nice guy, if I recall correctly. Cute Hawaiian. Never caught his name."

Bing-fucking-o! "And what about all the cash they found on him?"

He looked at me oddly. "Looks like you memorized that article."

I hesitated, collecting myself, and then replied, "Nah, just found it interesting, seeing as we were coming to Oahu at the same time it all occurred."

"Ah," he ahed, his pinky now curling over my pinky. "Yeah, I saw some of that cash. Lenny came from poor upbringings, like all of us. Guess he wanted to show off. But I don't think it was from drugs. Least that's not how he said he got it." Again, my ears perked up, along with certain other body parts. "I asked him about it, maybe like three weeks ago. He was flashing a big load of wampum. Said his boyfriend came into an inheritance and was sharing the wealth. Made sense. Lenny was a nice guy, and cute, personable. The kind of guy you'd want to make happy."

"Or maybe he was just impressionable, gullible, easily duped."

"Or maybe that, yes." He paused, his finger now pressing down into my crotch. "And speaking of heavy loads...um, want to see the employee lounge?"

I grinned and nodded, following him up and back inside. The lounge was in a rear corner, silver door, barely marked. We entered, trying to look inconspicuous. He led me through the place and into a small room. "Resting quarters," he commented. "Guests are strictly prohibited."

I leaned in and kissed him, his lips soft and wet, inviting. "And what am I?" I asked, breathing heavily into his mouth.

"Worth the risk," he replied, pulling me into him. "But we have to make it quick, sorry to say. Can't miss my plane."

Which was fine by me, as I didn't want to be missed either. In other words, we were naked in seconds, prone on the bed, me on top, pressing down hard on all that glorious dark flesh. My hand roamed his body, which was smooth as silk, caramel in color. I'd had my fair share of men before— well, maybe fair's not the optimal word—but Hawaiian was a new item on the menu. Needless to say, I made a glutton out of myself.

My mouth traverse his peaks and valleys, sucking on an engorged brown nipple, eliciting a groan and an arched back, not to mention a thick pick now prodding at my belly, vying for my attention. I quickly and eagerly relented and made my way south. A sticky bead of precome oozed up and over a wide mushroomed head, replete with its own fleshy turtle-necked collar. I took a lick and a hungry slurp, downing his fat woodie in one fell swoop.

"Oh yeah, suck it, dude," he moaned, pushing my head down and around it as a blissful tear trailed down my cheek.

He smelled of sweat and passion fruit soap, tropical and enticing, drawing my mouth from his cock to his heavy balls and pink, puckered hole.

"Bottoms up," I quipped, raising his legs in the air, allowing my mouth free range across his perfect ass. I slapped it, the sound pinging around the small enclosure. Then my tongue wound rings around his hole, zooming ever inward before diving in. Again, he moaned, bucking his butt into my face as he stroked his hefty prick.

"Yeah, fucking eat it, man," he rasped as I tongue-fucked him, all the while stroking my own pulsing tool.

Sadly, our encounter was short-lived. His flight was announced, the voice booming overhead. He stroked lightning fast. I hopped up between his legs, my own dick just above his, my hand matching him stroke for eager stroke.

"Shoot it, dude," I told him—and he did. His cock gushed, spewing a hefty load onto his belly and chest, followed quickly by three smaller ones. His body squirmed and writhed atop the sheets as he did so, his breath ragged as he moaned contentedly. And then my cock shot, my hot come joining his, splattering on his stomach until his skin went from tan to white.

"Fuck," I groaned long and low and deep as the come kept, well, coming.

"Fuck," he echoed, watching the spectacle.

With the last quivers and quakes and trickles, I stared down at our happy mess. "Aloha," I whispered.

"Why aloha?" he asked. "That means hello and goodbye."

"Exactly. That's about all we got."

He wiped his fingers through the sticky puddle we'd made. "Not all we got," he said, quickly hopping up and wiping himself off before giving me a soulful kiss and a wink.

We grabbed our clothes in a hurry, making sure he'd have enough time to get dressed and run to the sink. He went left, I went right—right, that is, into, Brandon, who was exiting the room next to ours.

He sniffed the air around me. "Better than a bathroom, I suppose," he commented, hurrying us out of the lounge.

"Did you find out anything?" I asked.

"Other than the fact that you're a slut? What would poor Will say?"

My stomach sank. Yes, we'd only known each other, for all practical purposes, for a few days, but still, it felt like cheating. Sort of. I mean, it was for a good cause. "It was for a good cause," I asserted.

He grinned and led us outside. "Far be it from me to cast the first stone, Chase."

"Plus," I added, assuaging my guilt. "I found out plenty."

I quickly filled him in on the Hawaiian boyfriend proof and the money alibi. He'd found out similar bits of information. Plus, one more: "The boyfriend drove a limo."

"Oh fuck," I said, this time not in delight.

"Indeed," he agreed. "An odd coincidence."

"Did your, um, informant say it was Liko?"

Brandon shook his head. "He didn't remember the name. Still, it seems unlikely that it wasn't Liko, what with all his apparent tie-ins with everything. Which also means that Lenny, as suspected, probably was professing his innocence for Liko's sake and not our own. Which also makes me think that he didn't know that his boyfriend was anything but a limo driver."

I shook my head and sat down on a bench outside. "Okay,

so Lenny, if he was innocent, which we're still assuming he was, was either not smuggling drugs, or, if he was, was duped into it by, more than likely, his boyfriend, which we're pretty certain was Liko. Meanwhile, Makani, the jailed dealer, claims that the so-called innocent and now-deceased Lenny was his smuggler, despite what we think."

"Right," Brandon agreed, sitting down next to me. "Plus, the press and the police think that the boyfriend is our missing pimp, Jed, not the aforementioned Liko. Which makes me wonder how someone who we think is so innocent could've been dating two such really bad men."

"Unless he was as stupid as everyone seems to think he was," I offered. "In which case, he was just slutty and very unlucky in love."

"This coming from the man who's slept with two men in three days."

I groaned. "Stop reminding me, please."

He grinned and raised his hand to hail a passing cab. "Fine," he said as she hopped up and climbed inside. "But when you hit three in four, it'll be official."

"What will be?" I asked, getting in behind him before slamming the door shut.

"You'll be an even bigger slut than I am."

To which I replied, "That would take seven in five, my friend."

He smiled, his mind trailing off to Lord knew where. "Ah," he sighed. "Yes, it would indeed."

***

We made it back to our hotel, alive, in one piece, and very much in need of a drink. We changed into our swim trunks— one knee-length, the other ball-length—and met the guys along our lovely stretch of beach. They looked entirely too relaxed.

"Having fun?" I asked, their lids briefly popping open to acknowledge our presence.

"How did the Hardly boys do?" Will asked as our chairs were placed on either side of them.

We ordered drinks first, then filled them in. Minus, of course, the sex part. Will shook his head from side to side and asked if Brandon and I wanted to take a walk?

Once out of Koni's earshot, we continued the conversation. "Well," Will said, "that's it then; you guys are out of all this. Pimps and murderers and drug dealers mean you two are back on vacation and I'm off mine."

"No way," Brandon whined. "I was promised some shopping and I'm going shopping!"

"So, go shopping," Will replied, his hand finding my own, making me feel guilty as sin, yet again.

"But if we can't go undercover, I won't need all the girly clothes," he complained with a pout.

"So, go buy boyly clothes instead," Will suggested with a heavy sigh.

"Those I already have," he retorted, arms petulantly over chest.

"Plenty of," I added.

"Exactly," Brandon re-added.

Will looked at the two of us and, once again, sighed, this time adding a shake of his head. "If it were anyone else, I'd pull out my badge and pull rank, but I know that won't work on the two of you."

"Meaning?" I asked.

"Meaning," he replied, "as soon as my back is turned, you two will be shopping and going undercover in the back of Liko's limo."

Brandon giggled. "Just don't turn your back in the bathroom; Chase seems to have a penchant for them these days."

I scowled at him, and said to Will, "Yes, you're probably right. So, let us go shopping and go undercover, find out what the police seem to have missed about Liko, and then we're out of this. Promise." I squeezed his hand until he relented. As if he had a choice, really.

"Fine, but you're being followed the entire time. Then that's it. Deal?" he said, less than enthusiastically.

"Deal," we both said, our fingers crossed behind our backs.

We returned to our chairs to find that our drinks had arrived. We chugged a round and ordered another. The tension began to melt away. Though, clearly, we hadn't won anything with that deal back there. Lenny was still dead and Jed was still missing, plus we had a new bad guy to contend with. And, if we discovered nothing, Will would be on the case solo, leaving me worrying for the rest of our vacation—it was a lose-lose situation if ever there was one.

There was a bright side, however. After a couple of hours of tanning and swimming, not to mention boy-ogling and a healthy lunch, much of it liquory, we were off on our shopping adventure.

When Koni started to follow us, we turned around with our best crossing guard stop-stance. "Where do you think you're going?" Brandon asked.

"Um, dress shopping, I suppose?" he replied. That much we'd filled him in on.

"Then you suppose wrong," he was told.

"Oh, come on," he protested. "I'll look far better in a skirt than you two old timers."

Will coughed. "Um, you're not winning any points, kid," he said.

"Oh, I mean, you'll need someone to tell you how great you look," he amended with.

"Better," Will said with a nod.

I looked at Brandon for some help, and got none. "Fine." I said. "But no dresses for you. Talk about corrupting a minor."

"As if I wasn't corrupted enough already," he wisecracked, now walking by our side. "What's one more vice in the greater scheme of things, anyway?"

"Shopping's an addiction, kid," Brandon told him. "Better to nip it in the bud now."

"What's a bud, dude? That like a craw?"

Will stopped in his tracks. "Oh God, I don't think I can take a whole afternoon of this. I'm going back to the beach. You, um, boys have fun shopping." He turned and walked away, shouting over his shoulder, "And stay out of trouble."

"Were it that easy," Brandon groaned, leading the way down Kalakaua Avenue, past the Outrigger Waikiki, the Cheesecake Factory—yum!—and on our way to shopping nirvana.

Waikiki is the Edenic version of Rodeo Drive, without all the plastic, bleached-blonde bimbettes. In just a one mile stretch of sidewalk, there's Fendi, Salvatore Ferragamo, bebe, Kate Spade, Bvlgari, Cartier, Juicy Couture, and Rolex, and all at ridiculously marked up prices. It was at moments such as these that Brandon's obscene wealth truly came in handy. Otherwise, we'd be back at the International Marketplace, trying on endless synthetic fibers and looking utterly dowdy.

We headed into Hermes first. If we had to go undercover, fuck it if we were going to be wearing granny hats over our heads. We entered the well-air-conditioned store, and my adrenalin started to flow. All the colors. All the variety. All the handsome queer store clerks. Be still my heart—and hard-on.

It was then we realized we were no longer in San Francisco. Three guys, even three obviously gay guys such as ourselves, couldn't shop for lady's scarves without drawing attention to ourselves. Surprisingly, it was Koni who came to our rescue.

"Aloha," he said to the cutest of the worker drones. "We need a birthday gift for our mother."

He coughed. "You three are, um, related?"

Without missing a beat, he replied, "Step-brothers."

That elicited a smile. "And what exactly would your mother like?"

Koni looked around the store. "Looks like you've got a lot of scarves."

The clerk looked around as well. "Seems the case, yes. Would you care to see some, young man?"

"Yes, please," came the reply, politely as possible, which was quickly followed by a whispered, "Asshole," when the guy was out of earshot.

Brandon snickered and walked up to the counter, while we followed close behind. Seconds later, the man emerged from the back, carrying an armful of scarves, each more beautiful than the next. A trickle of expectant sweat cascaded down my brow, despite the cool store climate.

"Easy, Chase," Brandon cautioned. "They're only scarves." I kicked him in the foot. He gritted his teeth and apologized. "Sorry, I should've known better."

"So," the salesman asked, "what does your mother like?"

We each pulled out our favorites, all of them quite different. "She's got eclectic tastes," I informed. "Mind if we try them on, to get a better feel for what would look best? On her, I mean."

He shrugged. "Suit yourselves." Clearly, we weren't fooling anybody.

"Beautiful," I said, looking at Brandon.

"Beautiful," he repeated, looking at me.

"Different," Koni mustered, looking at the both of us. "This may take some getting used to."

Brandon whispered in his ear, "Don't get used to it, kid. For now, you're only along for the ride. The limo trip is out of the question."

He frowned. "But I'm still getting the scarf, right?" he whispered back.

Brandon sighed and looked back at the clerk. "Wrap 'em up; we'll take all three."

Well now, this part of the story can go on for hours, obviously. The long and the short of it, however, is that the same scenario played itself out repeatedly from store to store, each one staffed, to our good fortune, with one gay man after the next, until we were sufficiently weighed down with numerous sets of sunglasses, shoes, sandals, stockings, bras (silk and frilly), panties (ditto), blouses, skirts, much-needed makeup, and, lastly, and new for the two of us, sarongs.

"All the locals wear them," Koni informed. "And, of course, the Japanese."

We chose three, each covered in floral patterns of different shades. They were form-fitting and strangely comfortable. Luckily, we were wearing them at the time when we spotted the limo pulling up in front.

"Liko," I said, in shock, as I ducked behind a mannequin.

Brandon and Koni shot in behind me. "Now what?" Brandon asked, peaking over my shoulder.

Liko was dropping someone off, someone coming into our shop. "Fuck," I whispered. "He's going to wait for her." Meaning, we were trapped.

"I have an idea," Koni whispered back. "Follow me."

Brandon and I looked at each other and shrugged. "Kids got more gray matter than the two of us combined," Brandon reasoned.

"Good point," I readily agreed, following our new leader.

We all squished into a fitting room. "Get dressed," he told us. "This will work out in our favor."

We stared at him, dumbfounded. "Huh?" I managed.

"Just do it," he told us, slipping on some sandals and one of the scarves and sunglasses. Brandon applied the makeup. That much we had experience in. With age comes wisdom, after all. And, sadly, frown lines.

We did as he had said, soon looking like three, well, sisters. Then, when none of the store employees were looking, we slipped out. Liko was leaning against his limo, barely paying us any heed. This I thought was a good thing. Escape, however, was not what Koni had in mind when he told us he had an idea.

"Excuse me," he said, in his best female voice, "is this limo taken?"

Liko looked up at us three women. "Sorry, ladies, I'm waiting for someone."

"Oh, such a shame. We've been shopping all day and can't walk another step. We'd certainly appreciate a ride," he/she explained, to my utter consternation.

It was then that Brandon joined in the plan. He reached into his brand-new Prada purse and pulled out his brand-new Prada wallet. The hundred-dollar bill caught the driver's attention. Its twin got the door opened for us. The poor woman inside the shop would have to find a new ride home.

We piled on in, our bags to the far end of the limo, our asses to the other end. My heart beat out a furious staccato rhythm in my chest. Koni turned on the speakers so that Liko could hear us. "To the Ohana," he told him, quickly turning off the speakers. Then he whispered to us, "It's a twenty-minute drive. We have that much time to get information out of him. Tag, you're it." Which meant it was our turn on stage.

"What should we ask him?" I whispered to Brandon.

He paused, thinking about it for a minute. "We're trying to find his connection to a missing pimp, an incarcerated drug dealer, and a murdered drug smuggler, right?"

We nodded. "Right," I replied. "None of which is going to be easy to work into polite conversation."

Fortunately, it was Liko who started the ball rolling. He knocked on the pane of glass that separated us. We turned the speakers back on. "There's an accident on Highway 1; I'll need to take a slightly longer route."

"No problem," said Brandon. "We're not expected for another half hour."

"Your husbands are waiting for you?" he asked.

"No, our, well, clients," replied Brandon. I stared at him in total confusion. "They paid for our shopping trip."

"You ladies are from here?" we were asked.

"Currently, yes," Brandon told him. "Working girls."

"Really? What kind of work are you in?"

"Think about it," Brandon said. "Three attractive women on their way to a tourist hotel. Bags full of merchandise we can't afford. Not like we're selling Amway products."

He didn't reply, not right away. Then, "Funny, I've never seen you three around before."

"We transferred. From Maui," I said. "Better, um, shopping here."

He laughed. "Yes, I can see that." Again, he paused, the

seconds ticking by like hours. "Just out of curiosity," he eventually said, "who do you work for?"

"We're solo artists," Brandon quickly told him, a look of terror mixed with pride on his heavily made-up face.

For some reason, the conversation ended at that point. Liko didn't respond to Brandon, and we didn't know what else to say. The ball had been tossed, but not returned.

At least not just yet.

We arrived at the Ohana a short while later. The limo pulled into a drive-up, and Liko got out, opening the door for us. Thankfully, he was still smiling. Our own smiles, however, were difficult to produce. "A pleasure, ladies," he said, slightly bowing as he waited for us to exit.

"Thank you again, um…"

"Liko," he said, shaking each of our hands. "And you are…"

"Judy," I said.

"Liza," Brandon said.

Koni paused. "Madonna," he said. "Catholic mother, you see."

A card was proffered. I looked at it. Just a phone number, nothing more. "In case we need a ride later?" I asked.

He shook his head sideways. "Nope, guess again."

He was making us state the obvious, just in case he was mistaken about us, I figured. "Employment opportunities?" I asked.

"Let's just say I might be able to guide work your way," he said, finishing the conversation by returning to his driver's seat. With a nod and smile, he cranked the engine. Rolling down the window, he added, "Have a good day at work, ladies." And with that, he was off.

Koni poked us in the ribs. "Gee, that was fun. Welcome to my world, ladies."

In all the confusion, I hadn't realized that he'd gone from being a male prostitute to a female one, all in the blink of a newly-placed eyelash. "Fun is not the word for it," I said glumly, grabbing my bags as I walked over to a bench.

My cohorts followed and joined me. "Look on the bright side," Brandon said. "We were right about Liko, at least. He's clearly mixed up in all this somehow. I mean, he wasn't offering us limo work, you know."

I grinned, despite the dire circumstances. "Madonna?" I asked our young friend.

"I don't look like a Cher," he informed.

"Trust me," I said. "You don't look like a Madonna either."

Brandon patted his head. "I don't know, maybe a little bit around the eyes."

Koni grinned. "See. And now we're hot on the trail."

The grin faltered. "Nuh-uh. We promised Will. One recognizance mission, and then we turn it over to the police. Besides, he was right; Lenny was murdered and Jed is missing— for a good reason, I'm sure. Now, we have an evil limo driver to contend with. It's all too much to handle, even for us."

I looked to Brandon for back-up. He sighed. "Yep, I'm afraid he—um, she—is right, kid. Time to turn this over to the professionals."

"You forget," he said. "I am a professional."

Sadly, it was something I hadn't forgotten. "For now, kid," I told him, "you're a professional tour guide. What's there to see around here?"

"You're joking, right?" he asked.

"Do I look like I'm joking?" Koni replied by pointing to my scarf, my sunglasses, and my sarong. "Oh yeah, sorry."

He laughed. "Look way down the street, cute dudette."

"Water, boats, tourists. So what?"

He shook his head. "Um, that's Pearl Harbor."

I looked up and squinted. "Ah. Well then, lead on."

Okay, per the pamphlet we picked up, Pearl Harbor and the USS Arizona Memorial are top Hawaiian tourist destinations, with over one and a half million visitors a year. Considering the sweltering heat, our recent sarong attire, and our newly acquired and now heavy purchases, we opted for a quick run-through. Needless to say, the Arizona Memorial is a sobering experience—and you know how much we hate being sober. Standing over a grave site where over a thousand men lost their lives is not at all enjoyable, especially since we were there as a result of Lenny losing his.

***

After our brief tour, we changed out of our disguises and hopped a cab back to our hotel. The sun began its decent, and the tourists were amassing along the beach. We ran upstairs and dropped off all the stuff we wouldn't theoretically be needing anymore, as we'd apparently accomplished our mission without even trying. Un-fucking-believable.

"Let's go down and watch the sunset," I suggested morosely, looking down at our wasted extravagances.

"Agreed," Brandon agreed, clearly thinking the same thought.

We made it as the sun hit the horizon, casting the clouds in a warm pink glow and turning the surf a golden orange. The air was warm, smelling sweet, as I raced to our familiar stretch of beach. Will was waiting for us, a smile growing wide on his handsome face. My heart skipped a beat at the sight of him. All was right in the universe again. Well, my universe, at any rate.

"How was the shopping?" he asked. "You guys were gone forever."

"Long story. Need sustenance," I managed, plopping down on the chairs he had waiting for us.

One fruity yet strong cocktail later, and we filled him in. "Wow," he said. "You did get a lot accomplished. Guess the ball's in the police's court now. I've also got some news, but you're not going to like it."

"Wait," I said, my hand up high. "I think another drink is called for then." Half-way through it, I told him, "Okay, spill it."

His smile went south. He looked to the ocean, his eyes not focusing. "Koni's friend, Buck," he said. My heart sank toward the cooling sand, preparing for the worst—and getting it in spades. "They found him this morning, floating in the Ala Wai Canal."

"Fuck," Koni cursed, his voice barely above a whisper.

"Those cameras around the house in the North Shore probably caught my image. Pass that around to enough places, and someone probably saw Buck talking to us the other night. Not too difficult to put two and two together," Will explained. "Guess the prior inhabitants really don't want to be found."

I looked over at Koni. His eyes were red and his nose was running. "Not your fault, kid," I told him.

"Yes, it is, and you know it is," he said—and I did. "We gotta find the guys that did this and make them pay."

"The police need to find them," I corrected. "We'll tell them about Liko and Jed, and let them handle it from here on out."

He shook his head from side to side. "The police don't give a fuck about some dead street trash and a no-good pimp."

I looked over at Will, knowing we were right to keep Koni in the dark about who he was and what he did for a living; there'd be no trust there, neither in him nor us. "It's been a long day, kid. Let's get some dinner and talk about this tomorrow, when our heads are clearer," I tried, rubbing his back with the palm of my hand.

He nodded, choking back the tears. "Fine, but don't forget that I know a lot of people like Buck, and I bet one of them knows where Jed is. The police could take forever to find him; I doubt it would take me all that long."

Again, I looked to Will, who gave me an almost imperceptible shrug. Koni was probably right, but it was better to be safe than sorry. In any case, I let it go. There was no point in arguing with him, not just yet. Instead, we walked back onto the beach and to the hotel next to ours, the Outrigger Waikiki.

"Is this Duke's restaurant any good?" I asked Koni. He nodded silently, his revenge-filled mind still obviously plotting. "Duke's it is then," I said, trying my best to sound upbeat. Trying, that is, and failing, miserably.

The restaurant was open on the beach side, all dark wood, comfortable, with pictures of the great Duke Kahanamoku everywhere. We walked to the front of the place and were quickly seated. The food was exceptional, the view of the darkening sky spectacular; the mood, however, was subdued. We were all thinking the same thoughts, none of them good. We ate our meals with little to say—free advertising, though: try the Hula Pie! —and then we finished and went back to our hotel. Koni didn't join the three of us on the veranda's rocking chairs; instead, he went upstairs and went to bed.

"Poor guy," Brandon said with a sigh. "I understand the guilt he must be feeling."

Will also sighed knowingly. "The life these street kids lead, it's a wonder any of them survives, even out here in paradise."

I sent my chair rocking as I stared out at the sidewalk, the tourists strolling by, oblivious to the nasty surrounding underbelly we'd recently come into contact with. "What do we do now?" I asked.

"I'll stop over at the substation on the way back to my hotel, tell them about our connection to Buck and Jed, see if they'll let me interview Makani over at the prison. Maybe he can shed some light on everything, though it seems unlikely. Plus, we still don't know how his boss was caught. Maybe that too will get explained. I'll come back over in the morning and fill you both in. Beyond that, take the kid snorkeling or something. Keep his mind off things. You three are officially no longer on the case. That's an order."

"Aye, aye, captain," I said, saluting him.

"With pleasure," Brandon added.

He left a short while later, a quick peck on my cheek and a squeeze of my hand. Brandon and I didn't last much beyond that. It had been a long and stressful afternoon, and we were exhausted, too pooped to pop, as it were. We promised ourselves a bad-thought-free day for tomorrow. No drag, no investigative work, no death and destruction.

We went to bed and fell fast asleep, awaking to a bright

perfect morning. I walked to our balcony and watched the surf roll in. The water, sapphire blue, was calm, reflecting the light off the already hot sun. The surfers had begun to amass further out, where the waves lifted them up and rode them to shore. I breathed in deeply, smelling the fresh air, the salty breeze, the aroma of breakfast just barely noticeable from far down below. Brandon soon joined me, somehow with cool mimosas in his hand, one for him, one for me. The door to the balcony next to ours opened; Koni walked out in just his boxers, his lean, hard body rippling as he yawned.

"Morning," he said. "It's a beautiful day in the neighborhood."

I grinned. "Perfect day for snorkeling, huh?"

He brightened even further. "Good day for it."

It would've been. Oh man, it would've been.

Cue that sinister music again. So fucking sorry.

We ordered breakfast and ate it on our balcony, watching the banyan tree come to life with innumerable small birds. All the while, I waited for Will to show up or to call, as promised. We finished our food, our mimosas, and a pot of coffee—and still no sign of him. The minutes ticked by. My heart began to beat faster. Something was wrong. I felt it in my bones. We expected him early, and early it was no longer.

"He'll be here soon," Brandon tried, as comforting as possible.

"I know, I know," I said. "Probably just sleeping in." I called his cell phone. There was no response. I tried twice more. Still nothing.

When ten rolled around to eleven, I knew he was in some sort of trouble.

We got dressed, the phone silent, no knocks on our door. My stomach filled with knots. "Something's not right," I eventually said to my friends.

"Nope," Koni agreed. "But what do we do?"

"Stay here. I promise, I'll be right back."

I ran outside and down to the lobby, jogging to the

substation a short distance away. The place was quiet, the bad guys still sleeping or in jail. I walked up to the counter and asked for an officer. One appeared a short while later, Sergeant Beles. I told him who I was and asked if he'd heard anything from Will.

He knew who Will was, but said he hadn't seen him for two days. I told him that Will came to the substation at about nine the night before. The sergeant flipped through a sign-in book, which they kept for anyone that came through. "Sorry, no. No record of his visit. You sure he was on his way here?"

I told him everything I knew. He shook his head, clearly disturbed. "I'll call the night-desk officer, Sergeant Sloan. If your agent friend was here, he'll be able to confirm it."

The sergeant left to go to his desk, leaving me alone in the sitting area. My heart madly pumped all the while. I was unable to swallow, to think clearly. I waited, and waited some more. Beles returned, his head shaking from side to side. "Sorry, he was never here."

"Fuck," I moaned. "That means he didn't make it. They know what he looks like. He was at Jed's hideout. There were cameras there. They picked him up. I know it."

I started to hyperventilate. The room began to spin. Will was gone. Captured. Possibly dead. The lights overhead grew dim, dimmer still.

Then everything went suddenly and completely black.

And that cued music reached its crescendo.

☀ REINFORCEMENTS CALLED ☀

I awoke in my bed. The shades were drawn, the room cast in pale light. "Must've been a bad dream," I said to myself, sitting up on my elbows with a mighty yawn.

"'Fraid not," came the startling reply from off to my right. It was Brandon. "You were gone a long time, so I came looking for you. You blacked out. The sergeant told me everything. He'll be in touch when they find Will."

I groaned. "If."

"They'll find him. Not good politics to let a federal agent go missing. Plus, he'll identify himself to his captors. No one wants that shit on their shoulders. They'll probably release him when they find out they've kidnapped someone with the F.B.I."

"Or bury him under twenty tons of beach sand," I countered with, a heavy frown now on my face.

"Nah, Will's a bright guy, sleeping with you the one exception. He'll be fine."

"Gee, thanks. I think." I paused, trying to collect my thoughts, scattered as they now were. I looked up at him. "What are we gonna do next?"

He smiled and rubbed my back. "Smart thing or typical-us stupid thing?"

"Lay both of them on me, just to be on the safe side."

"Yeah," he said. "That's what I thought you'd say. The smart thing, obviously, would be to let the police handle this. But, seeing as Lenny and Buck are both dead, and Jed is still missing, maybe that's not the best option."

"Meaning," I interrupted, "they need the help of two part-time drag divas and a street-wise prostitute/drug dealer?"

"Without their knowledge, of course. Pro bono work, let's just say."

"Of course."

He forced a laugh. "Hey, chin up, good buddy. We have several points in our favor."

"Such as?" I asked.

"Such as: they only ever saw Will, not us; we have fabulous new undercover clothes; we now have an in with Liko, who only knows our alter-egos; Koni has other street connections, who in the future will only know our alter-egos; and we have a secret weapon."

As he spoke, I raised a finger for each positive item. When he reached number five, my pinky only went up half way. "Huh? What secret weapon is that? Your sluttiness only ever helps you."

He punched me in the arm—so much for his tender side. "We have a secret weapon, dear Chase, and she's already on her way here."

I gulped. "You mean...you mean, my mom is coming?"

Again, he punched me. "No, idiot. Briana is coming. I called her as soon as we made it back here with your heavy, lifeless ass in tow. Between the three of us, we should have enough functioning brain cells to solve this puppy."

Ah, Briana. Brandon's sister. Just as conniving, ruthless, and beautiful. Brains to Brandon's brawn.

Meaning Briana, the smartest of our trio, not to mention soberest (mostly), was probably a smart option. Plus, if anyone could take care of themselves, not to mention us, it was definitely her. So, were we any safer? No. Comforted? Yes. Anyway, I couldn't argue; she was already miles over the ocean.

I hazarded a smile. "Good thinking," I told him. "If we're in this thing up to her asses, might as well include hers; it's bigger by far."

"Better hope she doesn't hear you say that," he cautioned.

"Point taken." Yes, we were duly and rightfully terrified of her. In any case, I looked at the clock; it was already two o'clock. It would take Briana a good five hours to reach us. "What do we do until she gets here?"

"If you're up for it, we promised the kid some snorkeling. I think we should at least give the police one day to do their best, anyway. Tomorrow, if Will doesn't turn up, and I'm sure he will, then we'll be in full force and devise a plan."

My stomach did a back-flip and then a routine on the uneven bars. How could I go enjoy myself when Will was missing? Then again, waiting by the phone, knowing it probably wouldn't ring, would be excruciating. And, truth be told, a small part of me believed what Brandon had said. Who would hold or kill a federal agent? These guys were bad, but probably not stupid.

"Fine, get the kid and let's go," I told him, forcing a pained smile.

"He's waiting next-door. I already arranged for a taxi. No fucking limos. The cab driver is outside," he informed, handing me a concealed cocktail.

Again, I grinned. "Speaking of brain cells, I think you used the rest of yours up during the last two hours."

"Tell me about it," he said, ushering me out the door. "I'm running on gin-soaked fumes at this point."

***

The three of us hopped inside the waiting taxi. Koni snuggled up to me. "Good to see you up and Adam, cute dude," he said.

"Thanks," I replied, mussing up his hair. "Now, let's hope the fish our ready for us."

To which Brandon promptly added, "Let's hope we're ready for us. I've never been snorkeling before. And muscles sink. You're just lucky you've got that big, old fat head of yours; you should float nicely."

I leaned over and socked him one in the arm. He reached over and smacked me upside the head. Koni sighed. "What the fuck have I gotten myself into? You're supposed to be the adults here."

"Says who?" Brandon asked.

"Yeah," I agreed. "Says who?"

We traveled the rest of the way in silence. It was a ten-mile ride to Hanauma Bay, along a tranquil highway, green mountains in the distance, beautiful homes on all sides. Arriving here takes your very breath away, the natural beauty so dazzling as to be other-worldly, especially since the bay was formed in an ancient volcanic crater, making it that much more stupendous to experience. Now a nature reserve, I'd read, the number of daily visitors is limited, the purpose more educational, preservation a key focus.

That being said, we were there to take our minds off of things, however temporarily. And education had never been high on our list of priorities. Call me shallow, but we were, after all, snorkeling in a relatively non-deep bay, so the description would be appropriate. In any case, we rented our gear, watched the safety video, and were off.

The water was warm, the bay a brilliant blue, shimmering in the mid-afternoon sun. Honu heads bobbed up not twenty feet out, and just below the surface swam trumpet fish, angel fish, and umuhumunukunukuapuaa—the Hawaiian state fish and international tongue-twister—plus dozens of other varieties of tropical fish, all in abundant colors and shapes, lurching in and out of the coral, some avoiding us, others curious and friendly, swimming by as if we were one of them.

It was, despite everything, an incredible day; though, of course, completely impossible to enjoy. Oh sure, for the sake of my companions, I put on a brave face, as I'm sure they did for me, but inside I was a bloody mess. Thoughts of Will chained in a room somewhere, or worse, filled my water-logged brain.

When we'd gotten our fill, both of the fish and the water they shat in, we packed up our stuff and watched the sunset from along a ridge overlooking the bay, the sun sinking rapidly in a fiery blaze, turning the sky a dusky pink. It was then that our brief reverie was interrupted by the ringing of my cell phone.

"Uh oh," I said, my heart pounding beneath my sunburnt chest. Then I looked at my cell's screen. "It's Will," I squeaked out in shock and profound disbelief.

He talked rapidly and in a hushed whisper I could barely hear. The conversation was one-sided and brief. The phone went dead, and that madly pounding heart of mine went kaboom.

"What happened? Where is he?" shouted Brandon.

I looked at him and then at Koni, and realized I still had to watch what I said. "They picked him up outside the hotel. Four masked men. They think he works for whoever turned in Makani and his boss, and is now trying to get to Jed, his captor. And, for sure, someone is after Jed. He's pretty certain that he convinced them that it isn't him. Still, either we find this person or they kill him. A trade off, Will said. And no going to the cops. He has no clue where they took him to, and the place has cameras everywhere. If they see any suspicious cars driving around, he's dead. And he's also fairly certain they have informants on the force, meaning there's no one we can trust."

"But we know that Liko is the bad guy, now," piped in Brandon. "Let's just trade him and be done with it."

I nodded. "Yes, that's what we think, but we don't know it for sure. Or, for that matter, why Liko would be looking for Jed. Or why he'd turn in Makani's boss. Plus, how do we get Liko to a secret hideout in exchange for Will, if it ever comes to that?"

"So, what do we do?" Koni asked.

"Will said we had three days to turn something up. He'll call me then with his whereabouts," I replied, my lungs and face now burning. "We bring Jed what he wants, he lets Will go."

"Meaning, we still need to go undercover." Brandon sighed. "This time with no alternative back-up."

I nodded. "Looks that way. Except there is one alternative."

"What's that?" Brandon asked.

I forced a brief yet knowing smile. "Our secret weapon fast

approaches."

"Ah," he ahed, the same smile appearing.

"This chick is that good?" Koni asked. "She some kind of superhero or something?"

"Or something," we both answered.

We left shortly after that, Koni walking in front as he looked to hail us a cab. Which is when Brandon leaned in to whisper in my ear, "Why didn't Will tell these kidnappers who he really was?"

To which I whispered back, "Trump card. Just in case."

"Just in case we don't get them what they want?"

I gulped and nodded. "But we will, dear Brandon. We will."

"Plus, there is a bright side to all this," he said, his arm tight around my shoulder.

"Which is?" I asked, my hand around his waist.

"Well, now we get to wear all those great new outfits we bought."

"Always the eternal optimist," I quipped.

"My glass, as you often say, is half full, Chase," he quipped back.

"Then let's get back to the hotel and fill it up completely. My optimism tank is running on empty."

"Thank goodness it runs on alcohol," he said, sidling into the cab that had pulled up.

"Amen for that, Brandon. Amen for that."

***

Briana arrived in the early evening, her cab pulling up to the Moana as we waited for her on the veranda. She smiled as she approached, her numerous suitcases trailing behind her, ass swaying like the palms overhead.

"What, no drink?" she asked, right off the bat.

Good Boy Scouts that we were, I handed her the one we had waiting. "As if," I replied.

She laughed. "I should've known better." She downed her

drink and craned her neck from side to side. "Nice digs. Seems like we're moving up in the world."

"Appears as such," Brandon agreed. "Minus the couple of murders, a kidnapping, and Chase's various shenanigans in certain men's bathrooms."

The smile left her face. "My room better be nice."

"Beautiful," he assured. "And semi-private."

She shook her head. "Nuh-uh. I ain't no truck driver. Meaning, I don't do semis."

"Fine," I quickly agreed. "Koni can sleep on our pull-out. You can have my room."

We introduced our ward to our frequent accomplice. "My condolences, kid," she said. "They don't play nice."

"So I've discovered," he agreed, his head bobbing up and down.

The bellhops grabbed her luggage and brought it up to her room. She sat in a rocking chair and breathed in deeply. "Nice place to retire to," she sighed.

Brandon and I laughed. Three people sharing one twisted brain. Scary. Then we filled her in on all the gory details. "Not good," I ended with.

"Nope. But seemingly par for the course. Bad news follows you two like flies to shit."

I grimaced. "Um, how about like limes to a daiquiri? Nicer imagery."

"Either way you put it, it sounds like you're in it up to your ears," she said.

"Then we'll stick with the daiquiri scenario. A much nicer way to go, if you ask me," Brandon chimed in with.

Briana laughed, her cheeks bursting forth a rosy red. "God, I missed you two. Luckily, I had a vacation coming to me at work. In other words, in between sleuthing, they'll be some pampering. Deal?"

"Do we have a choice?" I asked.

"Um, that would be a no. Now, tell me again everything you know so far, just in case you missed something?" she commanded, which we then promptly did. She paused when we were through, mulling it all over, and then started with, "So, if we go under the assumption that Lenny was innocent, then we can safely assume that he was set up for some reason. But why set up an innocent man?"

"To throw the police off the trail of the not-so-innocent?" I hazarded.

"Sounds reasonable," she replied. "The authorities would have both a dealer and a smuggler in custody, and if that smuggler wasn't really a smuggler, then the supplier would be safe, as would, in theory, the dealer's boss. Makani would get a reduced sentence and his cohorts would be in the clear. And Lenny would be a proverbial dead-end." We groaned at her choice of words. "Sorry, my bad," she apologized, and then continued with, "So, that leave's two related questions: who set up Lenny and who did in fact turn in Makani's boss, after the fact?"

Koni replied with, "I vote for Liko. Maybe the boyfriends weren't getting along."

Briana shook her head. "Maybe, maybe not. For one, it was Makani who turned Lenny in. I don't see a connection yet between Liko and Makani, nor do I see how Liko could've engineered that scenario. Plus, if we're going with the boyfriend thing, then it could've just as easily been Jed that did the setting up. After all, Lenny lived with Jed, not Liko. Seems to me, he had better access to Lenny. And, if it was one of the two boyfriends, I doubt they set him up over a lover's spat. My guess, there's some higher power involved in all this. Someone we don't yet know about."

Her saying this set something off in my head, the light bulb suddenly flicking on, however dim it was. "Wait," I said, snapping my fingers. "Will said that he thought the police were involved. If anyone had the power to set this whole mess up, it was them." And that set us to groaning, yet again.

"Fuck," Brandon swore. "If that's the case, then our job just got a whole lot more difficult. How do we investigate a police connection?"

Briana again gave her sage opinion. "For now, let's table that one. It's conjecture at this point anyway and probably way out of our league. I say we go to the prison and try to get in to see both Makani and his boss. If there's a missing piece to the puzzle, maybe they can provide it."

"Count me out," said Koni. "Me and prisons don't mix. Plus, you have more problems to contend with than their agreeing to talk to you."

"Such as?" I asked.

"Such as, only family members and legal counsel allowed. Plus, we don't know the name of Makani's boss. Even I don't know that."

"No," I corrected him, "we didn't know the name when we started all this. Maybe it's made the papers since then. And, I bet, the names of their attorneys have probably been reported by now, too. If we can't get in to see the culprits, then maybe their representation is the next best thing."

It was Koni who shook his cute, little head this time around. "But why in the world would an attorney tell us anything? What about client confidentiality, and all that garbage? Isn't what you're proposing illegal and immoral?"

We three nodded and smiled. "Of course, kid," I said. "But those are our specialties."

"Especially the immoral thing," Brandon added.

"Especially," Briana seconded.

"Ah," Koni ahed. "One of you is going to seduce the answers out of them."

"Piece of cake," Brandon said with a snap of his fingers.

"Oh," Briana said. "That reminds me, I'm starving. How about some room service and Internet access? Two birds, one stone."

She led the way, with Koni and me in the rear. "Wow," he whispered in my ear, "she really is like a superhero."

"Oh, hell yeah," I whispered back. "Or supervillain. Just depends on her mood. Meaning, don't piss her off. And if you do, warn us so we can duck and cover." He laughed. "No," I said, "I'm being serious."

"Oh," he ohed.

"Yeah, oh." I involuntarily shivered just thinking about it.

And then, minutes later, we were in my—now her—room. "Nice," she proclaimed, a broad smile on her stunning face as she quickly found the room service menu and ordered—all on our tab, naturally. Then she got down to business, the wireless keyboard on her lap and the television Internet access turned on.

Her pink polished nails ran rapid-fast across the device, and then, in the blink of an eye, we had our answer. "Voila," she said, pointing to the television screen. "Makani's boss is none other than…drum roll please…Edward Beles. Wait, that name sounds familiar."

"Oh fuck," the three of us guys said at once.

"Oh, right," she said, her index finger touching her nose. "Well then, another piece of the puzzle seemingly falls into place. There's the police connection then. Sergeant Beles at the substation and Edward Beles in prison. What are the odds that they're not related?"

"Slim to none, I'd wager," I answered, though we were quick to discover that this little tidbit of information never appeared in the press. "Guess the police would rather the islanders didn't know about this; it wouldn't look too kosher," I added, clearly stating the obvious.

"Look," Koni hollered as Briana continued scrolling through the articles. He jumped up and pointed to the TV. "It says here that both Makani and his boss are represented by the same attorney, seeing as the state of Hawaii is trying them together." He read further down. "Drum roll again…David Schwartz, attorney at law. Guess that's who we're seducing."

"Not we," piped in Brandon. "Me."

"Or me," Briana corrected, chin held up high.

"Hey, maybe me. Don't forget me," I pointed out.

The three of them laughed and ignored my appeal.

"Anyway," said Briana, still reading through her rapid research, "he's straight. Twice divorced. Now single. Both wives left him."

"Meaning, he's probably a schmuck," I reasoned.

"And probably easily taken in by a pretty face," Brandon added.

"But," Koni interjected, "don't you think we should hedge our bets, just in case?"

We all turned to look at him. "What's that supposed to mean?" I asked.

He pointed to Briana, then to me, then to Brandon, then to himself. "I mean," he replied, "maybe Briana should be joined by Judy and Liza and Madonna."

"Who's Madonna?" Briana asked.

"Me," Koni proudly informed. "'Cause I don't look like a Cher."

"Kid has a point," Brandon said. "Minus the Madonna option. I mean, give this lawyer three beauties to choose from. Increase our chances. Makes sense."

"As much as anything does, all things considered," Briana agreed, running to the door as her luggage and dinner simultaneously arrived. When we were once again alone, she unzipped the largest suitcase and flung it open. "Blonde, brunette, and redhead," she offered, three stunning wigs now dangling from her outstretched hand. "See how well I know you two?"

We hopped on the floor with her, Brandon grabbing for the blonde one and me for the brunette. Briana was clearly the fiery one in our trio, no doubt about that. "But how do we find this lawyer dude?" I asked.

A cough came from the bed. We three looked up, our wigs already snugly covering our scalps. "Um," said the young voice, "I think I have that one covered. But we'll have to wait until the morning, when this guy Schwartz's office opens up."

We shrugged, glad not to have to think of yet another plan by ourselves. Besides, Koni's ideas had all panned out thus far.

Then we wheeled Briana's dinner on to the patio, all al fresco like. She devoured her meal as we sipped from the bottle of wine she'd ordered. Koni, of course, settled for a glass of mango juice. Honestly, it's a wonder we'd never won the Big Brother of the year award. Then again, considering we still had our wigs on, maybe not.

"To successfully seducing a lawyer," Brandon toasted.

"And to getting Will back," I added.

"And to the massage I'm getting tomorrow," Briana additionally added. "You guys are already a big fucking pain in my neck."

"But you love us anyway," I reminded her.

"Less and less, boys. Less and less."

***

We rose the next morning, our, believe it or not, seventh day on the island. Time sure does fly when murder and mayhem surround you on all sides.

I heard a voice coming from the balcony, the sliding door now closed, muffling the sound. Koni was sitting in a chair, his legs up and feet on the railing while he talked on his cellphone. I looked at the clock on the nightstand. It was just after nine.

"What's the kid up to now?" Brandon whined, a pillow over his face.

"Beats me," I replied, and Brandon leaned over and punched me in the arm. "No," I shouted, "beats me, not beat me."

"Oh," he ohed, removing the pillow. "But the latter is so much more enjoyable."

"It's too early for your nonsense," shouted Briana from the adjoining room, the dividing door stupidly left wide open.

And then, "Oh good, you're all up," announced Koni as he reentered the suite. "Because I've got some good news."

"Mimosas are on the way?" Brandon asked.

"Well, yes, but only because you preordered them last night," he replied.

"Oh, yeah," Brandon yipped, rolling back over on his side. "Goody for me."

Koni sighed. "Anyway, the good news is that Mister Schwartz is meeting us at the bar at Duke's tonight. Seven sharp."

Brandon again rolled over and propped himself up on his elbows. "And how the friggin' fuck did you manage that?" he asked.

Koni grinned, his white teeth flashing amid all that glorious tan. "Easy," he told us. "When the mayor's office calls, you do as you're told."

I couldn't help but laugh. "Wait a minute," I said, "you pretended to be from the mayor's office and told him to be at Duke's tonight?"

"No, cute dude, I pretended to be the mayor himself and told him to be at Duke's tonight. Again, easy. Only, instead of the mayor, he's going to find you three, um, girls. A conciliation prize, I think they call it."

We stared at him in shock. Briana, too, from inside the door. "I need a drink," she said.

"Me too," Brandon and I echoed.

Our prayers were answered a split second later, the mimosas, strong coffee, and pastries being rolled in as if on cue. We took it all on the balcony, staring at the sun as it made its way skyward, billowing white clouds rolling in from far out at sea, the beach still empty, waiting patiently for the tourist onslaught.

"So, what do we do until tonight?" I asked.

"Divide and conquer," Briana suggested.

"The U.S. already owns Hawaii," I reminded her.

She punched me from my left, Brandon from my right. "No, dumbass," she said, "I meant our limo-driving friend, Liko. Somehow, we need to figure out his connection to all this. Since you and Brandon already have a connection with him, I say you should give that number a call and set something up."

"And what will you be doing?" I asked her.

She paused, clearly finalizing her plan. "Me and Koni here

are gonna find out as much as we can about Liko from behind the scenes."

"We are?" Koni asked, taken aback.

"Yep," she replied, "as safely as possible. Then we're getting facials and hot stone massages."

"Oh," he ohed, now all smiles. "I mean, we are."

"Good," she said, wolfing down a tasty looking guava danish. "Then we'll meet up somewhere for an early dinner and then head on out to Duke's."

"Um," I tried, "your day sounds just a tad more fun than ours."

"Finally," she told me, "an intelligent comment. Now, finish your breakfast so we can doll you up and make you look pretty...as possible."

I looked over at Koni, and said, "See, kid, I told you to be scared of her."

"Ah," she ahed, her hands raised in triumph. "A second intelligent comment. Will wonders never fucking cease?"

***

First thing we did, obviously, was call the number that Liko had given us. He picked up immediately and remembered us right away—as if we were easy to forget. He said that if we wanted to talk some business, he'd be free in an hour and to meet him at the corner table in the International Marketplace food court.

"Think you can find that?" he asked.

I looked at Koni, remembering it all too well. "We'll see you in an hour," I told him.

So, with breakfast reluctantly over and our plan seemingly put into play, we began our, well, transformation. We opted for the sarongs again, figuring they did us well the first time around. Instead of the nifty scarves on our heads, however, we wore our nice, new wigs, opting for the scarves around our necks instead, to hide our telltale Adam's apples. Faces, arms, and chests were neatly shaved. Naturally, Brandon had little to do in that department, since he practically majored in manscaping. Lastly, Briana applied the war paint to our faces, the fake eyelashes the finishing touch, and, voila, instant Judy and Liza.

Then we hugged each other goodbye. "Good luck," we told them.

"Keep 'em tucked," Briana replied.

And we were off.

"So," I said as we made our way across and down the street. "What's the plan?"

He shrugged. "Not a clue. Guess we wing it. Pump him for as much information as we can get and then beat a hasty retreat. At least we're meeting him in a relatively safe place."

I nodded and led us into the Marketplace. He was sitting off to the corner when we arrived, slurping on a dripping ice cream cone, looking like the cutest pimp I'd ever seen.

"Ladies," he said, proffering us two metallic chairs.

We sat across from him, nervous smiles plastered across our make-up-caked faces. "Thanks for meeting us."

"Thanks for calling," he replied. "Now, what can I do for you?"

Obviously, he was forcing us to make the first move. "We, um, we're in need of a, um, new agent," I said, lobbing the first volley.

"An agent, huh?" He grinned, his teeth perfect and white. "You're in luck then. I'm in the market for some fresh talent."

"Lucky us," Brandon/Liza said. "Business must be good."

The grin widened further. "Business is booming. Seems the competition has suddenly gone belly up." His choice of words dropped a pit the size of a grapefruit down in my stomach. "And it's hard to find Caucasian help around these parts. You two will do well with me. Promise."

We nodded, our smiles now cemented to our faces. "Sounds like a good deal," Brandon said. "Do you mind if we ask a few questions before we sign on the dotted line, though?"

"Shoot," he said. Also not the most appealing word, by the

way.

"Well, not to be condescending, but you picked us up in a hotel limo. If business is so good, why the need to moonlight?"

He put his mitt of a hand over Brandon's. "Think about it," he replied.

Suddenly, it hit me. "Good cover," I blurted out. "And you get to meet lots of potential, rich, lonely men."

"Smart girl," he said. "You'll go far."

"She already has," Brandon quipped, earning him a kick beneath the table. "But we have one misgiving," he quickly added.

"Which is?" Liko asked.

"We've never had an, um, agent before. How does it all work?"

"Simple," he said. "I find you work, you do the work, I take a thirty percent cut. You work your own hours, as often as you like, minimum twenty hours a week. Most of my talent takes home enough that twenty is all they need. In addition, I protect my girls from, say, less than polite clients. Fortunately, most of the work is with Japanese men, who, looking at the two of you, I'd think could easily be handled. How does that all sound?"

In truth, it sounded like a great job, remembering I had none to go back to. "I'm ready," I proclaimed exuberantly, now earning my own kick beneath the table. In other words, I forgot that we weren't really looking for work, least of all the illicit kind.

"Great," he said. "I just have to test you both out, and then we're good to go."

"Test?" I asked, a nervous trickle streaming down my cheek.

"An easy one; fear not," he replied, lifting a hand up and snapping his fingers. In an instant, we were joined by two unassuming Japanese men, both in brightly colored floral shorts and nearly matching button down, short-sleeved shirts. "Ladies, meet Mister Yamasuka and Mister Lanasaki. Regular clients of mine. Impress them, and we have a deal. Otherwise, you're back to being, well, agentless. Nothing to lose, everything to gain."

He stood. We stood. My heart threatened to explode from within my sarong. This, of course, was not what we had planned. Nuh uh. Suddenly, I felt sick—especially since I was being led off by Mister Yamasuka and Brandon was going the other way with Mister Lanasaki. At least I though as much; they looked quite similar. I glanced over my shoulder at Brandon as he was doing the same to me. "Now what?" I mouthed.

"Keep 'em tucked," he mouthed back, echoing Briana's prophetic sentiments.

My john's car was waiting for us around the corner, a large Cadillac, all black. Apparently, said client was some sort of big shot. Ugh, again, there's one of those phrases I should've been avoiding. In any case, he opened the door for me, holding my hand in his as I got myself situated. No mean feat, mind you; those sarongs are tight, after all. Then we were speeding off.

"So," I said in my best girly voice, "my name is Liza. What's yours?" He sat there, stone-faced, staring ahead as he drove us to Lord knows where. "Not into small-talk, huh? Me neither." Still nothing. Not a peep. Heck, I wasn't even sure if he was breathing. "Do you, um, speak any English?"

"English, no," he managed, the car now driving up, up, up, around winding, tree-lined curves, the ocean popping into view from far down below.

"Scenic," I muttered, now talking to myself, seeing as he was the strong, silent type. Well, silent, anyway.

And then we were there: a sprawling, split-level house, well-manicured, obviously tended to with tender loving care. A small patch of grass hugged the front walkway. Plot-sized. I gulped audibly. I prayed that my first day as a hooker with a heart of gold wasn't also to be my last.

He walked around to the side of the car and helped me out before escorting me inside. The place was massive, richly appointed, very Asian, just like my host. I walked around and spotted the koi pond in the center. I bent down to have a look-see as he walked behind me, cupping my ass in the small of his palm. Instinctively, I turned around and punched his chest.

Time itself stood still in the moment after that. His eyes became mere slits. I was, I figured, a dead duck. And then, as if someone was looking out for me, the smallest of grins appeared on his otherwise lifeless face. I socked him one again. The smile grew wider. My client, it seemed, dug pain. Meaning, the upper hand, apparently and literally, was now mine.

I reached out and slowly unbuttoned his shirt, revealing a hairless chest, dense with taught, compact muscles. I tweaked a thick, pink nipple, twisting it ninety degrees. He winced as his shorts began to tent. Seeing as my own cover would soon be blown, the sarong capable of doing little to cover my own burgeoning appendage, I turned him around and leaned him against a wall. He obeyed, humming in rapt content.

I shucked the shirt off his back and raked my fake nails across the exposed flesh. Thankfully, the glue held. Thankfully still, he moaned in pleasure. I reached around and unbuttoned his shorts. They fell to the ground and he kicked them off.

"Going commando, I see," I said, my voice suddenly raspy.

He replied by widening his stance and bending further down, his lily-white ass jutting out, robin's egg balls dangling down. He was now stark naked, save for his sandals, and was nearly hairless, like a little boy. I spanked his ass, hard, harder still. His knees buckled and he groaned with a fiery intensity.

My hooker's golden heart was turning coal black. "A girl could grow to like this," I cooed.

My hand reached up for another spank as his legs went farther apart in anticipation. It was then that I spotted it. I bent down for closer inspection. "Someone's been naughty," I said, pushing at the butt-plug he had nestled up his ass. He responded by reaching down to stroke his schlong. Well, schlong in training, at any rate. The guy was hung like a tsetse fly.

I grabbed at the base of the plug and gave a pull, the cream-colored latex coming into view, which kept on coming, inch by rubbery inch. "Damn," I said with a whistle. "You're like the Grand Canyon of johns. No wonder you weren't talking in the car back there; this toy here was probably blocking your windpipe."

I gave it a shove back in, adding a slap across his ass for good measure. He howled in ecstasy, the sound echoing down the marble halls. I pulled again and then crammed again, pull, cram, pull, cram, until sweat poured down his back and his ass was ruby red from the abuse I was giving him with my free hand.

He pointed his needle of a prick downward as his legs began to tremble, the tight muscles quivering and quaking as he spewed like Mount Fuji. Splat, splat, splat he went as his rather hefty load hit the floor. He turned around. Luckily, I was still in crouch position, my own rock-solid prick hidden away between my thighs. He bowed with a grin and a wink, then shoved the plug back in, his eyelids fluttering for the briefest of seconds.

He disappeared around the corner, returning with a stack of paper towels and a wad of cash.

"Clean mess," he commanded, handing me the towels and the money as he got dressed.

Since cleaning up a stranger's spunk isn't much of an aphrodisiac for me, my boner quickly and gratefully diminished. I stood back up, found a trash can, and got rid of the evidence. That was that. Well, almost. Besides my payment, he came back with a tip: a gaudy necklace, dripping in rhinestones. I bowed and tried, as best I could, to thank him, but he was already out the door and on the way to the car, with me running after him.

We rode back in silence. No surprise there. He dropped me off where he'd picked me up. Not a smile, not a word, nothing. Well, not nothing. I did have the stack of bills, a kitschy trinket, and the lingering scent of butt-plug to remind me of my day's work. I waved at him as he pulled off.

"Sayonara," I yelled, and turned around. Much to my great relief, Brandon was already standing there, smiling and nodding.

"Do I hear wedding bells?" he asked.

"No, fuckwad. That's that screw loose inside your head you're hearing, rattling around in that vacuous cavity of yours."

I hugged him long and hard.

"How much did he give you?" he whispered in my ear.

I pulled back and counted my pay. "Holy hell," I said with a whistle. "Five hundred. You?"

"The same. And all I had to do was let him suck my toes while he jacked off."

"Then we were lucky," I said.

"Very," he agreed. "In more ways than one."

I tilted my head. "How's that?"

"Besides the cash, which is gonna pay for four much-needed hot stone massages, we also have new information on Liko."

"Ah," I said, wrapping my arm in his as we started our short walk back to the hotel. "I almost forgot. Guy's rich, no doubt. I'm sure the sweat off his talents' backs paid for those perfect teeth of his."

"Yep, no doubt. Plus, with Jed out of the way, at least temporarily, it would seem he has a monopoly on the Japanese trade around here. Hence his need for us. He's probably expanding while he's got the chance," he said.

"Which means," I added, "that we can trade him for Will. It's gotta be Liko that's after Jed and who killed poor Lenny. Maybe Lenny had too much information on him, and maybe Liko had the perfect opportunity to off him: while he was running from the cops."

"That's a lot of maybes, though. And that doesn't explain how he set Lenny up for the smuggling, or his connection with Makani. Also, one other troubling thing: the other day, when he drove us to Jed's hideout, he seemed to know where we were going, trying to get us to stay clear. If he knew where Jed was all this time, why didn't he just turn him over to the cops, or worse, kill him. Either one would've got Jed out of the pimping picture for good."

We reached our hotel and started to our rooms. "Fuck," I said with a heavy sigh. "So, then someone else might be after Jed. But who?"

"Guess we'll have to wait and see, Chase. We still have two

days left before Will is supposed to call. And maybe Briana and Koni discovered something this morning. Maybe we'll even score big with David Schwartz tonight."

Again, I groaned as we made it back to our room. "That's two more maybes then, and that's four too many. Still, at least the evidence is mounting. Now, we just have to figure out a way to turn over Liko to Jed in exchange for Will. And that's not going to be easy, no maybes about it."

We de-saronged, un-make-upped, and re-bathing suited ourselves. "Chins up, dear one. We got off two Japanese men and made a thousand smackers in under an hour, all without being caught. The Hawaiian gods are clearly smiling down on us."

I punched him in the arm. "Chin," I corrected him. "Chin up. Not chins. Fucker. But you're right; so far, so good. Now, we just have to enlist a certain attorney's help without him knowing it, and we're one step closer to rescuing Will."

"And pray that David's got a bigger dick. That last one was scary small. No wonder the guy didn't crack a smile the entire time," he informed as he wrote a note to our friends to meet us along our usual stretch of beach.

"You shoulda checked his asshole out then. Guy was probably so plugged up that a smile might've set the gears irrevocably in motion. Mess-y."

He stared at me and shuddered. "I don't want to know, Chase. I don't even want to know."

***

It was nearly noon by the time we made it to our now-familiar umbrellas. The sun was high overhead and killer strong, the ocean cool and a radiant blue. We ordered drinks and lunch for four, hoping our friends would arrive shortly.

"We have to call Liko soon," Brandon told me with a grimace, much to my shock and dismay.

"Why the fuck so?" I asked, staring down at my feet as they

disappeared beneath the pleasantly warm sand.

"Because Judy and Liza are the only connections to him. They can't just vanish now. Plus, we obviously passed that test of his."

"With flying come."

He groaned. "Gross, but true. Meaning, we're now in his employ."

"Great, a real résumé booster. I'm sure the offers will be pouring in."

"On the bright side," he said, choosing to ignore my wit and dripping sarcasm, "our alter-egos make good lures. Liko said that he'd be there to protect them. What if the there is at Jed's?"

"Hard to picture that as a bright side, but I see your point. And who knows, maybe Liko offers health insurance and vacation pay."

"See," he chuckled. "Already one step closer to retirement, Chase."

"Or and early grave, Brandon."

We were interrupted by, "What's this about graves?"

It was Briana, looking radiant as ever, not to mention smug. Koni was at her side, the same knowing grin stretched from ear to diamond-studded ear. The chairs, as always, magically appeared, and our foursome once again convened.

"What's with the stupid-ass smiles?" Brandon asked. "Did the fleet just pull into port?"

She turned to glare at him. "You have a smudge of lipstick on your teeth, oh butch one. If you'd care for round two of the verbal parleys, maybe you should wipe it off first."

"Cease fire," I shouted. "We surrender."

"Finally," Koni muttered.

"Temporarily," Brandon muttered back.

I quickly changed the subject, filling them in on what we'd learned, omitting the part where we got off two teeny-weenied Japanese guys. "Did you two have any luck today?"

That, apparently, was the reason for the grinning. "Well, if you call sitting in Liko's living room luck, then yes, we had some luck today?" Briana crowed, practically glowing.

"Huh?" was all Brandon and I could manage, our eyes wide, mouths agape.

"Let me tell it, let me tell it," Koni pled, jumping up and down, and nearly knocking over the waitress with our food and drinks.

"Okay, okay," Brandon shouted. "Just watch the booze."

Koni sat back down, taking a massive bite of his burger and a huge chug of Coke before relating their day to us. "Okay," he began, gulping it all down. "So, I got on the phone this morning and started asking around if anyone knew anyone who works for Liko. Turns out, he only pimps out the local girls, which is why I'd never heard of him before. Jed's more of an equal opportunity scumbag, so him I knew about. Anyway, it took a few calls, but I finally reached someone who works for him."

"But not as a hooker," Briana interrupted, causing Koni's smile to turn upside down.

"Um, my story," he reminder her.

"Oh yeah, sorry. Please continue," she said, starting in on her chicken and mango salad, which shut her up for a few chews.

He paused. "Okay, where was I?"

"Friend, not a hooker, works for Liko," I reminded him.

"Oh, right. Jackie. She used to deal drugs for Makani, actually. Then her mother found out and made her quit. Now they run a house cleaning service together."

"Heartwarming," Brandon said, sipping at his liquid diet.

"Not really; they steal from most of their clients. But at least they don't deal drugs. Her mom's got some twisted morals, I guess you'd say."

"Yeah," I said, "those we know about." Briana and Brandon both kicked sand at me. "Sorry. Continue," I told him.

He took another gargantuan bite and super sip, and did just that. "So, I called Jackie, made some small talk, and, lo and behold, not only does she know Liko, but she's at his house at that very moment."

"Fortuitous," Brandon said.

"Huh?" our young friend huhed.

"Lucky," I interpreted.

"Yeah, lucky," he agreed, finishing off his lunch on his third and final chomp.

"And getting even luckier," Briana added, causing another mean stare from Koni. "Oops."

"Can I finish, please?" he asked, clearly enjoying his new-found seniority. We nodded silently. "Anyway, so Jackie, I know she's got this weakness. See, she might not sell drugs no more, but that don't mean she doesn't take them when her mom's not looking."

"And her mom wasn't at Liko's today, right?"

His grin was wide, dazzling, contagious. "No. Home sick. What's that word? Oh yeah, fortuitous. So, I told her I had me some good shit to share. Now, if it was me, I'd have asked why I wanted to share some good shit, but she just heard good shit and share, and she's inviting me over in a heartbeat."

"But you don't have any shit," I reminded him. "Not since Makani got busted."

He chuckled, as did Briana. "Arm and Hammer, best shit on the market. Luckily, I could still scrape together some real and true blow, enough so she'd feel some effects. Besides, when you think you're getting some good shit, your body reacts like it is, at least sometimes."

"Either way," Brandon said "you've made it into Liko's."

"Exactly," Koni said. "And then she gives us his address. Easy as poi."

"You mean pie," I said.

"Not in Hawaii. Anyway, so me and Briana, we hop a cab and tell him to wait for us out of sight for thirty minutes. And then comes the first surprise."

"Liko had a big house?" I interrupted, my own smug smile rising up my cheeks.

"Understatement," corrected Briana.

It was Koni's turn to kick the sand. "Yeah, understatement. Place was huge and oceanside. Big bucks."

"You said first surprise," Brandon interrupted, leaning in, his interest now piqued. "What was the second?"

Koni continued. "So, she invites us in. I tell her Briana's a friend of mine and she's cool. Jackie just shrugs, her eyes, her body movements, telling me she was hot for the blow. She takes us into the living room. I spread the shit out on the glass table. Chick shovels the shit up her nose. Fine by me; we had what we came for in the first five minutes there."

"What? What?" I practically screamed.

"Pictures," he replied, all cool, calm, and collected like. "Dozens of 'em, nicely framed on every table."

"Fuck," Brandon said. "Let me guess: him and Lenny, right?"

"Yep," Koni told us. "Every last one of them. So, I ask Jackie who the cute dude is, and she says it's the owner's boyfriend. Guys are tight. Big time in love."

"Fuck," Brandon reiterated. "And lovebirds don't cut each other's throats and dump them in the Pacific, right?"

"Back to square fucking one," I said.

"Almost," said Briana.

"Yeah, almost," Koni agreed. "See, I figured that Jackie knows two people we're interested in."

"Liko and Makani," I said, offering up the short list.

"Yep. So, bonus surprise: I asked her about our old supplier, Makani. I figure she knows about as much as me, but what the hell, no harm in asking. Only, Jackie was closer to the dude than I was, and this was news to me. See, this island is real small. Everyone knows everyone else. Shit, most of us are related somehow or another."

Brandon's and my face lit up. "No joking?" I asked. "You mean Jackie and Makani are related?"

"First cousins. And blood being thicker than water, she knows shit about him. Shit that a half a bag of blow later, we now know."

Again, I shouted, "What? What?" I know, our lives our better than a soap opera, right? Days of our Leis.

"Well," he said, almost at the end of his tale, "she said, just between me and her, Makani knew he was going to get busted. He was tipped off three weeks earlier."

"I don't get it," I said, "If he was tipped off, why didn't he just scram?"

"To where?" Koni replied. "Plus, by then, he knew that the police were already watching him. If he tried to leave, he'd have been nabbed."

Brandon snapped his fingers. "Ah," he ahed. "Now it makes some sense. If he knew he was going to be busted, he'd have some time to find a patsy, someone he could finger for a lighter sentence without casting a watchful eye on any of his real associates."

"Lenny," we all said in unison.

"And," I added, "it was about three weeks prior to his arrest that Lenny started flashing his money around. So, if it wasn't Liko that set him up, it must've been Jed. Jed has immediate access to him. Jed had cash to plant on him. Jed could fuck him and get the traces of cocaine up his ass."

"So," Brandon also added, "we at least, more than likely, know who set up Lenny. But why would Jed do that? What's his connection with Makani? And if someone tipped off Makani, why not his boss, Edward Beles? And who ratted out the boss and why? Pretty dangerous to do such a thing, I'd imagine."

"Deadly," Koni said. "Fortuitously, we may have our answers soon enough."

"David Schwartz," we all said in unison. Cue the scary music again. Not because bad shit was about to happen, but because we were now officially all on the same wavelength. Four lunatics, all connected.

"So," Briana chimed in with, "that leaves one more burning question."

"What? What?" I hollered for the third and final time.

She grinned, chewing on her last bite of salad and taking a swig of her cocktail. "Who, pray tell, is making the massage appointments? That pain in my neck is traveling all the way down to my ass."

I pointed to Brandon, who replied, "I did it when we got back from our meeting. Four hot stone massages at the Royal Hawaiian in one hour, then we come back and get changed, then dinner at the Hula Grill upstairs from Duke's, then we meet/stalk one Mister David Schwartz."

"Wow, impressive," she said. "You planned all that on your own, Brandon?"

He leisurely shook his head from side to side. "Concierge. I was taking a quick shower while he did all the work. Our morning made me feel, well, dirty."

"Really?" she asked. "What exactly did happen this morning?"

"Someday, dear Briana, we'll tell you" he replied. "Someday."

Never, dear Briana, in a million years, I thought. Never.

***

We downed another round of drinks, then walked the short distance between hotels. The Royal Hawaiian, also known as the Pink Palace of the Pacific or the Pink Lady—because, duh, it's pink, all pink, from the mission-style bell towers all the way across its wide expanse of posh luxury rooms—is the second oldest hotel in Waikiki, our own hotel, the Moana, being the oldest. Now, normally, you'd think that an all pink hotel would appeal to my, well, gayer sensibilities, but you'd be mistaken. There is something to be said for the notion of too much of a good thing. Brandon is a good case in point. Still, the place was lavish, in an austere sort of way. Mostly, I found it kind of dark and sobering. And we all know my opinion of sobriety. On a side, related note, the hotel has a bar that claims to have invented the Shirley Temple—as if a virgin drink is something you'd want to lay claim to.

In any case, we weren't there to sightsee; we were there for a well-deserved break from the turmoil we found ourselves in. Did I feel guilty about getting a massage while Will was being held prisoner somewhere? Yes. Did I let that stop me? Come on now, I think you know me better than that by now. In other words, hell to the no. Besides, we had a ton of time to kill, for lack of a better word, until our evening rendezvous, and I figured it's what Will would've wanted. Um, okay, it's what I wanted; so shoot me. Figuratively speaking, I mean.

We quickly found—now get this—the seven thousand square-foot Abhasa Spa in the right wing of the hotel, complete with treatment cabanas in a well-manicured garden setting. Tinkling, new-age crappy music welcomed us as we entered, as did the equally tinkling, new-age attendant dressed in a white, blousy two-piece ensemble that billowed as he walked up to us.

"Welcome," he said, sounding like he'd just taken a bottle of Vicodin or had been shot in the butt with a horse tranquilizer.

"Thank you," we replied as peacefully and serenely as possible.

He checked our names off and ushered each of us into our own private cabanas. "Undress, please," he whispered to me. "Klaus will be with you shortly. There are towels to your right. Help yourself to the ice water with cucumber strips."

"Um, anything stronger? My liver gets confused if it's not assaulted every few hours."

"I can cut a lemon if you like," he replied in all seriousness.

Seeing as the exertion might kill him, I politely declined. Besides, I had an emergency mini-bottle of gin in my pocket, compliments of our suite's mini-fridge. And yes, I fully intended on getting one of those when I returned to the mainland. God willing. I mean, talk about convenience.

In any case, I spiked my cucumbery water and hiked off my tank and dropped my knickers in about two shakes of a lamb's tail. For those of you not so mathematically inclined, that's about double the blink of an eye. I then wrapped myself in a towel and hopped up on the table, just before my masseur entered the room.

"Hello, my name is Klaus." He sounded like a gay version of Arnold Schwarzenegger.

I nodded and smiled. "I'm Chase."

"Chase. Odd to have verb for name. Is short for something else?" he asked.

"Chase. It's short for, um, Chase," I replied, clearly confusing him.

"I see," he said, but I didn't think that he did; all the blood in his brain was apparently fueling his massive chest and bulging—seriously bulging—biceps. "First I give you light massage, then I place hot stones on back and legs, then between toes, then rub tension out of tired muscles with the stones. You relax. You like."

"Or you'll break my neck?"

"I no break neck. Maybe crack neck. Rub neck. No break neck." His funny-bone had obviously been replaced by muscle. And then more muscle. Wrapped in muscle. He then rubbed some oil into his mitts and began to gently work my neck and shoulders. "You are full of tension up here, Chase."

"Yeah, about that, you see, my boyfriend, well, kind-of-boyfriend, was kidnapped by an evil pimp after my kind-of-boyfriend's prisoner, an accused, but probably innocent, flight attendant/drug smuggler escaped from custody and then was, um, um, never mind." I paused to catch my breath. "Yeah, so, I'm kinda tense."

"You mean Lenny?"

I jumped up and onto my side. "That you fucking understood?"

"Most of it," he replied, cracking a hint of a smile. I think. Though it might've been a spasm, from all his bulging muscle, as it bulged and then bulged some more.

"How did you know I was talking about Lenny? And how do you know Lenny?" I asked as he pushed me back down. I felt much like a swatted fly.

His hands worked their way down my back, to my thighs and calves, then to the arches of my feet. I exhaled sharply, feeling the stress drain from my muscles—not the bulging type, mind you. "You said flight attendant/drug smuggler," he eventually told me. "Can only be Lenny. But Lenny was no drug smuggler. The press, the police, they are wrong."

"I know," I said.

"Lenny's not bright enough to smuggle drugs."

"I know. I know."

"Too nice, too."

"I know. I know. Salt of the earth."

He paused, confused at the compliment. He placed the stones along the length of my body, small ones in between my tootsies. They were hot and heavy, though oddly comforting, pressing down on and heating up my pressure points. My lungs emptied and then filled. I sighed contentedly.

He began rubbing the stones into my flesh. In between grunts, I asked, "Again, how do you know Lenny."

"Small island," he replied, pausing as he worked me over. "Mostly, I know his boyfriend."

The bells and whistles went off. "Liko? You know Liko?"

Now it was his turn to grunt. "No. Who is Liko? Jed, I know Jed."

The bells and whistles started to sound like gongs—big, metal, deafening gongs. Then it hit me how he'd know Jed, seeing as there was probably only one way. I had to tread lightly, I figured, which wasn't my forté. "Um, Jed, right. Haven't seen him for a while."

The stones dug in deep, hot and unrelenting. "No," he said, "me neither."

He wasn't giving me what I wanted, so I upped the ante. In other words, I lied. "I used to work for him. You?"

He laughed, finally. Though even that sounded like a grunt. "Ja, that's how everyone knows Jed. No friends, just employees."

No friends, just employees. Did that include boyfriends? "So, Lenny used to, um, work for Jed, too?"

"Ja, ja. This is how they become lovers. Though I think Lenny was using him. Jed had nice apartment, big car, lots of money."

And finally, it seemed, Jed returned the favor, using Lenny to help out Makani. But why was still the question. "Ja. I mean, yeah. Big apartment. Big empty apartment. I hear he's still missing, though."

The laugh/grunt returned, and my body started to feel like a lump of Play-Doh. "Nein, not missing, I hear through the vinegrape. Just moved shop. Jed likes his money too much; his employees follow him to new stomping grounds."

My heart began to go pitter-patter from deep within my chest. If Jed wasn't missing, then he was findable. Meaning, Will was findable. Meaning, we might have other options for his safe return. "New stomping grounds? Funny, I was just about to look him up. For work, I mean."

The stones were removed, one by one, as his hands again worked down my body. "I hear he's somewhere near La'ie now. Lying low after trouble at the North Shore."

That trouble being us, apparently. And Will. "Thanks for the information," I said. "We boys have to stick together."

"No boy," he corrected, slapping my ass good and hard. Mostly the latter. "Klaus all man."

"Ja," I agreed. "All man."

One final laugh/grunt and he was done¬¬—thank goodness, as my poor body couldn't take much more. He left me alone to get dressed, my mind now reeling. Though that could've been from the body oil fumes. I emerged soon after, joining my friends in the courtyard outside.

"Man," Brandon said upon seeing me, "now that was perfection."

"Perfection," Briana echoed, her face quite tenseless.

"Sheer perfection," Koni agreed.

I shook my head. "Dicknobs. That hurt like fucking hell. Next time I see a stone, I'm gonna give it a good swift kick." I sat on the grass, trying to avoid looking at the all-encompassing pink. "Oh, and Lenny was a hooker who used Jed, who's now working out of La'ie, wherever the fuck that is."

"North from here, along the western coast," Koni informed,

before adding a, "Huh?"

"Yeah," said Brandon. "Huh?"

"What happened in there?" It was now Briana's turn. "All that new-age crap give you channeling abilities?"

"No," I replied. "That behemoth back there used to work for Jed. From hooker to masseur— like that's never happened before. Anyway, chatty Klaussy spilled the sauerkraut. Lenny met Jed when he was working for him. He liked the lifestyle and moved on in, apparently."

"Ah," Briana ahed.

"What ah?" Brandon asked her.

"Ah," she explained, "Lenny lives with Jed, but loves Liko."

"But Liko's loaded, too," I reminded her.

"Doesn't matter," Koni said. "He probably met Jed first, and there's no breaking up with Jed if Jed doesn't want to be broken up with. I told you guys: Jed has a rep. And a bad one. Meaning, no double-crossing. Either in work or play."

"Ah," Briana ahed, yet again. "And before you ask—ah, as in, ah, maybe that's why Jed set Lenny up to take the fall."

"Maybe," Koni allowed, "but if he knew about Lenny and Liko, it would probably be Liko in hiding now and not himself. Plus, no one knew where Lenny would be just before he met his untimely end, not even Jed, who was at the North Shore at that time. Something's definitely missing here. That puzzle you guys keep mentioning still has some big gaps in it."

"Kid's right," Brandon said. "So, we have to hope that our attorney friend tonight has some of those pieces."

"And is willing to hand them over," I added. "However unlikely that seems."

We remained there in silence, our brains officially exhausted. Still, at least we knew where Will was probably being held, and that gave me the tiniest iota of hope.

It was Briana who finally broke the silence. "Anyone up for a shower. I smell like a fucking musk ox."

"Oh good," Brandon said. "I thought that was me."

She glowered and marched off, the three of us trailing close (ish) behind her. "Now you did it," I whispered in his ear. "She's mad."

"Shit," he groaned, hollering after her, "Dinner's on me tonight." She continued onward without a peep. "And drinks," he quickly amended with. And still there was nothing, though I could've sworn I could see the heat radiating off her. "High end labels, no well-brands," he smartly offered.

She paused for a moment. "Forgiven," she muttered, then again moved forward. "For now."

We breathed a sigh of relief.

Koni leaned in and whispered in my ear, "Are we really that scared of her?"

"Yes, they are," she shouted over her shoulder.

"Ah," Koni ahed.

"Yeah, ah," I agreed. "Fucking ah."

🌴 Lawyers Screwed 🌴

The shower was great, the cold water like heaven against my steaming skin—though the oil still lingered. In other words, I felt and smelled like a wet salad. And, to top it all off, we still had to play girly dress-up. Okay, so normally I might not have minded that, but to do so in order to intentionally trick a straight man, well, even that was out of my realm of common decency.

"Yippy," shouted Brandon from the adjoining room. "Girly dress-up." See, Brandon has no decency—common or otherwise.

I put my robe on and joined my three friends, all of us glowing from the oil, and stinking just slightly less than before our showers.

"Only for Will's sake," I proclaimed, allowing Briana to pick out my short skirt and tight blouse before adding the fake boobs, fake eyelashes, and fake hair.

"Yep, for Will's sake," Brandon half-heartedly agreed, diving into the pile of clothes before emerging with the sluttiest outfit he could color coordinate.

Despite his pleading, we put our high-heeled feet down and didn't allow Koni to join in the festivities. He could come to the bar and order a coke, but "Madonna" would not be joining us. He frowned, but, with little choice, soon relented. Especially when we told him that he could order anything he wanted off the Hula Grill menu.

In retrospect, we should've just let him go in drag; it would've been a hell of a lot cheaper.

Within ten minutes, we were seated at a balcony table with a spectacular view of the beach down below, a myriad of swaying palm trees, and the sun as it made its gradual decent, turning our al fresco sojourn into a multi-media extravaganza. Okay, so I may have gayed it up a bit there, but, considering our dreaded mission in just about an hour's time, I had to find a bright side, if only for my sanity—what little I had to begin with.

The restaurant itself was like a comfortable home that was missing its façade, the main dining room looking more like a beach house than anything else. And, man, the menu looked yu-fucking-um.

Koni, heeding our generous offer, ordered the Coldwater lobster tail. Brandon groaned, but bit his lip. Briana, our power diva, ordered the baby back barbecue ribs, with Brandon opting for the healthier fire grilled ahi steak. My mouth watered at the selection, but each time I tried to order something rich and delicious, my so-called friends reminded me of my tight dress, which would only continue to get tighter the more I ate.

Glumly, I told the waiter, "North Shore vegetable stir fry, please. Made without butter."

The same so-called friends nodded their heads in agreement with my healthy yet bland choice. I kicked each of them under the table. Accidentally, of course. And accidentally again when, thirty minutes later, they ordered pineapple coconut crème brulee for three, but urged me to go with the sorbet trio. My dress was happy; I, however, was not.

And then seven o'clock rolled around. "Show time," Brandon muttered, paying the bill, his smile vanishing in an instant.

We trudged out, our meals going sour in the pits of our stomachs. Duke's bar was just downstairs and noticeably fairly quiet, what with everyone eating dinner, and all. So, we pulled up four stools and stared out at the crowd, with the beach and ocean just beyond.

"What's this guy look like?" I asked.

Koni grinned. "I think I remember seeing his picture in one of the local rags a while ago. You're in for an unusual treat."

"Cryptic response," I said. "What, does he have one leg? Three ears? A Siamese twin dangling off his side?"

He nudged me in the ribs and nodded his head toward the side of the bar. We all followed his gaze. "Oh," I ohed, feral drool instantly forming at the corners of my mouth.

"He's a lawyer?" Brandon whispered.

"Apparently," Koni replied, also sotto voce. "Maybe it was a back-up occupation—in case the Mister Honolulu pageant fell through."

"Mister Hawaii," I corrected. "Or make that Mister World, because he's rocking mine."

We all sat up straight. Well, considering half of us were in drag, make that vertical. Then three of us reapplied our lipstick. So yeah, the word straight definitely wasn't correct. And then fixed our dresses and repositioned our wigs. Again, definitely not straight.

David ordered a drink and sat down two stools over from us. He looked our way ever so briefly, then stared at the entrance, obviously waiting for the mayor to arrive. Good luck with that, I figured. Out of the corner of my eye, I watched him as he fiddled with his drink and repeatedly checked his watch. When twenty minutes went by, and with him obviously growing more and more impatient, I went for broke. "Did your friend not show up?" I asked, leaning across an empty barstool.

He forced a smile and replied, "Probably just running late."

"Yes, probably," I said, batting an eyelash—and praying it wouldn't fall off. "Well, you can join our little party, if you like. I mean, it beats sitting there waiting all by yourself."

Again, he looked up and over, taking each of us in, one at a time. We must've looked an unusual foursome, but he relented just the same. "Sure," he told me, sliding over with a glowing grin that made even the sun jealous. "Just don't be mad if my friend eventually does indeed show up."

"No problem," we all somehow said at once, causing him to jump.

"Sorry," I apologized for the four of us. "Sometimes, are

minds are strangely in sync." I then introduced each of us in turn, his hand reaching out for a shake all the way down the line.

"Strong grip," he said to Liza/Brandon.

"I work out," came the reply, along with a nervous smile.

We all then turned to stare at him, clearly at a loss for words. Perhaps, we should've planned beyond our not-so-chance encounter. That meant only one thing: we had to grease the wheels. Thankfully, we were sitting at a bar; there was ample grease in every bottle.

"So, David, you're in luck." I said offhandedly, thinking fast.

"Really, Judy, how so?" he asked, leaning in, his breath as sweet as a bee's ass.

I forced a smile and crossed my newly-shaven legs. "Today's my birthday; everyone has to buy me a round."

My friends looked at me in relief, since their minds were as twisted as my own and they apparently knew what I was up to. "First one's on me," shouted Briana, again causing poor David to jump. Luckily, he didn't object. Then again, we didn't give him much of a chance. Briana ordered the tallest, kick-assingest concoction they made.

Wheels in motion, the cogs now all greased and rarin' to go, we were set.

One drink down—rapidly down—and our ensemble was noticeably cooler, calmer, and collecteder. David fit right on in, chugging his potion and eagerly waiting for the next one. It was obvious, by then, that his "date" had stood him up, so why not hang with this fun bunch? Which is why we moved to a nearby round table, our drinks following us, and proceeded to get rip-roaringly shitfaced. And no, not Koni. See how adult-like we were? Okay, ignoring the dresses and the wigs, see how adult-like we were?

So, let's torpedo ahead, all systems go, lower the hatches.

Five rounds later—I think it was five, but it was hard to count by that point—we were completely and utterly wasted, and David was our new best friend. I mean, who wouldn't want to be friends with two Hooters waitresses, a nuclear physicist, and an American Idol contestant who missed it by one to make it on the show. Luckily, he was too drunk to ask any probing questions, or we might've been completely screwed.

A nice cool breeze blew in off the coast, making the tiki torches flicker just outside the restaurant, their flames dancing in David's deep brown eyes. How, you may ask, did I know this? Well now, with each passing drink, his chair scooted closer and closer to my own, his knee bumping and grinding against mine, his hairy forearm brushing against my rather bare one. Drunk as I was, none of this went unnoticed, neither by me nor my motley crew. Jealous as they were—and who could rightly blame them?—at least our plan was working. And this time, I did indeed tuck and tape, and tape again, meaning my throbbing prick would remain thankfully well-concealed.

Several hours into our evening, he leaning in, his breath syrupy and potent, and whispered, "Are you having a nice birthday, Judy?"

"What the f…oh, oh yes, I am. Best birthday ever," I replied, suddenly remembering my original ploy, not to mention my female(ish) voice.

"But I haven't given you your gift yet," he again whispered, his soft, full lips gently tickling my tender ear.

"Yes, you did," I reminded him. "You bought a round, oh, a good couple of rounds ago. I seem to recall they were flaming and nearly caught my dress on fire."

He chuckled and pointed to my charred shirt sleeve. "They did catch your dress on fire. And we didn't have to pay for that round. Anyway, I meant the other gift, the one back at my apartment."

"But how could you have gotten me a gift? You didn't even know me before tonight?" I paused, my eyes locking on to his. "Oh," I ohed, figuring out what he was getting at. "Is it something I can unwrap?"

He smiled and nodded. "Uh huh."

"Okay," I told him. "Besides, it's bad luck to turn down a

birthday gift." Even when it's not your birthday, and you're not really someone named Judy who's not really a Hooters waitress. Meaning, in terms of luck, I was already pushing mine to its limit.

So, I excused myself to go to the bathroom. Briana and Brandon/Liza quickly jumped up to join me, as girls frequently and inexplicably do.

"I can't believe it," I practically squealed behind closed doors.

"I know," Brandon said, reapplying his/her lipstick. "He picked you over us. So, he's either farsighted or too drunk to realize." I jabbed him one in the ribs. "Very lady-like," he added.

"Um, girls," Briana wisely broke in with. "May I remind you that we're here to garner information, not bed-notches."

My stomach sank at the comment. "Oh yeah." I groaned. "Fuck, now what? He obviously wants to sleep with Judy, and Judy is only skin deep. Or dress deep, as the case may be. Is be. Is." I was confused. And drunk. "I think I should've stopped three rounds ago."

Brandon smiled, his ruby red lipstick glinting in the overhead light. "Ah, the prefect excuse then. Too drunk to fuck. Just drag, no pun intended, the information out of him and cuddle until he falls asleep. Then run, as fast as your Ferragamo heels can carry you, out of there. Problem solved."

I took what he said in. "That could work," I reluctantly agreed, looking at Briana for backup.

"Or clobber him over the head and ransack his place until you find the information we're looking for. Then run, as fast as your Ferragamo heels can carry you, out of there," she offered.

I took into consideration what she said as well, then replied, "I think I'll go with the cuddling."

"Suit yourself," she said with a shrug, leading our trio out of the bathroom.

Our two "male" companions sat there patiently waiting. When David saw me approaching, he jumped up, said his goodnights and nice-to-meet-yous, grabbed my hand, and led me out of the restaurant. We quick-stepped it through the hotel and back to the main strip, the fresh air feeling great on my flushed skin. Suffice it to say, so did his grip in mine. Great and nauseating at the same time. It was a heady mixture, to be sure.

He lifted his hand up and hailed a passing cab. A minute later, we were on our way. A minute after that, I was at a complete loss for words and sobering up mighty fast. A minute after that, his roving palm was on my knee and those supple lips were nibbling on my earlobe. I held him off with small-talk and lightning fast reflexes; he laughed, but took the hint. Thank God. Though, by then, it didn't seem like He was listening anymore.

The cab, fortunately, didn't have far to go. David's apartment building was maybe fifteen blocks away, a towering mess of glass and steel, slick and new and obviously costly to inhabit.

He greeted the doorman with a perfunctory nod before leading me upstairs. Way upstairs. Thirty floors later, we emerged at his high-rise abode, the furnishings spectacular, the view even more so. Him included. He had me in a lip-lock in seconds, his mouth pressed firmly on mine, his hands roaming up and down my flimsy dress.

"Um," I tried, in between heavy breaths. "I, um, may have had too much to drink tonight, David."

"Ditto," he dittoed, his mouth traveling up and down my neck and over my clavicle.

Cleary, he wasn't familiar with this tactic. "No, I mean, I don't think I'm, er, up for this tonight. Couldn't we just talk and cuddle?"

He pulled away, a mischievous smirk playing across his face that only added to his overall handsomeness. With a wink, he blurted out, "I already know."

"Huh?" I huhed. "Know what?"

He moved away to sit on a couch, one of several, all in tan suede. (No red wine in this apartment, I figured. Anyway, again, he looked up at me, still smiling widely. "Judy, I graduated twentieth in my class."

"Oh, okay. Well, that's pretty good. Congratulations."

"At Harvard Law School."

I scratched at my wig. "Ah, well, that's really good then, I suppose." I hadn't a clue where he was going with all this, but at least he stopped mauling me and was talking instead.

"Meaning," he continued, "I'm smart enough to know a man in a dress when I see one."

I gulped, choking on my spit. He jumped up and patted me on my back. "It's okay. No worries, dude. You see, I like that." The last three words came out raspy, husky, full of, if I wasn't mistaken, desire.

"You...you like guys dressed like girls?" I managed. "But you graduated twentieth in your class at Harvard Law School."

Again, he laughed. "Which means I like guys in expensive dresses, but it doesn't change the facts."

"But, but, you're straight. You're wearing a wedding ring."

He held up his hand and pointed at the ring in question. "Was married, twice. Until they found out about my, well, pastime. See, gay transvestites don't exactly bring in high-priced clients, nor do they make for happy husbands, especially ones that look better in their wives' clothes than they do."

Again, I coughed. "Wait, you wear dresses, too?"

He stroked my wig, his hand running down my dress until it landed on my tucked and taped prick. He grinned, keenly aware of what I'd done. "Yes," he eventually said, "I like to dress up like women, just like you do. And I like sleeping with guys who dress up like women, especially sexy guys like yourself. Only, this island is pretty small, so running across men like yourself, or like myself, is a pretty rare event."

"Which is why you were so eager to join our little party tonight."

"I prayed you'd ask," he admitted, leaning in for a hot, sultry sucking on my lips.

He broke the kiss first and walked in for a tight hug, sighing in my ear. With my head now on his shoulder, it was then that I spotted it, or, rather, them: manila folders spread out on a glass and chrome desk. Work folders. Bing-fucking-o. "So, David," I whispered, "do you wanna get plowed by a guy in a dress tonight?"

"Oh yeah," he moaned, his cock growing stiff in his khakis as it butted up against me waist.

"And do you wanna get plowed by a guy wearing a dress while you're in a dress?"

He pulled away, his face an inch away from my face, a look of out-and-out lust spreading from ear-to-ear. "Oh yeah," he repeated, his breath now ragged. "Please."

Which meant we now had a Plan C, no cuddling and no conking on the head needed. "Sounds like fun," I said. "So, go make yourself pretty, 'cause I'm about to plow your ass something silly." All twentieth in his class acres of it.

He practically tore to the bedroom. "I'll hurry," he panted over his shoulder.

"No," I shouted back. "I mean, take your time. Let's so how beautiful a girl you can be."

He laughed. "Deal." And then he closed the door behind him.

"Deal," I repeated, waiting a cool minute before sidling over to his work area.

The folders were neatly labeled, case after case, most of them thick with legal papers. I scrambled through each one, trying my best to keep them in the order I'd found them in. But nothing, nada, zip. No mention of Edward Beles or Makani.

"How's it going in there?" I shouted through the door, checking on what little time I had left.

"Half-way there, Judy," he hollered back, his voice already two octaves higher, meaning we were now both tucked in tight, more than likely.

I hurried over to his desk and flung open his filing cabinets. My attorney(ette) was a busy man (girl). And well-organized. Anal even, and color coordinated. Edward Beles's file was rightly near the front. I propped it open and immediately was confronted with an odd piece of information. Odd and definitely disconcerting. It was also, sadly, all I had time to discover.

"One more minute," he cooed from behind the door.

I shoved almost everything back the way I'd found it and hopped over to his couch, my lady-like legs crossed and the smile returning to my lipsticked lips just as he emerged, the proverbial butterfly emerging from its cocoon.

David made a surprisingly beautiful woman. God that sounds weird, even coming from me. David made a surprisingly beautiful woman. I mean, really, how many people get to say something like that in their lifetime? Or want to, even? In any case, he had long, shapely gams, covered as they were in at least one pair of dark pantyhose, with bulging calves that flexed as he strode over to me in his three-inch heels. His dress was short, satin, and champagne colored, shimmering in the light. His waist was narrow, his chest padded and broad, his arms sinewy, gloved, to hide the hair. The blonde wig hung low and curled, framing his impeccably made up face, replete with ruby-red lipstick, a hint of blush, and long, luxurious, black eyelashes.

He reached his hands around my waist and pulled me in, the air around us now saturated in Chanel. I stood there and thought that this was one first I could somehow live without. And yet, surprisingly, this new and unexpected fetish of mine was strangely exciting.

"You're very, um, uh, pretty," I managed.

"Thanks," he said, his voice now soft, feminine. "So are you."

Very weird. And even weirder to come. Literally. Will, I thought to myself, please know that I'm doing this for you. And maybe just a tad for my pulsing cock, which was simply begging for release by then.

He grabbed my hand and led me to his oddly masculine bedroom, kissing me before flopping down on his back, his eyes hungrily roaming up and down my body. I took the hint, unzipping my dress and letting it slide to the carpet. He groaned. "Leave everything else on," he pled, kicking off his heels before gliding out of his hose. Next, he hiked up his skirt to remove his pink, satin panties, which, I quickly noticed, had some sort of rubber front padding. In other words, his prick was now free and gladly springing to life, rolling in a circle as it pulsed with life, growing inch by steely inch. And then it was my turn to groan. His fat cock, long and turgid, made for an unusual sight, nestled as it was against his dress.

He grinned at my obvious admiration, then lifted his knees up and out, his beautiful, crinkled, pink hold winking up at me. I bent down for a cursory lick, causing him to arch his back as he writhed on the high-threadcount sheets. I spread his cheeks apart and dove in. Once good and wet, I asked, "Ready for the real thing, pretty lady?"

"Sweet talker," he replied, reaching over for a rubber and some lube.

"Sweet asshole," said I.

"Oh," he purred, "I bet you say that to all the ladies."

"Um," I umed with a slight, involuntary shudder. "O-kay."

Choosing to change the subject, which was confusing the shit out of me, I slid on the rubber, my prick now jutting out from the side of my panties, and slicked us both up, one then two lubed digits gliding up and in, getting him good and ready for the looming onslaught.

I pressed the head of my cock up against his portal. Knock, knock. I was in. He was tight, his ass sucking me in until I was flush up against his smooth ass, balls banging flesh. His hiked-up skirt and my too-tight bra only barely registered in my semi-bothered brain; instead, I focused on his impressive tool and tantalizingly taught hole. Not his wig, not my wig, not the smudged makeup, the dangling earrings, or the wadded-up pantyhose on the floor.

Okay, screw it, the whole scene was a big drag mess, and so I fucked him fast, furious, and hard, willing the whole thing over and done with. All the while, he moaned and groaned and bucked and rocked, stroking his cock slowly, oh so slowly, clearly trying to make the moment last. Fuck-fuck-fuck. Bad karma, bad.

So, I took matters into my own hands. Well, hand, really. Meaning, I took his tool for him and stroked like mad, all while I pounded at his gratefully hardening prostate. Romantic, no. Expedient, yes. Besides, it was knowledge I was after, not romance. And knowledge was just what I got. In spades. Aces of spades, to be exact. Yep, cue the doom and gloom music again, 'cause what I learned wasn't any good. No sir, no how. Well, with David, at any rate, no ma'am, no how.

"Yes, yes," he howled, spewing streams of man-sap and fairly ruining his beautiful frock.

"Yes, yes," I sighed in return. Yes, thank God this over with. My kink, you see, un-kinked—it went, um, straight as a fucking arrow, in fact.

He cleaned us both off and begged for some night-time company. I told him I needed to get back; my friends would be worried. I had plans in the morning: I was donating a kidney. Anything to get the fuck out of there. He relented and called a cab. At last, I breathed a sigh of relief as I put my dress back on. Gladly, he got re-boyed while I was doing just the opposite. Then I gave him a quick hug and a kiss and hightailed out of there, the cab waiting for me as I emerged into the sticky night air.

I made it back to our room in one piece, thank goodness, and my friends were waiting for me on the balcony with an already open bottle of merlot, also thank goodness. "Thank goodness," I said, lunging for a glass before downing it one fell swoop, then quickly going for a refill.

"That bad?" Brandon asked.

I shut my eyes and tried to erase the memory. No luck. "Ask me again in ten years. Maybe that part of my brain will be wiped clean by then."

"So, the night was a total bust?" Briana asked.

I shook my head from side to side and let me eyes wander to the dark ocean down below, the white froth of the breaking waves still in evidence. "Yes and no," I replied.

Brandon groaned. "Let's start with the yes then."

"Okay," I started, "I was able to find the file for Edward Beles, the big boss."

The three of them sucked in their collective breaths. "And?" they all asked.

"And right on top there was a letter that he received in prison." I frowned and finished off my wine. "It was unsigned, but the gist of it was that Jed had turned him in to the police just after Makani was arrested."

"Ah," ahed Brandon, "so that's why Jed is in hiding. There's a pissed off, incarcerated drug lord out to get him." He paused and scratched his head. "Fuck," he added. "But we're supposed to turn whoever is after Jed over to him in exchange for Will. How can we do that if it's Edward Beles?"

"Wait," added Koni, "that doesn't make any sense. If Jed turned in Edward Beles, then he already knows who's after him, more than likely. Meaning, there can't be anyone to exchange for Will. Plus, why would Jed turn in Edward anyway? I know for a fact that Jed doesn't deal in drugs. The two sleaze-bags don't even seem to have a connection, as far as I can tell."

"Maybe Jed was trying for some sort of leniency after Lenny was caught, giving up Edward so that the authorities would leave him alone," I offered. "After all, in theory, Lenny worked for Makani, who, in turn, worked for Edward. The police would've certainly tried to tie Jed into all that, him being Lenny's supposed boyfriend, and all."

"Could be," Koni agreed. "I mean, Jed might not have been associated with Edward, but he probably knew who he was. Remember, this island is wee small and all the bad guys at least know about each other. And turning in someone you're not associated with wouldn't be bad for your business, at the very least."

Brandon shook his head. "But turning in someone with even a modicum of power can be bad for your health."

And then I shook my head, yet again. "Only, if Jed turned

Edward in, like the note said, he had no reason to think it would get back to Edward."

"Maybe," added Briana. "Or maybe not. I mean, if there's a bad presence on the police force, you'd think Jed would know about it. He also has money and power, it appears, so he's also probably got some knowledge of these sorts of things, even if it's only hearsay. Meaning, if he turned in Edward to save his own skin, he'd have to know that there'd be a chance that Edward would find out and try to get back at him, even from behind bars."

My head now sunk into my hands. "In other words, we're royally screwed. Edward Beles did read that note if David had it in his possession, so it is Edward or his goons that are after Jed, more than likely. But then Jed would know that, and would also know we'd have no one to exchange for Will. It just doesn't make any sense. Either Jed is playing us for some unknown reason or he doesn't know that Edward is after him."

"Ah," came Brandon's familiar ah. "Which could mean that someone is trying to lay the blame on Jed for Edward's incarceration, but Jed really isn't the guilty party, after all."

"A set up," Koni said. "Someone with a bone to pick with Jed."

"Ah," Briana too now ahed. "And we know who that probably is."

"We do?" I asked.

"Yeah, we do?" Brandon echoed.

"Ah," I eventually echoed, apparently, it being my turn to ah. "Liko. Getting Jed out of the picture means one less pimp on the local scene. Plus, they were both dating Lenny, so there was probably no love lost between the two of them. And, if Liko really was in love with Lenny, as we suspect, he probably hated Jed just enough to want to set him up."

Briana sighed. "That all makes sense, but it doesn't do us a hell of a lot of good. I mean, besides being mere speculation, there's nothing we can prove to Jed. And I'd hate to exchange an innocent man. Not to mention, how would we even get Liko to Jed's, even if we wanted to?"

To which Koni added, "Also, let's not forget about Lenny. We still have no idea who killed him. Jed was up north when Lenny was killed, Makani and Edward were in prison, and Liko, as far as we can tell, was in love with him. Not that that totally frees him from speculation, but I'd say it would go a long way. Plus, no one could've known about Lenny's escape."

"Which means," I added, a sour grimace on my face, "there's a fourth person we don't know about, someone with an axe to grind with Lenny and who had at least brief access to him just before we found him floating in the ocean. But who?"

"Fuck," Briana said with a snap of her fingers. "Sergeant Beles, our apparent police connection to all this. Who tipped off Makani that he was going to be arrested? Stands to reason, Makani's boss's own brother would do such a thing, if he was one of the bad guys."

"Fuck," I reiterated. "And Lenny escaped just outside the station house. He never made it to Liko for safe keeping. Meaning, the police killed him. Meaning, they killed Buck, too. Meaning, we're next, if we don't keep a low profile."

"Wait," Brandon added. "Sergeant Beles already knows us, and we already told him everything we knew. Not good, dudes. Not good. Anyone with information related to this is getting themselves killed, and we have a boat-load of it now. I'd be surprised if Chase and I aren't already next on the hit list."

"So, what do we do?" I asked. "Times running out, for Will and perhaps us."

We sat there, the sound of the distant breaking waves occasionally shattering the silence. "Well," Briana exhaled, startling the rest of us, "since no one else is stating the obvious, I'll be the brave one: we're just going to have to rescue Will. There's no one to trade him for and we can't go to the police."

I allowed myself the briefest of smiles at hearing her say this. "And it's not like we don't know where to start looking," I added. "Klaus told me that Jed is near La'ie. All we have to do is ask around. Maybe, we'll hit upon him before Will calls us."

"And if we don't?" Brandon asked.

My smile suddenly vanished. "Then we trade him for Liko. I mean, maybe Liko didn't kill Lenny, but he's definitely not all that innocent either. A pimp for an F.B.I. agent sounds like a fair trade to me."

"But how do we do that?" Koni asked.

"Difficult, but not impossible," I replied. "Judy and Liza now work for Liko. Liko drives a limousine. What if some rich bozo ordered up two Anglo hookers to go up to La'ie? And what if Liko had to take them there? Then we get up to La'ie undercover with Liko in tow. Simple."

My cohorts nodded, but looked unsure. "Then what?" Brandon asked, party-pooping all over my plan. "Even if we somehow managed to find Jed's hideout, how do we get Liko there along with us? And, even if we do manage that, how do we convince Jed to trade Will for him? Need I remind you, dear Chase, we have no real evidence against Liko, especially nothing that will make it look like Liko is out to get Jed instead of who really is, namely the incarcerated Edward Beles."

"Ah," I ahed, one final and glorious time, the smile now in full radiant force. "Not nothing, Brandon. We do, in fact, have one piece of evidence." From my bra, the one David gratefully made me keep on during our less than enjoyable—mostly—sexcapade, I removed a lone slip of paper. "Whoever wrote this did so to set Jed up. If we can prove it was Liko, then even if it is Edward that's after Jed, it's only because of our dear pimping limo driver friend. Meaning, we do indeed have something to trade with."

"And if we can't prove it?" Briana asked. "If we can't prove that Liko wrote the note?"

I poured the remainder of the wine and admonished her, "Glass half full, Briana. Glass half full."

***

To be on the safe side—chicken-shits that we are—we

pushed the dresser in front of the door and all slept in one room, waking up early to put our plan into action. Well, and to fortify ourselves with chocolate chip pancakes and mimosas. Anyway, yes, the plan was convoluted, and no, it wasn't easy, but it was all we had to work with.

Thankfully, we now had Briana, who Liko had yet to meet. Donned in her red wig and Jackie O. sunglasses, she was as incognito as we could possibly get her. She called down and ordered a limo, requesting Liko as her driver. Then she was off, as were we, to meet him, face-to-face.

"It's okay that we're going to the beach while she's risking life and limb, right?" I asked.

"It's what she would've wanted," Brandon replied, leaving her a note where to find us upon her return. "Though better to inform her of this after the fact."

"You guys are scared of a girl that barely reaches your chests," Koni chided.

"Meaning, her fists are at crotch-level," I reminded him.

"Oh, right." He grimaced. "I forgot."

So, we headed down, breathing in the fresh ocean air as the elevator opened up to reveal the new day. Yes, we were nervous, but at least we were now doing something to try and get Will back. And something was definitely better than nothing. Granted, when we rescued him with rich, sultry tans, he might not see it that way, but, as I always say, it's better to look good and feel terrible than to look terrible and feel good. Okay, I don't always say that, but I planned on doing so when Will eventually asked me how I could go sunbathing while he was being held in captivity—locked in a dank basement, gnawing on a grisly cow bone.

The chairs, as always, appeared seemingly out of nowhere, with our feet disappearing into the warm sand within seconds. I stared out at the sparkling blue water, the waves calm, rolling peacefully in, as couples held hands and walked through the tumbling, cool surf. I felt a pang in my heart, a throbbing in my chest. Brandon looked over and noticed my frown. "This will work," he told me, rubbing my hand.

"Pretty iffy," I replied.

"The best plans always are."

I laughed. "That don't make a lick of sense."

"No," he laughed back. "But, as George Michael says, you gotta have faith."

"The same George Michael who's been arrested for cruising men's bathrooms and passing out in his car while on drugs?" I asked.

"Okay, bad example," he allowed with a shrug. "Still, it's going to work."

Then Koni leaned in, and just simply had to ask, "Who's George Michael?"

"Oh, dear God," I groaned. "The fetus is bugging me again, Brandon."

My friend kicked some sand his way. "Shut up, fetus," he cautioned.

Koni harrumphed, but otherwise did as we told, only barely whispering, "Geezers," below his breath.

I smiled just the same, glad to at least have the company of comrades in arms, plus our newly-served second mimosas of the day.

Thirty minutes later, Briana made her triumphant return, her itsy-bitsy, teensy-weensy, yellow polka-dot bikini barely covering what little of her there was. "Glad to see you were worried about me," she told us, taking the seat we had reserved for her.

"Will this make up for it?" Brandon asked, handing her a frosty Piña Colada in a large hurricane glass with a thick slab of pineapple wedged on the rim.

"It's a start," she replied, the smile returning to her pretty face.

"So?" I asked eagerly, turning to look her way.

"So," she responded, "it's all set. I pretended to play the bumbling assistant looking for company for her bosses. Billionaire bosses. Which perked Liko's ears up right quick."

"Then you told him that the company would need to be in

La'ie sometime tonight, for whatever fee deemed appropriate?"
I asked.

Her smile widened. "I could see the dollar signs flash above
his head. Naturally, he said he knew of two girls that would be
perfect, and then offered to drive them there himself, telling me
he got off work at three o'clock and then asking if that would
work. I told him that would be fine, but only if these associates
of his met a certain criterion."

"Meaning, Anglo and looking exactly like us, of course,"
Brandon interjected.

"Yep. Exactly. Liko paused, but said that was fine. I bet he's
out looking for you two even as we speak. Better give him a call
before he finds two other girls like you," she said, downing half
her drink in celebration of her obvious success.

I nodded and jumped up. Liko didn't have our cell phone
numbers, nor would he ever. I called him from the lobby pay
phone. Needless to say, he was delighted to hear from me.

"Judy," he practically squealed. "I was just thinking about
you and Liza."

I bet. "How sweet. So, how did our little test go?"

He laughed. "Like gangbusters. Mister Yamasuka and Mister
Lanasaki are hard to please. They said they couldn't wait to see
you both again."

"They know that many words of English?" I asked, only
barely joking.

"Cute. Very cute. Hey, while I have you on the line, I have a
job for you ladies. Rich clients, up in La'ie."

I paused for effect. "We can't get up there," I told him. "No
cars."

"I'll take you," he quickly informed. "Good for business,
anyway. Expanding the territory. Beautiful drive, too. And big
bucks. See, I told you, Liko will take good care of the two of
you."

"Yep," I cooed, "you sure did. So, what time will you be
picking us up?"

I could practically hear him smiling from across the line. "A little after three. Same place as before. That work for you two?"

"Like a charm," I replied. "See you then."

After a quick phone call, I ran back to our chairs to find my friends chomping at the bit. "Well? Well?" Brandon practically shouted.

"So far, so good," I told them, plopping down with a heavy sigh. "Plus, I figured out a way to get Liko to Jed's, should the need arise."

"How's that?" Briana asked. "Drugging? Clobbering? Drugging and clobbering?"

I winced and replied, "Um, sounds like someone needs to get some aggressions out."

She reached over and socked me one in the arm. "Yes. Are you volunteering?"

"Anyway," I said, wisely changing the subject as I rubbed my sore spot, "no, no violence needed. I mean, you told Liko to drop Judy and Liza off at a local Starbucks, right?"

"Right," she agreed. "He drops you off and picks you back up when you call him. My so-called bosses like their anonymity. He said he could wait until noon the next day."

"Exactly. So, if all goes as planned, and we find Jed, we call Liko and tell him to pick us up there. Then we make the swap. Him for Will."

"But it'll be his word against ours when the confrontation occurs. And why on earth would Jed believe two hookers? Again, we have no proof that Liko wrote that note," Brandon argued.

To which I argued back, "No proof. Not yet. But wait, I think we will."

Koni looked our way, his head swinging from side to side. "Um, so I don't suppose you'd like to share this side plan with us, would you?"

"Nope. Not yet. Still working out the logistics," I told him. "But fret not, little one, you'll be there to see it come into fruition."

"He will?" Brandon asked, surprised at our young friend's

inclusion.

"Yeah, I will?" Koni asked. "But how? I still don't get this part. Liko is driving you and Brandon up. He doesn't even know about me and Briana. Thank God."

"And he never will, hopefully. But Brandon and I need you in La'ie."

"To help find Jed?" he asked.

"To help find Jed, yes. Odds are good, he has people working for him on the streets up there. People you might now. People who hopefully know where to find him."

"Huh," he huhed, his smile now evident, glowing like the shining sun. "You guys really do need me."

I reached over and patted his mop of hair. "Of course. Look at us. Could we possibly do this without you?"

He laughed. "Actually, it's a wonder you two can tie your own shoelaces."

I raised my feet to show him my laceless sandals. "Exactly," I concurred.

"But how do I get up to La'ie," he thought to ask.

"There's more than one limo driver in Oahu, and after I got off the phone with Liko, I hired one for you and Briana. He's picking you two up thirty minutes before Brandon and I get picked up."

"So, we'll have a head start," Briana added.

"Exactly," Brandon said.

"Yes, exactly," I agreed, suddenly staring at Koni, who had a strange look on his face. "What is it?" I asked him.

I roused him from his thought. "Oh, um, probably nothing. Just something I was thinking about. La'ie is a super small community. I don't know, maybe five thousand people at most. Why would Jed set up shop there?"

I shrugged. "Is there something there to attract tourists?"

He scratched his head, then smiled. "Oh yeah. Big time. The Polynesian Cultural Center is in La'ie. Huge place. Run by the Mormons."

"Huh?" I huhed.

"Yeah, huh?" Brandon echoed.

Koni nodded his noggin. "Yeah, sounds weird. But Brigham Young University Hawaii is up there, and they own and run the Center. Most of the performers and employees are Mormon students from Polynesian countries, and they're there on scholarship. Place turns a big-ass profit too. Meaning, mucho tourists."

"Mucho tourists with money to burn," Briana added.

"And for Jed to rake in," I also added.

"Now, all we have to do is find him," Brandon added to our additions.

I shut my eyes and buried my head in my hands. The sum of all this wasn't going to be easy to come by, I figured. Not by a long shot.

✨ Mormons Duped ✨

We ate lunch on the beach, waiting for our appointed hours with destiny. The meal, needless to say, didn't sit well with us. Though the drinks, needless to say, were fabulous and consumed in their entirety. And then, all too soon, we were back in our rooms getting dressed—Brandon in a short, short one piece frock, and me in a long, long two-piecer. Luckily, if we were still able to use such a word without getting struck by lightning, we weren't really going to La'ie for business, at least not the kind Liko had intended for us.

Briana and Koni left with a hug and a kiss and a promise for a quick reunion. They'd go up north, do some quick recognizance work, and meet up with us soon after we were dropped off. After that, we'd again be a foursome in search of our missing fifth, namely Will.

"Some vacation," I murmured, a short while later, trudging down the street, sticky sweat dripping down my pancaked forehead.

"Least we're seeing the island, though," responded Brandon, uncharacteristically, a strange smile appearing on his already-tanned face.

I turned to look at him. "Huh?" I huhed. "Oh wait, you just took a pretty blue pill, didn't you?"

"Two," he replied. "Want one?"

"Two," I also replied.

"Smart. They do take the edge off." He handed me the miniscule saviors, which I downed in one relieved gulp. "Better?" he asked.

"Couldn't be any worse."

He glanced down and took himself, then myself, in. "Well, it could be. Our dresses could be off the rack. Blech."

I grinned, despite the circumstances. "That the pills talking or are you just trying to make me feel better?"

His grin widened. "What do you think?"

I nodded my head, as did he. "The pills," we replied as one.

A minute later, we were walking into the now-familiar International Marketplace. Our smiles turned upside down when we spotted our new boss in the food court, his hand up and waving, his mouth stuffed with masticated hotdog.

He stood when we approached, offering a hand and a crumb-filled smile. I shivered, despite the fact that, yes, he was still adorable. "Ladies, a pleasure," he mumbled, still chewing as he gulped down his lunch.

We forced our own smiles to return. "Same here," I said.

Small talk clearly over, he started to lead us on our not-so-merry way.

"Wait," I semi-shouted.

He paused and turned. "Wait? Can't. Clients are expecting us."

"I mean, wait just a minute, please. We, um, we have a small matter to attend to."

"We do?" Liko asked.

"Yeah, we do?" Brandon asked, his head tilted to the side, all confused-puppy-like.

"Yes, we do," I reiterated, willing my still-in-the-dark friend to go along with my bright, shiny plan.

"Oh, oh yeah, we do," Brandon agreed, taking a seat and crossing his lady-like legs, trice covered in nylon. Trice, now there's a word not often used. Like lull and, um, cull.

I joined him and bade Liko to sit. He grumbled, but did as we asked. "Fine, just please hurry. Time is money."

"Exactly," I readily agreed, removing a piece of crisp, white paper from my brand-new Prada purse—calfskin, beige, three sparkling rhinestones along the side. Heaven. A stylish silver pen was quickly added alongside. "And money is the name of the game," I added, trying my best to keep my voice even. And womanly. Though by then I was willing to settle for one of the two, the latter being the safest bet, at that very moment.

In any case, he sighed, his eyes turning to mere slits, and said, "Um, FYI, I hate games."

My veins turned to ice, despite the intense Hawaiian heat. "Not a game then," I quickly corrected with. "Just business." I slid the paper toward him, the pen close behind, my heart beating furiously in my padded chest. "Something Liza and I thought you could sign. I mean, after all, we've never had a, well, um, agent before. Call it a letter of employment."

He grinned, sort of, and let loose a truncated chuckle. "Let me get this straight," he said. "You want me to sign a letter of employment? Put my name on a document with the intention of prostituting the two of you? Are you nuts?" He whispered all this, the smile tight, the words barely working through gritted teeth.

Brandon looked at me like I was insane. I held his hand and continued. "No, of course not, silly. In fact, you don't even need to sign your name to it. We just want something in writing that says you'll be there to protect us. You don't even need to be specific about what you're protecting us from."

Brandon piped in with, "Um, yeah, it's just that we'd feel better if we had more than your word on that one point, seeing as we've only just met you, and all. I mean, we are, in a way, putting our very lives in your capable, strong hands."

His face loosened, the full smile gratefully returning. Three cheers for Brandon! And fully medicated, no less. "I see," he said. "Fine. Just a short note. Nothing legally binding. Or illegally." He laughed at his lame joke. So, did we, leaning in to watch him put words to paper. Fifteen words, to be exact. But that was fine. I looked down and recognized three of them. This was exactly what we needed.

I quickly grabbed the paper away from him, and then we dashed to the waiting limo. We drove in silence, cutting up and over along Highway 63, which soon hugged the coast as we traveled north to La'ie along Highway 83. I watched the scenery whizz by, dense green flora on either side of us, the crystal-clear ocean down below, small houses, pristine lawns, an explosion of colorful flowers both high and low. Small communities with impossible to pronounce, vowel-laden names appeared and then disappeared in nearly the blink of an eye: Kane'ohe, Kahalu'u, Ka'a'awa, and Hau'ula. I tried to concentrate on the beauty of it all, and not on our approach to Will's hopeful whereabouts. I tried, of course, and miserably failed. Will, as you can guess, was never too far from my troubled mind, pretty blue pill or not.

Three quarters of the way there, Brandon poked me out of my reverie. "What was with that paper?" he whispered in my ear.

At last, my smile returned, unforced. "Insurance," I whispered back, clutching my purse. He looked at me in bewilderment, but I offered no more. If the time came that we'd need said sheet of paper, I was thrilled that we had it. Still, I prayed that the need would not arise because that would mean we were up Shit Creek. And, God, do I hate to paddle.

Within minutes, we were pulling into La'ie. Signs for the Polynesian Cultural Center and the Mormon Church were posted everywhere. Except for a few small businesses, these two seemed to be the only game in town. Liko pulled up to a corner Starbucks. "This is the place," he proclaimed over the speaker. "The lady who hired you two said she'd be by to pick you up in about ten minutes. Want me to wait around?"

"No," I shouted, then caught myself. "I mean, no, that's okay. We'll be fine. We have done this before, you know. But thanks."

"Suit yourself," he said. "Oh, and you'll each be getting paid a grand. I take thirty percent. Ask for the money up front. And call me when you're ready to be picked up. If you have any problems, I'll be nearby. Okay?"

"Okay," we both agreed, letting ourselves out of the limo.

He pulled away without another word. "Employer of the year," I muttered, coughing out the dust he left in his wake.

"Fucking fuckwad."

Brandon chortled and sat his tightly-encased ass on a nearby bench. "Still," he said, adjusting his wig and his boobs, "so far, so good."

The comment didn't go unheard. "Not quite," said the familiar voice.

We both turned our faces to the side. Koni and Briana were standing to our right, their heads moving from left to right.

"What does that mean?" I asked, the sound of dread creeping in.

"It means," Koni replied, "no leads. In fact, no people, hooker or otherwise."

"How can there be no people?" I asked.

He motioned with his head and his finger for us to follow. We did as he asked, the four of us walking a few short blocks away from the coffee shop. "This is why," he said, motioning out across the vast parking lot that lay before us.

"Oh," I ohed. "It looks like half of Hawaii is here." And I wasn't exaggerating. The Polynesian Cultural Center parking lot was jammed with cars and tour buses, acres of them, it seemed. I scratched my head. "But then, where does Jed drum up his business?"

"Good question," Briana replied. "And there can only be one answer."

"Which is?" I asked, still clearly in the dark.

She pointed beyond the parking lot. "Poor students, rich tourists. You do the math."

Brandon and I nodded in understanding. "Got it," he said. "Good cover, too. I mean, who would suspect a Mormon?"

Briana touched her finger to her nose. "Exactly. So, is anyone up for a little Polynesian culture?"

We paused. "Um, do they have booze in there? Beer, wine, fruity cocktails?" I asked.

Koni snickered. "Dude, place is run by the Mormon Church. What do you think?"

"I think," I replied, "that this drag ass should stay out here, just in case."

"Just in case what?" Briana asked, already pulling Brandon and I forward.

"In case, um, in case a daiquiri truck drives by. Judging from the crowds, or lack thereof, they'd need our business," I tried.

"Honey," she retorted, tugging harder, moving us ever closer to the entrance, "with customers like you two, they'd be able to retire. In a week."

"Good point," I said, preparing for the Mormon onslaught. Sadly, she was no longer listening by then.

***

We paid the exorbitant entrance fee—well, Brandon paid for us—and entered the park—though at forty-two acres, it was more like a town: a town broken up into communities of islanders from the Central and South Pacific Ocean, most of them students, most of them Mormon, and none of them looking like they'd ever even set foot in Utah.

"Just when you think you've seen everything," Brandon soon commented as we approached an area representing Tonga to watch an able-bodied man climb a coconut tree in order to retrieve, like duh, a coconut. "He doesn't look Mormon to me."

The man climbed down and split the coconut in half—with a rock and his bare hands! Then he drank the milk. "Strong fucking Mormon at that," I added.

"With a big dick," Koni also added.

I gaped down at the man's well-covered crotch. "You got x-ray vision, kid?" I asked.

He laughed and turned my way. "Wishful thinking, but no. His name's Ben. Big Ben, they call him. In the trade."

"Ah," I ahed. "Coconut tree climber by day, street walker by night. Great résumé builder."

"Though I'd imagine that the latter pays the bills better," he retorted. "In any case, I wondered what happened to him; I haven't seen him out working for weeks."

"Should've looked up rather than out then; guy's a born climber," Brandon commented as we continued onward, just to make sure our run-in with Ben wasn't coincidental.

We walked along the side of a green lagoon, happy tourists floating by in wide canoes, snapping pictures as they passed the villages of Hawaii, Samoa, New Zealand, Tahiti, the Marquesas, and Fiji. We too strolled through each of these, taking in the free shows, the island crafts, the expensive tourist food, and—yuck—booze-free drinks. And, as expected, we caught sight of quite a few of Koni's ilk, which is why, just to be on the safe side, we covered our young friend up with a straw hat and sunglasses, to keep our mission under wraps. Still, he recognized each of them in turn, filling us in on their stories, none of them happy, not by a mile.

"Guess we were right," I finally said, an hour into our cultural journey. "Thousands of tourists parading by every day, ripe for the picking."

"And no cops," Koni pointed out. "Jed must be raking in some heavy dough up here."

"Yep," I agreed, "but that doesn't help us in locating him. I mean, I doubt most of them know where he lives, and I doubt even further that they'd be willing to fill us in, even if they did."

Brandon turned to Koni, and asked, "Any ideas, kid?"

He paused and played with the meager hairs on his chinny-chin-chin. "Maybe," he soon said, and then informed, "but we have to find some flour first."

"Flour, huh?" asked Brandon, arms crossed over brawny chest. "Are we gonna bribe one of them with a freshly baked cake?"

"Cake, no. Bait, yes," he replied, cryptically. "Let's just split up and meet back here in fifteen minutes. There's gotta be flour around here somewhere. I doubt they truck all this crappy food in."

We did as he asked, each of us wandering off to a different corner, sniffing for baked goods as we did so. I returned empty-handed, my companions already standing at the designated spot.

"No luck," I informed. "Lots of cake and cookies, but no flour."

"Same here," said Briana.

"Ditto," sighed Koni.

Brandon smiled and produced a hefty white bag from behind a nearby tree. "Will this do?" he asked.

My friend rarely amazes me anymore. Still, finding a pound of flour in fifteen minutes was impressive, even for him. "Who'd you have to suck off to get that?" I asked.

He dropped the bag to the ground in a puff of white smoke. "How insulting," he replied, his hand to his barely-there heart, his head tilted away in mock injury.

"Okay," I corrected. "Who'd you let suck you off then?"

He turned his face back our way, the briefest of lascivious smiles appearing. "Horny baker who spotted my Adam's apple. We forgot to wear scarves today, Judy."

My hand involuntarily shot up and ran down my throat. "Fuck," I coughed out, the flour cloud rising as I rummaged through my purse for some sort of cover-up.

"Yeah, for that I would've gotten two pounds of flour," hacked my slutty best friend. "In any case, what's this shit for, kid?"

Koni removed a cookie from his back pocket. It was in a clear baggie. He ate the cookie, naturally, and then ripped the bag of flour open. Filling the baggie with the white powder, he stated, proudly, "Bait, as promised."

Three imaginary light bulbs appeared over three not-so-imaginary heads. "I take it that some of your friends in the field have a drug problem," Briana quickly surmised.

"Understatement," Koni replied. "That's why so many of them turn to tricking in the first place—to pay for their nasty habits. In any case, a big bag of powdered coke, like this one here, should be good enough to get us some valuable information."

"Wait," I interjected, "but it's not coke, it's flour. And whoever we sell it to is going to know that as soon as they try it out, which they'll probably do before they buy it."

His smile doubled in size. "Yeah, cute dude, unless the person we sell it to is only buying it to resell it. Someone who doesn't do drugs. Ever. Someone who can turn a hefty profit without having to wiggle his big willy."

"Ben," the three of us said in unison.

"Ben," he echoed, his noggin bobbing up and down. "Sure, he can climb a tree, but that's about all he can do, other than shake his money maker. Give him another option to make some quick cash, and he'll take it. Luckily for us, he really does practice this Mormon stuff. Meaning, no stimulants. Meaning, no coke."

"Um," I umed, "don't the Mormons frown on prostitution, too?"

"And homosexuals. Still, a guy's gotta make a living. Ben figures he's just using what the good Lord amply gave him. He also has no problem selling drugs to non-Mormons. Weeds out the evil non-believers, he figures."

"One problem, though," I said. "He already knows you, and it'd look suspicious if you were selling drugs in La'ie, all of a sudden. My guess is, it would get back to Jed, which we definitely don't want to happen."

"True," Koni agreed, "but he definitely doesn't know either Judy or Liza, and neither does Jed, thank goodness."

I grimaced. "Great, first I take up prostitution, and now drug dealing. This vacation just keeps getting better and better. Maybe after dinner we can do some slave trading."

"Technically," he corrected, ignoring my griping, "it's flour dealing, which I doubt is a crime. Besides, Ben's dumber than dirt. This should be easy for the two of you. Just sell it to him super cheap and then somehow get him to tell you where Jed is hiding out."

"Somehow," I reiterated. "How somehow?"

"Use your feminine persuasions," he tried.

"But I'm not a woman and he's gay anyway, right?"

"Stop being so difficult. The worst you can do is fail, and

then we'll just be back to the old drawing board."

I sighed. "Fine. But remember, the guy cracked a coconut open with his bare hands, so the worst that could happen is not, as you said, fail. The worst that could happen would be that my head would be next on his list of items to split."

"Or mine," Brandon added.

"As if anyone could put a chink in that thick thing," I said.

"Asshole," he sneered.

Briana piped in. "Please, not now. Mamma's got a massive headache. Just take the flour, strike up a bargain, and find out where Jed is hiding."

"But…"

"No. Go. Now."

We bowed our heads and slunk away, the baggie of flour well-hidden in Brandon's purse. "Geez, what's her problem?" I whispered.

"Must be her time of the month," he whispered back.

We ducked just in time, the small coconut whizzing by us at alarming speed. "Shut up and go," we heard shouted from behind us. Needless to say, we did as we were told.

Ben was sitting off to the side, reading his bible and sipping on a box of milk. Wearing nothing but a leather wrap-around, he made for an unusual site. And yes, I know, considering what we were wearing, look who's talking, right? Anyway, he looked up when we approached.

"Next show's in a half hour, ladies," he informed, a wide grin on his handsome, dark face, a trickle of milk trailing down his chin.

We smiled in return and stood facing him. "We caught your last one. You're amazing," Brandon cooed, sending our patsy's grin into overdrive.

"Just doing the Lord's work," he replied. "However odd it is that it's up a tree."

"Funny you should say that, young man," I said, just as the Lord, at that very moment, shot down a beam of inspiration to yours truly.

He stood up and set his bible down on the rock he'd been sitting on. We towered over him in our high heels. "And why would that be funny?" he asked, his grin only slightly fading.

"Well now," I began. "We're from Salt Lake City."

"Utah?" he asked, now staring up at us in wonderment. "I've always wanted to go there, to be among my people."

"Our people," I told him.

"You're Mormons?" he asked.

To which Brandon replied, "We're Mormon's?" And then quickly amended with, "I mean, yes, we're Mormons. Osmonds, in fact. Distantly related."

"Yes," I agreed, nodding my head. "Very distantly. And we're just back, in fact, from doing missionary work. A breather before we head on home."

Brandon looked at me like I was nuts, but nodded his head just the same. "Yes, tell the dear boy where we flew in from, sister," he said, only slightly nudging me in the ribs.

I racked my brain trying to think of an appropriate city, the Lord's beam rapidly dimming. "Bogota," I blurted out.

"Columbia?" Ben asked. "You two ladies did missionary work in Columbia?" He looked at us in surprise.

"Yes," Brandon chimed in. "Central America is so desperately in need of the gospel." I nudged him back, hard. "Er, South America, I mean. We spread the word from one impoverished hamlet to the next. Wretched place. Just wretched."

Ben nodded at us sagely. "I'd imagine. And dangerous, too. I mean, for two such, um, dainty women such as yourselves."

Dainty. Now there's a complement neither of us would've expected. Still, we played it to the hilt. "Yes, very. Poverty, violence, rampant drug dealing."

He coughed and momentarily looked away. "Well," he eventually said, "at least you made it back in one piece."

We vigorously bobbed our heads up and down. "And made it through the airport without getting arrested," I said, then quickly put my hand over my mouth. "Oops," I added for effect.

Brandon, catching on to this part of my plan, slapped me on my arm. "Now, Judy, we're not supposed to talk about that."

"What?" Ben asked, his eyes now wide. "Talk about what? Why would you get arrested at the airport? Is Mormonism illegal in Columbia?"

I looked at Brandon, our eyes locked in silent speech, as if to say, is it okay to tell him our secret? Well, that's what we wanted it to seem like, at any rate. And then I smiled and said, "Show him, Liza. I think we can trust our new friend here."

He/she paused and then slowly unzipped his/her purse. We looked around, to make sure the coast was clear, and then quickly removed the baggie of flour for Ben to see, and then just as quickly shoved it back inside.

"Is that what I think it is?" Ben asked, a bead of sweat now running down his smooth cheek.

"Uh huh," I replied. "Top notch, first-rate Columbian cocaine. Our host family had no money to repay us for helping them find salvation. They gave us this instead."

To which Brandon added, "And it would've been the height of rudeness to decline their most generous offer. It was all they had. Luckily, two Mormon missionaries such as ourselves didn't arouse suspicion at the airport." He gulped for effect. "It was all we could do to make it through security without fainting dead away from fear."

Ben's head was now bobbing along with our own. "I'd think so," he said, clearly calculating his next move. "But what are you going to do with it now?"

"Sell it?" I said with a shrug. "And give the money to the church, of course."

He laughed, clearly thinking, bingo! "How would two missionaries go about selling a bag of coke? Who would you sell it to? And what if the police caught you? You could both go to prison for years."

"Dear me," I said, clutching my (fake) chest.

"Yes, dear us," Brandon agreed. "Do you have any other

suggestions, young man?"

He pretended to mull it over. Lull and mull, two words you don't hear much of. Oh, and, of course, the aforementioned cull. "Well, seeing as we're all Mormons, I could sell it for you, and then donate the money to the church."

I sighed and exhaled, a smile returning to my face. "But won't it be dangerous for you, young man?"

"Not as much as for the two of you," he replied. "I know this island better. I'm sure I can find someone to sell it to without fear that the police will find out. And, as you said, it's for the church."

"Amen," Brandon said.

"Yes, amen," I agreed, watching as my friend again removed the baggie from his purse, and then added, "But, just in case, I'd feel better if you gave us your cell number." He looked at us with a mix of curiosity and alarm. "You know, so we could check in on you, make sure everything went smoothly. I don't think I could live with myself if I thought we got you into any sort of trouble."

Ben paused, his hand tentatively reaching out to take the baggie. "We insist," Brandon insisted, then whispered, "We'll give you the cocaine for your number. Otherwise, it just wouldn't feel right." He bounced the baggie in his hand, to visually show Ben the obvious heft of it.

And that was all she wrote. "Deal," he practically shouted, snatching it out of Brandon's grip before shoving it inside his leather skirt. Then he reeled off his cell number as I wrote it down. He ran off soon afterward, clearly thinking he'd scored, big time. Little did he know that all he scored was the ability to make a nice-sized cake.

Brandon, collapsing on a rock, looked up at me, and asked, "What the fuck just happened?"

I smirked and patted his bewigged head. "Still haven't figured it out yet?"

"What?" he asked. "Is there more to the plan? You lost me about halfway through."

I motioned for him to follow me to a nearby pay phone. A minute later, I had his answer for him. "That was indeed Ben's cell phone number he gave us," I told him.

"And?" he anded.

"Wait, let's regroup first. It might make him suspicious if he gets the call now."

"What call? What are you talking about?"

I ignored the question and ambled off. Brandon followed close behind as we met up with Briana and Koni. "Well?" they asked with expectant looks on their faces.

"Yeah, well?" Brandon also asked.

They looked at my friend and scratched their heads. "What does that mean?" said Briana. "You two were together, right? Don't you know what happened, Brandon?"

He hid his face, and mumbled through his hand, "Not a fucking clue."

They looked at me, then at him, then back at me. "Well, cute dude, what happened? Do we know how to find Jed or not?"

I shrugged. "Possibly. We'll know in a few minutes. But first, we have to find a rental car company. Just in case."

Brandon punched me in the arm, followed soon by an even harder wallop from Briana. "Stop being so damned cryptic," she said, with Brandon and Koni nodding the same sentiment.

I smiled a wide and beguiling grin, clearly delighted at my rare upper hand. "You get more flies with honey," I suggested.

"Okay," Brandon replied through gritted teeth. "Tell us your plan, honey, or I'm going to let the next one fly upside your head."

I ignored the comment and turned around, walking back the way we'd entered. The three of them sighed, but trailed close behind. Luckily, there was a rental car company in the center of town. It was small, with just a few cars, but we only needed one, and one was all they had available. Then I found a payphone down the street.

"Now," I finally told them, "we find out where Jed is. Or not." I smiled, but before anyone could hit me again, I read from the piece of paper I'd written on and started dialing. He answered on the second ring, thank goodness, because my heart was about to pound right through my (padded) blouse.

"Who's this?" Ben asked, immediately.

"Jed," I replied, curtly, my voice even, deep—though I hadn't a clue as to what he sounded like.

Ben coughed and stuttered out, "Jed? Um, yeah, Jed, how can I, um, how can I help you?"

Clearly, he wasn't accustomed to hearing from his employer. "Meet me at my house in fifteen minutes. I've got a job for you."

Again, he coughed. "Yeah, okay. But, um, you never like us to come to your house. Never. Remember?"

"Don't tell me what I do and do not like. Just get over here." I hung up before he could reply, and looked at my friends with a look of out and out satisfaction. "Yes," I told them, "in answer to your question, we know where Jed is. Or at least soon will."

They looked at me in utter and well-deserved astonishment. It was Brandon who bowed his head first and began a slow clap. "Bravo," he said. "And all done with nothing but fat cells in that pee-sized brain of yours."

I grinned, despite the back-handed compliment. It was, of course, the best he was capable off. "Thanks," I replied humbly. "Now, we follow Ben straight to Jed."

"Then what?" Koni asked, thereby bursting my bubble. Which is usually booze-soaked and fairly impenetrable.

I faltered. "Beats me. One plan per day is all I can muster. We were fortunate to get that much. I'm kind of like a leap year in that regard—I come around once every four years. So, tag, you're it."

They didn't reply, figuring, I was certain, we at least had a promising lead. So, we got into our beat-up rental car and stared at the entrance to the Cultural Center. Sure enough, not a minute later, Ben emerged, walking quickly to his even-more-beat-up mess of a car, a scowl on his face, his barely-there outfit replaced by shorts and a tight tank.

We gave him a minute head start and followed a couple of car lengths behind. Thankfully, the roads around La'ie were narrow and curvy, so he had to drive slowly, despite the obvious rush he was in. None of us said more than two words, tense as we were, afraid of the unknown, of what we were going to do next. Terrified at the idea that Will was almost in our grasp, but seemingly unreachable.

And then, a short while later, and after umpteen turns, a house loomed up ahead. It was on cul-de-sac, a dead end. Gulp. Ben pulled in to an arced driveway, while we pulled off to the side of the road, behind a tree, out of sight.

He hopped out of his car and ran to the door, then knocked and waited. And waited. And waited some more. One minute, two, three, five, ten. Nothing. The lights were off, no one was home. He scratched his head and sat on the front stoop. Another five minutes, and he drove off. We ducked behind a tree and watched him zoom back the way he'd arrived.

"Well," I said with a heavy sigh, "at least he won't find out that Jed really didn't call him."

"Not immediately, but probably at some point," Briana added.

I nodded. "Hopefully, after we rescue Will, when it won't matter that someone is obviously playing games with his worker bees. In any case, this truly does bode well for us."

"Because no one's home and we have free reign of the place?" Koni asked.

"Exactly," I told him, a relieved smile forming on my face. "If Will is still in there, we can get him out and be gone before anyone is the wiser."

Brandon grimaced. "So, Einstein, you have a key to this place?"

My smile vanished in a heartbeat. "Please stop raining on my pride parade, dearest one."

"Then get off your float, dipshit," he responded, "and come down to the real world. The door is locked, for sure, and there has to be surveillance cameras everywhere, just like there was at his last hideout. For all we know, there are armed guards lurking about, ones that don't answer the door unless someone's trying to force it open. Meaning, we've made it to the pearly gates, and the angels are away on vacation. Indefinitely."

I snickered. "Yeah," I said, "as if you'll ever be facing those."

He punched me and started walking up the road to the house.

"Where are you going?" Briana shouted after him.

He paused and turned around. "Three sisters and their teenage brother. Lost. Their car broken down on the side of the road."

"What's that?" she shouted back. "The plot of some book you're reading?"

I poked her with my elbow. "He doesn't read," I whispered out of the corner of my mouth.

"I heard that," he yelled back. "And no, it's not the plot of some book. It's the plot of right here and right now. Real life plotting. Someone had to come up with something. Might as well be me. So, let's go. Time's awastin'."

Reluctantly, our unhappy group approached our supposed leader. "But what if, as you say, the place really is guarded, under surveillance?" I asked.

He shrugged. "So what. They have no idea who we are. If asked, we're lost, just like I said. Not like we look like we're up to no good, not in these outfits."

Which was true. Just as he said, we were three gussied up broads with a teenage-looking dude in tow. Not exactly the rescue cavalry.

We approached the front door, my heart thumping, my breath ragged. We knocked. We waited. Nothing, just as with Ben. I looked at Brandon; he looked at me. "Well?" I asked, glad to relinquish authority.

"Side fence," he said, already heading that way.

The house was nice-sized, the fence ultra-high, solid wood, no gaps in the slats. Place cost some ultra-big bucks, the occupants obviously not hurting for cash. There was a door leading to, we figured, a yard; it was latched, shut good and tight. We knocked loudly. No reply. And no surprises there.

"We could try huffing and puffing," I suggested.

Brandon groaned. "I'm all up for blowing, but not a solid-wood fence." He looked around and spotted our salvation. A decorative rock sat in the corner of a well-manicured garden. He ran over and rolled it our way. "But climbing might do the trick."

"And doing the trick is your specialty," I commented.

He let it go, but not without a punch to my arm first. Then he climbed up, his hands just reaching the top rim. We three bent down and hoisted him up, until his padded chest hung over the other side and his legs dangled down.

And then, "Oh fuck," said he.

"Oh fuck what?" asked we.

And—cue the dreaded oh fuck music—the gate swung in, Brandon along with it. And we knew in an instant what our friend was oh fucking. For there, standing before us, were two of the biggest, meanest, unfriendliest looking Hawaiians I'd ever seen. Dressed in black suits and black sunglasses, they were no happier to see us than we were to see them.

"Aloha," I managed with a limp-wristed wave.

"What the fuck are you doing?" the larger of the two behemoths asked.

"Our car broke down," Brandon responded from high up above.

The Hawaiian glanced his way and asked, "So, you're breaking in to call a tow truck? What, no cellphones?"

We had no answer for that one, least not a good one. Clearly, our plan wasn't that, um, planned out. As usual, it was Briana to the rescue, batting her eyelashes as she pushed out her ample bosom. "Sorry, we're not from Oahu. We didn't know who to call. We were only hopping the fence because no one answered the front door, and we wanted to see if that was because someone was out back and couldn't hear the doorbell."

I grinned, moaning internally. "Yes," I agreed. "That's why we, um, didn't use our cellphones. Sorry. Can you, um, can you help us?" I too batted my eyelashes and also pushed out my ample, albeit fake, tits.

The Hawaiians grimaced and turned their attention back to Briana. They shook their heads and slammed the door, flinging Brandon out and down, thankfully onto a soft(ish) bush. "Ouch," he grumbled.

We helped him up. "Hey," Briana shouted at the door. "That any way to treat a lady?" I pointed to Brandon and myself. "Three ladies," Briana corrected. I pointed to Koni. "Three ladies and a, um, three ladies." Still, there was no response.

"Wait," Brandon whispered. "Those black suits, I see them around San Francisco all the time. Maybe those goons aren't dressed like bodyguards."

"Huh?" I huhed.

He ignored my huhing, and shouted, "Three ladies on their way to church. The Mormon Temple."

Again, we waited, the silence nearly deafening. Then a sound, a click. The door creaked open, the Hawaiians still standing there, expressionless. They craned their necks down to stare at us. "You four are Mormons?" the bigger one asked, the faintest of smirks appearing on his otherwise stony face.

"On a retreat," I tried. "From Salt Lake."

Their faces now lit up. Well, like a twenty-watt bulb, but at least it was a start. "You don't look like Mormons," said the smaller of the two. "Dress wise."

"There's a good reason for that," I said, praying some logical reason would present itself.

"Which is?" I was asked.

"Fire," Brandon blurted out.

"Fire?" both Hawaiians asked. "You're dressed like that because of a fire?"

And that sent my mind to racing, the logical idea, somehow and miraculously, presenting itself. "Yes," I replied. "Fire. Our, um, hotel caught fire." They looked at me dubiously. "Just a few rooms. Electrical problem. But our usual clothes got smoke-ridden. And you know the kind of stuff they sell in Waikiki." I pointed to our outfits.

They nodded. "A sin," opined the bigger one.

Considering what we paid, yes it was, but not in the way he meant it. "Yes, a sin. In any case, we were on our way to the Temple and got turned around. Then our car broke down over there. Perhaps it was God's will we ended up here, beholden to the kindness of strangers. Mormon strangers, if I'm not mistaken."

At last, they shot down scary full-on smiles, which stretched wide across their dark faces. "Takes one to know one, right?" the smaller one asked. "But where are your husbands?"

Ah, the volley was tossed, at last. And now we had the home-court advantage. "Three single sisters chaperoned by their brother," I said. "Adopted brother, I mean." I hoped they were too smitten to realize that the three so-called sisters looked nothing alike.

The door opened wider, revealing a massive courtyard, well-groomed, lush with plant life. The Hawaiians split apart, opening up a tight alleyway between them. For the briefest of moments, I felt like Moses, the sea parting to let us in to the Holy Land. "We'll call a tow truck for you, ladies. The master of the house is away, briefly, so your stay must be a short one," said the smaller of the two. Though it was a bit like comparing the Alps to the Rockies.

To which the larger one added, "And then perhaps we could meet afterwards, say for dinner?"

We three sisters looked at each other and nodded. "That would be lovely," Briana agreed.

They smiled, lowering their menacing sunglasses. "Great," the larger one said. "Now, if you'll give us a moment, we'll go call for the truck, then we'll make plans for later. Okay with you?"

We nodded, walking into a large sunken living room and then depositing ourselves onto two leather sofas. In an instant, we were alone.

"So, this is what a lion's den feels like," I quipped. "A lot more luxurious than I would've expected."

The four of us sat there staring at each other, waiting for one of us to come up with something brilliant. Sadly, we'd all had our daily brainstorms and were frightfully tapped out. Then again, it wasn't brainstorms that were going to save us.

Not this time.

Perhaps not ever again.

Because it was at that very moment that the owner of the den, the lion named Jed, made his appearance. Four sets of eyes bulged and a couple of sets of now-thankfully-concealed Adam's apples bounced up and down. Our host scanned the room. "Who the fuck are you?" he asked, his voice echoing off all four walls, deep and threatening, sending every nerve-ending in my body on edge.

Like deer caught in the headlights, we froze. "Um, our car broke down," I tried.

"Your car broke down? A bit off the beaten track, weren't you?" he asked, an obvious sneer on his angular face. Jed was handsome but cruel looking, short and bulky, someone you wouldn't want to run into down a dark alley. I knew in an instant that he didn't believe us, and that flirting would be a lost cause.

I tried again. "We were looking for the Temple and took a wrong turn, then our car broke down. Your men are calling a tow truck for us."

He sat down across from us, his legs crossed, his head thrown back. "Strange," he eventually said, startling us. "My men were told not to allow anyone inside, ever, under no circumstances."

The men in question had entered the room, but remained silent. They knew they'd done wrong, and looked, much to my worry, nervous. They outweighed him three to one, but were cowering like scared sheep, making us appear like lambs to the slaughter.

"Sorry," Brandon said. "We'll wait for the truck outside then."

We took our clue, the four of us standing and inching away from the couches. Jed let us get to the edge of the living room, but not an inch more. "Nope," he said.

We froze, hearing the click of the gun. We turned and saw it pointed our way, moving from side to side, aiming for each of us in turn. "You'd kill three defenseless women and a young boy?" Brandon asked. "On their way to church? Bad karma."

He laughed. "Trust me," he replied. "My karma's already fucked. In any case, I don't think you were heading for church. In fact," he continued, now standing up, moving closer, closer still, the whites of his eyes narrowing, "I think you somehow found this place on purpose."

My legs shaking, my heart madly pounding, I countered with, "But we don't even know you."

He chuckled, the gun quivering in his grasp, sending a cold chill down my spine. "True. But it's not me you came to see. Nor my men, I'd imagine." The men in question cast their eyes downward; we stared ahead, terrified that the gun would go off at any second, one of us taken out before our very eyes. He continued. "No, I believe you're looking for a certain guest of mine. He too was looking for me a few days back on another part of the island, for reasons still unknown. You must be pretty good friends to be willing, and able, to come searching for him here. Don't you know who I am by now? The bad guy? The one your mothers warned you about?" Again, he chuckled, sinister as all fuck.

I moved an inch toward him, realizing I had to play the ace up my sleeve. It was now or never. And never wasn't much of an option. "Will," I offered.

"Will," he echoed. "Now we're getting somewhere."

My friends looked to me, the terror evident in their faces. But I knew something they didn't know. That is to say, had something they were unaware of. "Yes, we came to get Will. He called and said that if we could find the person that was out to get you, you'd make a trade. Will for that person. And someone most definitely is out to get you."

Jed nodded, the gun only slightly pointed away now, but still raised, still a heartbeat away from our annihilation. "I allowed the call. Seemed fair. I could've killed your friend, but been none the wiser about who, as you say, was out to get me. At least in the short run. And someone is out to get me, for sure, also as you say. You all aren't the only ones trying to find me, to put me out of business, or worse. Still, I knew it wasn't him, because I didn't know him. And this island is small, and I already know just about everyone I need to know. And I don't know you four, either. That's not to say you're not my enemies, but it seems unlikely. In any case, you were supposed to wait three days, and then we'd trade the information elsewhere. You broke the rules. Tsk, tsk."

I forced a smile. "Will said he'd call in three days. Yes. But we have the information now, the person now. And this is the only place we can offer him to you."

"In my home, temporary though it may be?"

"In your home, yes. Or, more importantly, while we're all together. In person," I told him, my voice quaking, my knees knocking, try as I might to keep them ramrod-straight, to hold me up.

He shook his head from side to side. "I don't buy it," he said, the gun again rising, causing me to jump. "If you all are just tourists, as your friend, Will, tried to explain, a group of tourists somehow embroiled in the arrest of my ex, Lenny, then how did you find me so easily? Twice now, at two different houses? The cops can't even find me. And yet here you are. In my fucking living room. Doesn't add up."

"Doesn't need to," I replied, praying he wouldn't shoot me for my insolence. "I know who's out to get you. I can prove who's out to get you. And I can hand him over on the proverbial silver platter. Provided we get Will back, as you promised, in return. Beyond that, we have no connection to you, never have, hopefully never will again."

He leaned on the back of a leather chair, rubbing the side of the gun with his outstretched palm, the smile still there, the eyes running from me to my friends and back again. "Pretty brave for a little lady such as yourself. Not to mention one without a gun." He paused, obviously pondering his next move. "You don't have a gun, do you?" Again, there was that laugh.

I laughed as well. Flirting might not have helped, but sucking up couldn't hurt. My friends took the hint and laughed along with me. "No gun," I replied. "Just a certain person you're looking for. That is to say, who's looking for you. To get you, as you say. Put you out of business, one way or the other."

He sighed. "Fine. A trade then. This person for Will. Even Steven." He set the gun down by his side. "Now, where exactly is this person?"

Everyone turned my way, allies included. I reached into my purse and removed my cellphone. I looked up at Jed. "No funny business, promise. I just have to call him and give him the address. He'll be here in fifteen minutes, tops. Then we make the trade."

He nodded his head. "If he's not here in fifteen minutes, the four of you are dead. One by one. Pop, pop, pop, pop. Understand? Oh, and if the person you're calling tries anything, again, pop, pop, pop, pop, and an extra pop for your friend downstairs. Yes?"

A lone bead of sweat trickled down my forehead. "Yes," I agreed. "He'll be here." Please, dear God, let him be here.

I dialed him, at last unafraid of his having my number show up on his cell. Did I feel the slightest twinge of guilt at setting him up? Oh, hell yes. Still, it was either him or Will—meaning, I could live with myself for doing this. He was, after all, still a bad guy, pimping people that were just barely out of their teens, plus Lord only knew what else.

He picked up on the fourth ring, my chest pounding, my head throbbing. "Who's this?" he asked.

"Judy," I replied. "We need help. They don't want to pay."

"Fuck," he groaned. "Fine, I'll be right there. What's the

address?

I held my hand over the receiver as Jed mouthed it to me, and then I repeated it back to Liko. "Hurry," I said, trying to keep my voice even. "These guys are scary."

"Yeah, yeah," he said. "Keep it calm. I'll be right there."

I hung up. The room was eerily silent. We all stared at each other. "He's on his way," I announced.

"Who's on his way?" Jed asked. "I mean, who exactly?"

I smiled, not ready to play my trump card just yet. "Wait and see," I replied, instead. "But this is the man who is out to get you. I'm certain of that much."

Jed shook his head. "You're playing with fire, lady. Just spill it."

I smiled, moving my head from side to side. "Please, just wait until he gets here. Everything will be obvious then."

We all sat down, saying nothing, staring at the ground, anywhere but at the gun. Five minutes, ten, fifteen. The doorbell rang, right on time. I allowed myself a breath. Liko had come, as promised. The trade would happen. It would. It had to.

One of the goons opened the door and escorted Liko in. His face went white when he realized where he was.

"You bitches tricked me," he coughed out, trying and then failing to beat a hasty retreat. Naturally, he was no match for the two towering Hawaiians.

"Liko," Jed said with a nod of his head.

"Jed," Liko said, held in place, his eyes steely, beady, full of hatred.

"So, you two do know each other?" I asked.

Jed laughed. "Of course, we do. Small island. Same business."

"Same boyfriend," Liko added, lips pursed, rage rising up his neck in a red flush.

"You knew that, too?" I asked.

They both looked at me. "Yes," Jed said. "But why do you know it? Just who the fuck are you?"

I coughed, changing the subject. "Doesn't matter. Let's just make the trade."

Liko struggled with his captors. "What trade? What the fuck's going on?"

Again, Jed laughed, good and hard. "They brought you to me," he said, looking around the room at our odd gathering. "Just as I planned."

Koni and Brandon and Briana and I stared at him in shock. "Huh?" we all huhed.

To which I added. "How did you plan it? We barely planned it. And only just recently at that. Care to explain?"

His laughter abated, the gun again pointed our way. "Are you sure you want to know, little lady?"

I gulped. "Never mind."

"Yeah," Brandon seconded. "Never mind."

"Yeah," Koni thirded. And then, "Yeah," Briana fourthed.

"Too bad," said Jed, "because I'm going to tell you anyway. And then, well, I'm going to have to kill you. All of you." He pointed the gun to Liko's head. "And especially you. Then your friend Will. And that will be the end of this little mess."

It was then I went for broke. Out of options, I blurted out, "I don't think the F.B.I. will like that too much. And then this little mess, as you call it, will most definitely turn into one giant one."

It was then that the room went deadly silent.

Deadly, obviously, not being the best choice of words.

✳ **Missions Accomplished** ✳

"What?" was all Jed could say.

All heads turned my way, as did, fuck, the gun.

"Will," I managed. "Is a federal agent. Not only that, at this very moment, the concierges at three separate hotels have letters containing our whereabouts: one letter will be mailed to the local authorities, one to the state, and one to Will's boss, should we not come to claim them in exactly two hours. All three mention you by name, Jed. And, like we keep hearing, this island is small enough that you'll have nowhere to run to, nowhere to hide. You kill us, and you seal your own fate."

Jed stared at me, his mind obviously working out his next move. "Get him from downstairs," he soon said to one of his henchmen. "Quickly."

I held my breath, neither looking right nor left—though I knew for certain that it was Koni staring the hardest at me. A minute later, Will at last appeared. I looked up, locking eyes with him, my heart pounding, boom, boom, boom. "Sorry," I said. "I had to tell him."

He nodded, obviously understanding.

It was all I could do to not run up and hug him, to hold him in my arms and tell him that everything would be okay. Jed, unfortunately, crushed the moment. "Fine, let's start from the beginning then. Maybe we can still work something out." He looked, for the first time, nervous. Thank goodness for that.

"Fine," I echoed. "Let's hope so. In any case, like we told you, we're in no way out to get you. We were just looking to save Will, who, in turn, was looking for Lenny, until Lenny turned up, well, you probably already know how Lenny turned up."

He looked at me, his face twisted in uncertainty. "No," he said. "How did Lenny turn up? Did the police finally capture him?"

The question was unexpected. True, the news still hadn't broken, but I assumed that Jed was either responsible for Lenny's untimely end or at least tangentially tied to it. It was Liko, however, that spat out a reply. "Fucker," he blurted. "You were setting him up all along. And now he's dead because of you. I saw them drag his body off the boat. I saw what you did to him." He stifled back tears as Jed's guards held him in place.

Jed shook his head, his eyes momentarily shut tight. He opened them again and stared at his captive. "No, Liko. I didn't kill Lenny. I set him up, yes. I had to. The orders came down from up top. Makani needed a scapegoat, someone not bright enough to know that he was being set up. Not until it was too late."

Liko's eyes flared. "I knew, asshole. I kept telling him that there had to be a reason you kept showering him with cash. It couldn't have been out of generosity. You like your money way too much for that."

Jed grinned, sending a cold blast of hatred through my heart. "No," he said. "I told him it was because I didn't want him to leave me for you. True, to a point."

Then it was my turn to pipe up. "Makani knew he was going to be busted, so you gave him some leverage by offering up Lenny. But you weren't counting on Liko's stepping in to try and bring you down because of this. But that's just what he did. He wrote a letter to Edward Beles in prison and told him that it was you that set him up after Makani was caught. He couldn't save Lenny from prison, but he could, at least, get even with you for eventually putting him there. Sadly, that's not how things went down."

Jed's grin grew wider. "Smart lady, but how do you know all this?"

I stared at him in shock. "Wait," I said, picking up on

something, putting the pieces together. "You knew, too? You knew that Liko had written the letter?"

The grin grew to a chuckle. "Fortunately, there's a certain lawyer that has an, um, itch that I can help scratch. So yes, I saw the letter. And I knew who wrote it. Knew who had to have written it. There was only one person stupid enough to try and set me up. Or desperate enough."

"Liko," I said, staring at the person in question. "So, when you picked up Will the other night on his way to the police substation, you figured that was your chance to even the score. But why not just pick up Liko in person?"

Jed moved from his leaning position, pacing instead, the gun still pointed our way, moving back and forth to each of us in turn. "My, my, such a smart girl," he said. "I hoped as much, anyway. You all found me so easily up at the North Shore, then so easily got information from that idiot Buck, so I figured you'd somehow figure out Liko's association with all this and would bring him to me. And look, here you are, and here he is. Bravo."

"But why?" Brandon asked.

"Yeah, why?" I echoed. "Again, why not just pick him up yourself? Why go through all this?" I motioned around the room, then at the gun.

"Ah," he ahed. "So, you don't know everything then, do you?"

I paused, afraid to show him some Achilles spiked heel I was unaware of. Instead, I shined a light on his own. "I knew you were holding a Federal agent, which is something you obviously didn't know."

He stopped pacing, his grin turning to a scowl. "Like I said, smart girl. So now, what do we do about all this?"

"Stick to the plan," I said. "We trade Will for Liko. Sounds like you would've gotten to him sooner or later anyway. Guess it's sooner now. And, just as I said before, Will is all we ever wanted."

Jed's smile only briefly returned. "So, we make the trade, and then what? You all leave and never darken my doorstep again? Your friend, Will, here would have to turn me in eventually. Kidnapping, attempted murder, prostitution, drug dealing. The list goes on and on—and will get me life in prison, for sure. I could just kill you all now and take my chances, right?"

Will, at last, spoke. "No, I can't turn you in. I wasn't on this case, officially. And there are certain, well, aspects of it that wouldn't look good on my record. Besides, Lenny is already dead; there's nothing I can do to change that. You boys can work it out however you like, and leave us out of it from here on in."

Again, Jed paused, once more aiming the gun away from us. "A stalemate," he said. "I can't let you go and I can't keep you. So, I guess I have no choice." I gulped, praying he'd decide on the latter. "Fine, go," he eventually relented, shaking his head back and forth. "But if you come looking for me again, trust me, it'll be me who finds you the next time. And it'll be the kid who goes down first."

My blood froze as he walked over and the held the gun to Koni's head, playing with the trigger as the kid in question gulped and sweated. This I wasn't counting on. We, after all, could wash our hands of all this and leave the island. It wasn't so easy for our young friend. "Deal," Will said, and we all nodded our agreement.

Jed spoke to one of the goons, who promptly escorted us out. Easy as that. Hostages to free men—um, drag queens—in no time flat. We walked quickly to our car, in silence.

With the door shut, I was at last able to breathe again. "Fuck," I said. "I can't believe that worked out."

"It almost didn't," Will said, grabbing my sweaty hand in his. "That could've gone down either way."

"But it didn't," said Brandon. "It went our way."

Briana coughed. "Except Lenny is still dead and we aren't any closer to figuring out who did it. Plus, there was that mysterious comment Jed made."

"You picked up on that, too, huh?" Will asked, after a quick introduction. "So, you don't know everything then, do you? Everything you all did to rescue me turned out okay, but only by sheer luck. Jed had all the pieces beforehand, knew everything you knew. But he still knows something we don't. Something obviously key."

"He didn't know one thing, though," I said. "Thank goodness." It was then I turned to look at Koni, who was sitting in the back seat in between Brandon and Briana. His face was contorted in a steely grimace. "Sorry," I told him. "We couldn't tell you about Will."

He turned my way. "I thought we were friends," he managed in between gritted teeth. "You tricked me into helping you."

I sighed. "No, Koni. We are your friends, but we knew you'd be scared off if we told you about Will."

"Fuck yeah," he said. "I'm a teenage drug-dealing prostitute, and you led me and all my friends right to the front door of the authorities. You think living behind a convenience store is bad, try prison."

"We're sorry," Brandon chimed in with. "We had no choice."

"There's always choices," he retorted. "You just made a bad one. And your next one will be to drop me off at the store. Your case is over; you can go home now."

He tilted his head back and shut his eyes. The conversation was, apparently, finished. I looked to Brandon, who shrugged. Will leaned in to my ear and whispered, "Let him go. The case isn't over. Not yet. He's safer this way."

I too closed my eyes, just before I cranked up the engine and drove off. Will, of course, was right. But that didn't make it any easier. I hoped, once he cooled off, that Koni would forgive us. In any case, we were just lucky no one had gotten hurt, especially Koni. And not counting the two already dead men and the one soon to be, namely Liko. And, yes, that too weighed heavily on me, truth be told.

***

We dropped Koni off, as he had asked. He didn't say another word to us or even look in our direction; he just walked away, out of sight, breaking our hearts as he did so.

"That sucked," I said to my friends. "Big time."

"But better safe than sorry," Will reminded me.

Brandon tapped him on the arm. "Why's that? Like he said, case closed. We're back on vacation now, what little of it is left."

The three of us looked up at Will, who replied, "Yes, you are. If that's what you want." He tilted his head, the meaning of his statement not lost on any of us.

"Oh shit," said Brandon.

"Ditto," said I.

"You don't have to help, if you don't want to," added Will.

"But help with what?" I asked. "All roads seemed to lead to Jed. And that's now a dead end, so to speak. Can't we just turn it over to the police? Maybe they can unravel this from here on out."

He shook his head from side to side. "No can do. Can't even let them know I've been rescued. I have a feeling that the missing piece to this mess of a puzzle can be found down at their headquarters. I'll let my superiors know that I'm okay, but that's it. Unfortunately, I can't let this end, not just yet. Lenny's killer is still out there, and Jed needs to be brought to justice, somehow, without risking Koni's safety."

"Or our own," Brandon reminded him.

"Goes without saying," he said.

"Fine, just don't go without saying it," Brandon replied. "In any case, for the time being, we're all safe and sound; can we at least go get a drink and catch some warm Hawaiian rays? This day has worked my last gay nerve."

"Amen," Briana shouted.

"Sing hallelujah," I added.

To which everyone did.

***

We dropped off the rental car, got undressed, then re-dressed as boys, and made it to the beach just as the sun began its meeting with the horizon. The drinks arrived moments later, with the four of us facing the ocean, side by side, at long last. I held my frosty cup firmly in one hand, the other holding Will's. For the first time in days, I felt relaxed.

Almost.

"I better call in to home base," Will informed us, "before they send any more agents in than they already have."

He whipped out his cell and dialed. We listened to the conversation as the sky turned red. Though one sided, we didn't like what we heard. No sir, no how. And the red just as quickly turned to black.

"They didn't know you were missing?" I asked, after he'd signed off.

"Nope," he replied. "They knew I was on vacation, so they weren't alarmed that I hadn't checked in."

"Doesn't make sense," Briana said. "Chase reported everything to the police. Even if Sergeant Beles is on the wrong side of things, he'd have to report your kidnapping."

Will scratched his head. "Very true. Something doesn't add up. Again."

"Especially that last thing they told you on the phone," I said.

He continued scratching, throwing in a nod for good measure. "You picked up on that, huh?"

"Hard to miss," Brandon replied.

"And yet we missed it up until this point," Will wisecracked.

"Well now," I said, "It's not like Liko told us he was a police informant. Hard to work that into a conversation."

To which Will added, "And one that's about to testify in the state's largest land development scam."

"Ah," Briana ahed. "But that does make a bit of sense. In fact, it explains a lot."

"Um, care to elucidate?" I asked.

"Think about it," she replied, taking a healthy chug of her creamy concoction. "Why would a pimp need/want to also be a limo driver?"

"To drum up business?" said Brandon. "That's what we came up with before. I mean, that makes sense. Rich, lonely men looking for companionship, striking up conversations with the well-connected limo driver."

"Sure," she said with a nod. "But remember, that microphone over your head is always on, unless you remember to flick it off."

I laughed, despite myself. "Limo driver, pimp, and blackmailer, too, right? He must have very complicated tax returns." I took my own fortifying chug of booze, then added, "But you're right, that makes even more sense. The guy has much more money than just the limo driver/pimp thing would allow for. Blackmailing puts him in a whole new stratosphere."

Brandon nodded as well—and, naturally, chugged, as well. "But police informant? How did he add that to his growing roster of dubious titles?"

"Protection," Will informed. "That small island thing. So long as he keeps a relatively low profile, the police tend to ignore his more ignoble deeds. Which is why, I figure, he sticks with the Japanese business trade. They probably make less of a stink when they're pissed off, probably requires less of his involvement. Fuck and fly home, and all that. Pay him off, if need be."

"But again, why police informant, all of a sudden?" I asked.

"Leverage," I was told. "He's still a pimp. Still gets into hot water, from time to time. It also explains why his record came up clean. The police probably keep it that way on purpose."

"So, the hot water gets cooled off when he trades information?" It was Briana's turn to ask.

Will nodded. "Seems as such. Only, this time, it appears the information was too big for his own good. He either testifies or the water turns to scalding."

"Fuck," I fucked. "Not good."

"Nope," Will agreed. "Not good at all. This is a huge case, and it all turns on his testimony."

"Which he can't give if he's missing," I added.

"Or dead," Brandon tacked on.

"And he's at least one of the two right now," I added some more, already building on shaky ground. "So, does that mean what I fear it means?"

We all sat there in stunned silence, desperately trying to think of anything other than the inevitable. "Sorry," Will eventually said. "I have to try and rescue him. I mean, before, when it was just him and Jed playing things out, with Koni's safety on the line, I let it go. Had to let it go, even if it was killing me to leave Liko there like that. But now, now I have no choice. I have to try and save him. Then I still have to try and figure out who killed Lenny. And why my disappearance went unreported." He stopped listing the impossible, and then turned our way.

"What?" Brandon asked. "Do you want our help without asking for it?"

"I can't ask for it; you know that," he replied, a tortured look on his otherwise handsome face.

"But you can imply it, right?" asked my friend.

Will stared at us, adorably batting his eyelashes.

"Fine," I relented, staring out to the ocean. "We'll help. Just so long as we try our best to keep Koni safe. Meaning, Jed can't find out about our involvement in Liko's rescue." I paused and looked his was. "Is that even possible now?"

He nodded and smiled. "Possible, probable, and doable," he replied. "The way I see it, Jed really was holding me in the hope that someone would figure out that Liko was out to get him, and then trade him for me. He also must've found out that I wasn't a cop. Thankfully, word didn't make its way to him that I was an agent."

"But who did he think you were then?" Briana asked.

"Just a friend of Lenny's who was trying to prove his innocence. I couldn't tell him that Lenny was dead, because that's something I couldn't have known, theoretically. That was also lucky for us, seeing as Jed didn't know it either. In any case, he believed me. Thinking back on it now, I guess he had little choice. Plus, he was planning on killing all of us in good time, I assume."

To which Brandon added, "Until Chase spilled the beans. I don't suppose there really are three letters floating around out there, are there?"

I blushed, and replied, "Smart as that would've been, no."

Will reached over and patted my head. "Still, it worked. Thank goodness. You saved all our lives."

The blush spread, the thrill of it finally working its way to my usually-addled brain. Then I turned to Brandon. "You so owe me one, dude."

He shook his head. "You'd think so, right? But look at all those nights I saved you from boredom. The way I see it, we're even now."

"I'll take that as a thanks."

"Take it any way you like, sweetie." He turned to face the darkening ocean, finished the remnants of his drink, and then whispered, "Thanks."

"Ditto," said Briana, raising her now empty glass.

"Um," umed Will. "Yeah, thanks, but..."

I turned again to look at him, his head tilted in that adorable puppy-dog way. "Fuck," I groaned, yet again. "And I so usually like your but, but what was that one for? Or do I want to know?"

In the short time I'd know Will, I'd found that he wasn't one to beat around the bush. In other words, this particular bush must've been more like a fucking dense forest. Needless to say, I wasn't too far off the mark.

"We have to recue Liko," he reiterated.

"We know that," I too reiterated.

"Only we can't risk Jed finding out what we're up to," the reiteration continued with.

"And we know that, too."

"And that's where that but comes in," he told us.

"Ah," ahed Briana.

"Ah," echoed Brandon.

"What ah?" I asked, clearly lost—as usual.

"He means," Briana said, "that we did our jobs all too well. Jed doesn't know you and Brandon, but he knows me and Will."

"But he does know us...oh...he only knows Judy and Liza." I paused and digested what was being implied. "So, that means it's up to Brandon and me to rescue Liko, if we don't want Jed to associate any of this back to Koni. Am I getting warmer?"

"Piping hot, Chase," replied Will. "Right on the spot. Only, I can't ask you and Brandon to do this."

"So," said I, "we need to volunteer our services, without your theoretically knowing about it."

"Theoretically, yes," he replied.

"But we can't sneak up to that house again. They'll be looking for some sort of rescue attempt. Plus, Jed and his posse are probably long gone by now, on to another hideout, since the last one was found," I offered.

Will nodded. "Oh, he's gone, alright. He'd be stupid to stay. And he's definitely not stupid." He paused and grinned, his perfect teeth glowing in the light of the silvery moon, which had at last made its triumphant appearance. "But careless is another issue entirely."

I chuckled. "You know something he doesn't know you know."

"Exactly. Because, even though he's not stupid, his cohorts, as you found out, are easily duped."

I heard Brandon's tummy growling as my own joined in the chorus. "Um, since I sense another drink coming on, can we get some food to sop up some of the alcohol? I mean, I think we're going to need to be on our toes tomorrow," I opined.

"Yeah," agreed Brandon. "Then we can hear the rest. My brain needs a break from all this shit, anyway."

"Good idea," Will said. "Besides, there's nothing we can do

tonight."

We stood up and headed the few dozen yards to Duke's. We'd had luck with our plans there before; I hoped tonight would be a repeat performance.

So, arm in arm, Briana and Brandon walked on ahead.

Arm in arm, Will and I did, too

And we found a nice quite table off in the corner, away from prying eyes and ears.

Of course, we ordered drinks first. Strong ones. Then dinner. Then down to business.

"So," I began, drinks in hand. "What did you learn from Hawaiian Thing One and Hawaiian Thing Two?"

Will smiled and took a sip of his wine. "They were frequently bored and came downstairs to visit with me when Jed was out, which was often enough. Mostly, they tried preaching to me. Naturally, to keep on their good gargantuan sides, I politely listened, asked the right questions, and nodded sagely during their sermons. My guess was that they figured I'd be dead soon enough, so they better save my soul while there was still time." I shivered at the mere thought, while Will took another sip and continued. "But in between, I asked about the house we were in, and about the house at the North Shore."

"Why that?" Briana asked.

He grinned. "I figured, should I escape or otherwise get out of there alive, I might need the information for later."

"Later being now," I interjected.

"Yep," Will said. "Plus, I was curious how he kept his cover the two times that we know about."

"And?" anded Brandon.

"And," he continued, "he didn't need to rent or borrow them. The houses were broken into. Sort of."

It was my turn to interrupt. "And how does one sort of break into a house?"

The meals came, hot dishes of local flavor. We ate and drank with gusto. In between chomps and slurps, Will replied, "Jed's customers let him know when they're out of town, should he need to lay low for a while or if he needed to entertain rich clients that were looking for a discreet getaway. They left the keys hidden someplace that only Jed knew about. If Jed used the house, the key was replaced and turned upside down. The owner knew Jed has been there, and then called the police to say they'd been broken into."

"Genius," Briana said. "Then, if there's any trouble down the road, the owner could claim complete ignorance."

"Even better," Will added. "Jed brought his own security cameras. So, he never got caught unawares. A perfect set up. Free luxurious accommodations which are untraceable to the police. And he never used the same place twice, and he always had the next one planned ahead for, and then the one after that."

I snapped my fingers. "Holy crap," I nearly shouted. "We were in the next one, and you found out where the one after that is located."

He reached over and squeezed my hand, sending a warm flush across my cheeks. "Exactly, Chase," he said. "And it was super easy to find out. So long as I was willing to hear their Mormon teachings, they were willing to answer my questions, which I asked in a merely curious way. I never asked who owned the house or what Jed's connections to the owners were, so they didn't get suspicious. And when I said how amazing the house we were in was, they casually mentioned how the next one was even more unusual, built into the very side of Diamond Head, overlooking the ocean far down below."

"But how do we find it?" I asked. "There's gotta be dozens of houses ringing the mountain. Hundreds even."

He took a few more bites of his meal, nodding as he did so. "What set the other two houses apart, Chase?" he asked.

I tried to recall something that stood out about them. "Well, they were both remote, off the beaten path, houses the average person wouldn't be driving by."

"Yep. But the houses around Diamond Head, at least around its base, are all off the same one or two roads. Perhaps fenced in, walled off by trees maybe, but your neighbors could still see your comings and goings. Unless…"

"Unless you had no neighbors," I said, finishing his train of thought.

He smiled again, lighting up the entire room. "An old ranger station. As a public park, no one is allowed to live up there, but the property is still used for state ceremonies. It's closed for the next few months while the road leading up to it is being upgraded, the land manicured."

"So, no traffic at all right now?" Brandon asked.

"Not even reachable by car, for the time being," Will replied. "A perfect temporary hideout, if you have the right connections."

"Which, of course, Jed has plenty of," I said.

"Apparently," Will agreed. "In any case, that's where Jed is headed. Perhaps already is. And hopefully with a still-alive Liko."

It was then that are our little gathering went silent. Briana was pointing to the bar, which was sitting off at a diagonal to us. Though we still had it in our line of vision. That is to say, Briana did. We looked at what she was pointing at, and our jaws simultaneously dropped.

The bar had two large television screens above it. Generally, I figured, they aired sporting events. Only, whatever had been playing at that very moment had been suddenly replaced by the local news.

"Well," I managed, my neck craned around to watch in disbelief, "that explains why Sergeant Beles didn't report Will's abduction."

"Yep," agreed Briana. "Dead men tell no tales. But how? He must've been murdered right after you left, giving him no time to report anything to Will's superiors. Meaning…"

"Meaning," I interrupted, "he wasn't the bad guy either. Or at least not the one we were looking for. How many square ones can we be back to?"

We turned our heads away from the bar. "Not square one,"

Will corrected. "We do know more than we did before. Maybe, after we rescue Liko, we'll have the needed missing information. Because that guy seems to have more connections than Ma Bell."

"True," I said, "but how do we get to him? If the hideouts were well-guarded before, this one will be doubly so. We can't possibly sneak in this time."

"Then we don't sneak," Briana said with a mischievous grin spreading from ear to ear.

I noticed her staring off into the distance, and I followed her gaze. "Ma Bell," I echoed.

The rest of the table looked over as well. "What a lucky coincidence," added Will.

"What?" Brandon asked. "I see two guys in jumpsuits. What's lucky about that? We get to offer them some fashion advice?" He squinted, and then added, "Oh."

"Yeah," I said. "Oh. Way to go Einstein."

He grimaced and replied with, "Costumes, ugh. Last time I wore a onesie, I was in diapers. Anyway, how do we get them off their backs and onto ours?"

We paused, until Briana's smile grew even brighter. "Feminine persuasion," she purred as she stood up and pushed her chair away from the table. "If I'm not back in ten minutes, come rescue me."

"It's them I'm worried about," I hollered after her.

To which she hollered back, over her shoulder, "Good point."

We watched as the two telephone repairmen disappeared into a back room, with Briana following close behind. My heart thumped nervously inside my chest, but when it came to Briana, I generally had well-deserved faith.

Needless to say, I wasn't disappointed this time, either.

She emerged not eight minutes later, well within her allotted time, with a smile on her face and two pairs of workmen jumpsuits in hand. She dumped them on the table and downed the drink we had waiting for her. With a satisfied wipe across her full lips, she proclaimed, "Mission accomplished."

"But how?" Will asked, clearly unfamiliar with her prowess.

She grinned and cupped her tits. "Lethal weapons, boys," she replied.

"You showed them to the telephone repairmen in exchange for their work clothes?" he asked.

"Gets 'em every time," said she.

Will shook his head. "Wait," said he. "Just for the promise of seeing your, um, breasts, they gave you their clothes?"

She nodded up and down, then side to side. "Sort of."

And then I, too, nodded my head. "They're unconscious back there, aren't they?"

And again, she nodded. "Yep, so we better leave, while we're ahead."

We immediately downed what food remained—and drinks, of course—and skedaddled on out of there, an ample tip left on the table and two sets of jumpsuits in hand.

"I still don't get it," Will admitted, when we were back on the beach, heading to our hotel.

"Watch," she told him, then looked at Brandon and I. "Wanna see some titties?" she asked.

"Do we have a choice, sis?" Brandon groaned, kicking the sand with the point of his toe.

"No," she replied, pushing her jugs together to double her already ample cleavage. "Now, come closer." We reluctantly moved in. "Closer," she commanded. And we obeyed, getting within an inch of her bodacious ta-tas.

"Not too hard, please" I pled, just as she grabbed our heads and knocked them together.

"Ouch," Brandon howled, falling to the sand.

"I said not too hard," I yelled up at her.

"Trust me," she admonished, offering a hand to help me up. "You wouldn't still be able to stand if that's what I wanted."

I rubbed my noggin, and told her. "Thanks. I think."

She turned to Will, and asked, "Does it make sense now?"

He grinned, the smile reflecting the brilliant moonlight.

"They didn't know what him them?"

"Exactly," she said with a laugh. "Then I just had to remove these nice duds and beat a hasty retreat. All in a day's work, fellas."

"If you're from Shanghai," I told her.

"Or in Oahu and desperate," she corrected, and rightly so.

And with a final nod, we headed back inside our hotel.

***

Briana and Brandon, exhausted from the day's activities, practically ran to the elevator and back up to their respective rooms. Will and I held back. "Wanna go for a walk," he asked, a sly grin peeking out of the corners of his mouth, eyes sparkling all the while.

"A walk, huh?" I asked, already turning back around before kicking off my sandals and digging my feet into the wonderfully cooling sand. "Sure. A walk. I mean, because I don't get enough walking in a given day. Just a walk, though?"

He laughed and grabbed my hand. "Brandon is up in your room and Briana is up in hers. Mine is too far to get to in a reasonable amount of time. And, well, I have been locked up in a basement for the past several days, and a hotel bathroom seems less than, um, well, nice."

"Okay," I said. "Then a walk it is. A nice walk." I winked at him and threw him a sly leer, completed by my batting eyelashes and all the accoutrements.

He tightened his grip on my hand and led me down the beach. The moon was now high in the pitch-black sky, reflecting silver in the peaceful ocean that lapped at the shore to our right. Couples walked up and down the beach, arm in arm, leaning up close to one another. "Romantic," he whispered in my ear.

"Uh huh," I replied, turning my head into his, our mouths instantly meshing as one. "Nice," I moaned.

"Nice," he repeated, his big, strong arms wrapping around

me, pulling me in.

"I missed you," I sighed, my heart so full of emotion that I felt it would burst at any second.

"Ditto," he said. "And thanks for, well, saving me."

I grinned, my hand sliding in front of me to cup his burgeoning prick. "No worries on that front," I told him.

His grin mirrored my own, glinting in the moonlight, radiant. "Sweet talker."

"One of my strong points." I gripped his hand and fell into his embrace. "Now, when can I get a gander at that Billy club of yours?"

He chuckled and nuzzled on my neck. "You're right. That is a strong point you got there." He looked around, and came up with a reply quickly enough. "I'll show you mine if you show me yours." His head nodded behind us to several rows of surfboards. Rows you could climb in between. Rows cast in utter darkness.

"Naughty boy," I chided, hurrying him over.

"Guess I have my own strong points," he retorted, now running to the destination.

I stopped him just before we reached our trysting place, however. I had to tell him what I'd done to help rescue him. That is, what I and, of course, Judy had done. It wasn't, after all, sex for the sake of sex I'd had. In other words, I had to clear my conscience. Well, my recent conscience, at any rate. It would've taken a truckload of erasers to clear absolutely everything, if, in fact, I could even remember half of it.

He grinned when I was done with the sordid tale. "And I'm the naughty boy?" was all he could say.

Clearly, I was forgiven. Thank goodness. So, with a renewed spring to my step, and a boner as hard as granite in my shorts, we hopped over the chains and walked five feet in, with the boards towering over us, hiding us from prying eyes. He lifted his arms as I helped him off with his shirt. Mine followed suit before both were tossed to the sand. Two pairs of shorts followed, then two pairs of underwear, until we stood there, two naked naughty boys with nothing on but devious grins.

We could hear the voices of the people along the beach, of music from the nearby restaurants, of the surf not thirty feet away. None of that mattered; it was just him and me, the moon high overhead, causing his slick prick-head to glow like a beacon in the night.

"Damn," I groaned, sinking to my knees as he worked his rod in and down my throat, pumping my face with his crotch as I reached around to splay his cheeks apart, to tease his sweat-rimmed hole.

"Fuck," he exhaled, his sigh low and deep, like a growl, while he worked my face, and I began to finger his hole, first with one, then two fingers. In deep, up to the hilt. "Fuck," he repeated.

I popped his prick out of my mouth and stood back up, my fingers still entrenched in his butt. My lips found his lips, which were soft as down, his tongue swirling inside all the while. He reached below to stroke my dick. My free hand did the same with his. Slow and easy. All the time in the world.

Only, that wasn't the case.

We heard two voices approaching from behind us, and we froze, mid-stroke. They drew nearer. Two men, stopping at the edge of the row of boards. They'd come from the opposite side from where we had walked from. We couldn't see them. Thankfully, they couldn't see us, either.

They talked in hushed whispers. To our benefit, the breeze carried their conversation the few needed feet. It was difficult, but not impossible, to hear them.

"Where is he?" asked the first man.

"Fuck if I know," said the second. "We were just about to grab him, and he ups and vanishes. Someone must've tipped him off. Told him to stay low until the trial."

There was silence for a few seconds. "But that doesn't make sense," continued the first. "There's nobody but us. Unless Mister Yamasukas' got someone else on the payroll."

"No, that can't be it. If that was the case, that person

wouldn't have tipped the limo driver off. The only other person that Mister Yamasuka had on the payroll, related to all this, is dead."

The two chuckled, their voices growing only slightly louder. "Thanks to you," said the second.

"Fell right into my lap," laughed the first man. "Guy probably would've been offed after five minutes in prison, anyway. Fuckin' Hawaiian was dumber than dirt. Still, he served his purpose, right?"

The laughter abruptly stopped. "Only, one man down, the other missing. We finally got everything pieced together for Mister Yamasuka, and we can't finish the job. No limo driver, no payoff."

Again silence, and then, "Nah, he'll show up. Small island. And we got our tracers out everywhere. Can't lie low for too long. He'll show his head before the trial, and when he does, it gets cut, just like his boyfriend's."

The conversation ended. We heard the two men turn around and walk away. We moved in their direction, to the end of the row of surfboards, still hidden by darkness. They, however, were now cast in the light of the building ten feet up and over, they're uniforms clearly visible from behind as they disappeared back into the substation.

"Oh fuck," I cursed.

"You got that right," Will agreed. "A dead Hawaiian, dumber than dirt? Can only be one of them right about now. Which means…"

"Which means," I interrupted, "Lenny was indeed up to no good. Maybe innocent of drug smuggling, but not so innocent of other illicit activities. But what? What was he doing with all that money? And why was he set up as a drug smuggler?"

We moved back into the middle of the boards, away from nosy ears and eyes. We quickly got re-dressed, the mood clearly gone, then walked back to the beach and plopped our asses down in the soft sand, staring out at the moonlit ocean in front of us. "I think I get it," Will eventually said.

"Then that makes one of us." I sighed. "Please, continue."

He nodded and held my hand, his index finger caressing mine. "Lenny was dating Jed."

"Got it, and?"

"Kind of odd to be dating two competing pimps. Dangerous, in fact. Unless you had a compelling reason."

"Jed mentioned that Lenny liked money. Money that couldn't be made on a measly flight attendant's salary."

"Exactly," agreed Will. "But let's backtrack on that issue. Liko somehow finds out that Mister Yamasuka is up to some shady business, probably while Mister Yamasuka was in his limo at some point. Liko tries to trade that information with the police, but ends up being a forced witness, and one unaware that not all the police are on the up-and-up. Mister Yamasuka finds out that Liko is going to testify against him, but doesn't know what Liko knows or exactly what he's already told the police. Liko's a dead man, either way, but better to know what he knows before he's taken out. Now then, how do you found out what Liko knows without tipping him off that you're on to him?"

"A cute Hawaiian boyfriend?" I tried.

"Better yet, one that has inside knowledge of the competition, Jed. Meaning, one that's hard to pass up. A bird in the fucking hand."

I nodded my head, at last understanding. We had, it seemed, been trying to solve one case, when, in fact, there were two, minimum. "So, Lenny is recruited by Mister Yamasuka to pursue Liko in exchange for a hefty salary. Liko falls for Lenny and, we can only assume, spills some beans. But, before Lenny can tell Mister Yamasuka what he knows, his jealous boyfriend, namely Jed, frames him as a drug smuggler, thereby helping out Makani. Liko figures this out and, in turn, frames Jed with the incarcerated Edward Beles."

"Right," Will said. "Only, Jed has a certain lawyer for a client, who promptly warns him that Edward Beles is after him because of a certain letter he received in prison. So, Jed is on to

Liko, and Mister Yamasuka is on to Liko, only, we hand him over to Jed before Mister Yamasuka can get his dirty mitts on him, or that is, once Mister Yamasuka's stoolie policemen can get their dirty mitts on him before he can testify."

"Makes sense," Will said.

"It does?"

"Much as anything. Only, no one knows that there are multiple games afoot. Either way, though, Liko's a dead man, either by Jed's own devices or Mister Yamasuka's."

"And Lenny was dead either way, too. Mister Yamasuka would've gotten to him, either in prison or outside of prison. He knew too much." I paused and sighed. "Poor guy. How could he have known that the long arm of the law had a knife hidden up its sleeve?"

"So, now we know who killed Lenny," I offered.

"Yep. Mister Yamasuka, however indirectly"

"But how do we get to Mister Yamasuka?" I asked. "We have no proof, no evidence. A rich, Japanese businessman with, I'd assume, strong ties to the community. No one will believe us, or want to."

"Unless we really do rescue Liko."

"If he's even still alive," I said, my head now sunk low to my chest.

"My guess is he is. Liko's proven to be a smart cookie, thus far. And so has Jed. I bet those two will come to some sort of agreement that will be beneficial to the both of them. Liko, after all, probably has a ton of valuable information."

"But we have to reach Liko, and soon, just in case. I mean, we can't wait until the morning now; it's too risky. We have to get to Liko first, so he can testify against Mister Yamasuka."

"Looks that way," Will agreed. "Looks that way."

"Looks what way?" we heard, both of us turning our necks around, only to see Brandon and Briana standing directly behind us.

"I thought you both went to bed," I said.

"We did," Briana replied. "But then we got worried when

you didn't return, what with everything that's been going on, and all."

"Didn't you consider that Will and I were, well, doing what Will and I do when we're not with you?"

They both nodded. "Yep," Brandon said. "Only, that usually takes you about five minutes; you were gone much longer than that. So, we came looking for you, just in case."

"Thanks," I said. "I suppose."

They both sat down on either side of us, staring out at the rolling moonlit waves. "So, what looks what way?" Briana asked.

Again, I sunk my head down to my chest. "You don't want to know."

"Fuck," Brandon said, hearing the obvious dread in my voice.

"Yeah, fuck," Briana reiterated.

"Yeah," I said. "We tried. But then a new twist to all this presented itself."

"Fuck," Brandon repeated.

"Yeah, fuck," Briana, too, repeated.

"Yeah, fuck," I thirded. "Fuck, fuck, fuck, indeed."

🌴 Sarongs Bought (Yet Again) 🌴

So, we filled them in, their faces blanching beneath the moon's glowing rays. "Guess we'll be needing those telephone repairmen uniforms sooner than expected," Brandon groaned.

"Looks that way," I agreed, seeing his groan with a moan.

He saw my moan and raised me with a sigh. "Let's get going then."

And so, we got up, retrieved the uniforms, and got down to the task at hand. Sadly, we were holding a crappy hand, but the pot was so big, so important, that we had little choice but to keep on playing for it.

***

With the help of a map, and a cab driver who didn't seem to mind, or care, that we asked to be dropped off in the middle of a road, in the middle of the night, in the middle of an extinct volcano's mountainside, we found ourselves about a hundred feet directly below the house we were searching for. It was on the smallish side, two stories, dark, with evidence of stalled construction scattered around it, a road still in transition, uprooted trees waiting for a new home.

We flicked on our flashlights and began the trek up. The path was rocky, unkempt, difficult at best. We huffed and puffed and, fifteen minutes later, made it to just outside the house. As we noticed from the road, it was dark, but not from lack of electricity. The windows had been blackened out, covered from the inside with some sort of opaque paper. Still, hints of light poked out in small slits along the sides.

"Someone doesn't want to be seen," I made note.

"Or found," added Brandon. "Again."

I gulped. "Then they're not gonna be too happy seeing us."

"No," Will agreed, "they're not. Maybe we should turn around and go home. I can't ask you to do this. Too dangerous."

"Too late," I said. "We've come this far, might as well see it through. Besides, I think I have an idea."

"Oh goodie," Brandon groaned. "Because your ideas are always so spot-on."

I punched him in the arm. "Asshole. Do you have any ideas how to proceed?"

He looked around. "There a bar around here?"

I too looked from side to side. "Nope."

He shook his head. "Then, no, no ideas. Please, do continue."

I sighed, and said, "Look at the side of the building."

Our group all stared in that direction, the full moon illuminating what I was indicating. "The phone lines go in over there," Will said, already catching on as he tiptoed to the box before yanking on several of the wires. Then he returned to our little group. "Done."

"What?" asked Brandon. "Now they can't order a pizza?"

Again, I hit him on the arm. "Idiot. Now they need a telephone repairman. Two, in fact."

He looked to me, then to the jumpsuits we were holding, then back to me. "Oh," he ohed.

"Yeah, genius. Oh." I paused, shaking my head. "Now, let's wait a half hour, and then go make some noise by that telephone box. If we can't bring Mohammed to the mountain, we'll bring the mountain to Mohammed."

"You mean two mountains, right?" Briana asked. "Two big Hawaiian Mormon mountains?"

I smiled. I mean, at least one of my friends had some sort of brains. I was relieved it didn't have to be me anymore. Mine was severely overworked as it was. "Yep. And they'll be bringing us inside, soon enough."

We sat on the ground and counted the stars. That lasted about ten whiny minutes. Then we counted Brandon's tricks, which most definitely filled the remaining twenty. Then Brandon and I got dressed in our jumpsuits. They were comfortable, if not completely unstylish. A few seconds later, we were standing by the telephone box, making a racket as Briana and Will hid behind a tree with two large limbs as weapons, just in case. Though, in truth, the Hawaiians would've done way more damage to the sticks than the other way around.

As expected, not five minutes later, they came running out. Well, lumbering out, anyway. "Who the fuck are you?" the bigger one asked.

"Better question," I managed, trying my best to hide the fear in my voice. "Who the fuck are you? This is state-owned property. Closed for repairs. Vacant. Our monitors showed an unexpected interruption of service, and we came out to see what the deal was. What's your excuse?"

I stood there, arms akimbo, legs spread apart, trying—and failing—to seem bigger, more threatening. "Yeah," added Brandon, mimicking my pose as best he could, nelly queen that he is. "I'll just run back to our truck and call this in, if you like. They can send out security."

"No," the second one practically shouted. "I mean, no, no need for that. We, um, are security. This ranger station has been experiencing, um, vandal attacks lately. They sent us out to, um, to, um, prevent such attacks." The second so-called security guard nodded, as did we.

"Fine. No problems then. We just need to get inside to have a quick look," I said, going for broke.

"Inside?" the second one asked. "Why inside? The wiring is obviously out here." He pointed to the box we'd been messing with, the wires still dangling down.

"Because," said Brandon, thankfully coming to my rescue, "the, um, box is working fine. The disconnect must've occurred internally, at the source, in the, um, the basement."

"The basement?" asked the first behemoth.

"The basement," Brandon repeated.

"The basement?" echoed the second Hawaiian.

"The basement," I said, making it a complete go-around. "Should be a quick fix. Just lead us to it, and we'll be out of your hair in no time. Either that or a whole crew stops by tomorrow. We wouldn't want that, would we?"

They moved a few feet away to converse in privacy, returning a minute later. "Fine," the larger of the two agreed. "We'll take you down to the basement. But please make it quick. Our, um, our boss is inside, and he hates to be disturbed, so if you could be extra quiet, we'd really appreciate it."

"Extra quiet. No problem," I told them, the two of us already following them toward the front of the house. I turned around and gave our cohorts a thumbs-up, and, seconds later, we were inside the belly of the beast.

The place was dark, deadly quiet, the furniture covered in sheets. Only a few lights were lit, the windows, as we'd already seen, covered in black paper. We ignored all this and headed to the basement, silent as church mice. As if we'd ever encountered one of those before. The church variety, at any rate.

We climbed the stairs, down, down, down. One of the Hawaiians flicked a switch from the top. They didn't, thank goodness, follow us down. I stared up at them, a lump in my throat the size of Detroit. Trapped like a bug in a rug. Or a queen in a dungeon. Two queens, that is. "Thanks," I hollered up. "We'll be done in fifteen minutes, tops."

The smaller Hawaiian shook his head. "Fine. Stay here. We'll come back and get you. And, please, be quiet. No noise." He put his sausage-thick finger to his lips, the universal sign for shut the fuck up.

I nodded and mirrored the gesture. "No problem," I whispered.

But, of course, there was a problem.

There's always a problem.

Always.

We heard them lock the door behind them. Click. We waited a few seconds and checked, just in case the noise was the sound of our last collective brain cells going click inside our heads. Sadly, as suspected, we were officially, terrifyingly locked in.

"So close," I moaned.

"Which is only good in horseshoes and hand grenades," Brandon quipped.

"Got one?" I asked. "A hand grenade, I mean."

"I left it in my other pocket, sorry," he said. "Now what?"

Only the now what? abruptly became a what now?

Bang, came the first shot, quickly followed by another, both overhead, both loud and jarring. Thirty seconds later, two more, bang, bang.

"Fuckin-A," I shouted loudly, the sound echoing from one cement wall to the other.

"Shh," Brandon whispered, covering my mouth. "I doubt they're out of bullets. Hide."

Did I neglect to mention that the basement was ten by ten? No windows, no walls, no hiding places? Well, it was, and there weren't. "Where?" I asked, the question muffled by his sweaty hand.

Not that it mattered much anymore. Not two minutes later, we heard the door go click again. We threw our arms up, dropped to our knees, and I shouted, "Don't shoot us; we're too young to die!"

"And too pretty!" added Brandon.

"Our mother would be so proud of you," Briana shouted back down.

We looked up in stunned surprise. "Better a live sissy than a dead hero," I retorted as she and Will ran downstairs.

"You're okay?" Will asked, an obvious look of relief splashed wide across his face as he grabbed me in a big bear-hug.

"Seems so," Brandon replied. "Now, where's mine?"

Will reached his arm out and pushed Brandon into our group, soon joined by Briana, all of us smiling and clinging on, until I thought to ask, "Um, don't get me wrong, this is quite lovely and all, but, well, who was shot upstairs?"

To which Briana replied, "Everyone, it would seem. Jed, Liko, and both Hawaiians. Whoever did it must've come in the back door because we didn't see anyone. We heard the gunshots and came running, spotted them all upstairs and then found you both down here, all in a matter of minutes. Guess the shooters didn't know about you two, or cared."

"Holy fuck," I managed. "So, we weren't the only ones looking for them. Little good that information does us now. No more evidence, no more clues, all the suspects shot and killed."

It was then we heard a new noise: not a shot, as before, but a dragging sound from up above. We four tiptoed up the stairs and exited the basement, the only sound now our ragged breathes. And then the creak of a floorboard. We moved stealthily around a corner, and there he was, a trail of blood behind him, his skin now gray where once it had been a deep, dark tan.

"Liko," I managed, my voice cracking.

He looked up, but didn't recognize us—after all, he'd only ever seen us in drag before. We ran over, two on either side of him. He grunted, his head collapsing to the floor, his breathing shallow.

"Who did this?" Will asked.

Liko moaned. "Two men," he managed. "In masks."

"But why?" Will asked, though, obviously, we knew the answer already.

"Information," he grunted in reply. "Know. Too. Much." The words just barely made their way out from between his cracked lips.

"What information?" Will asked. "Tell us; we'll make sure to get them for this."

There was no reply, at least not right away. Then, with what little energy he had left, he coughed, and rather cryptically replied, "Check the koi pond." And with a final raspy exhale, he was gone.

We looked away, stood up, and walked outside. Will took out his cell and called the authorities. We bowed our heads, collecting our thoughts.

"Strange," Briana eventually said. "There's no koi pond around here that I noticed. Just these thin woods and this ranger house. And we were at Liko's already; there was no koi pond there either. Though, unfortunately for us, there's one in just about every hotel in Waikiki. Meaning, we're screwed."

We all looked to each other, three frowns and one knowing smile. "What's the shit-eatin' grin for?" Brandon asked.

"I think I know what koi pond he was referring to," I offered.

They stared at me in surprise. "You do?"

"Uh huh," I uh-huhed. "Mister Yamasuka has one inside his house." I blushed, looking at Will.

"Um, okay," he said, keenly aware of how I knew this, but gentleman enough to let it go. "That makes some sense, I suppose. Liko must've heard Mister Yamasuka say something about his koi pond at some point. Must be a hiding place. A watery safe of sorts."

"Agreed. But what if the cops already know about whatever is hidden?" Brandon asked. "If Liko was about to testify against Mister Yamasuka, then maybe he already told the police about the pond."

"Nah," Briana said. "Then he wouldn't have told us to check it out. My guess is, he was saving that bit of information. A final bargaining chip. Just in case."

I sighed. "Only, Mister Yamasuka, it seems, isn't interested in bargaining anymore." I looked back at the house, instantly remembering the carnage. "Still, it's of no use to us. Liko was our only connection to Mister Yamasuka. I wouldn't have the first clue where that house of his was. Not like I was writing down the directions on our way up there. And I seriously doubt he's listed in the phone book."

"Nope," Briana agreed. "But Will could find it out. He could call his superiors and ask."

Will shook his head. "I could, but then we'd be possibly tipping the bad guys off that we're on to them. There's too great a risk that they would find out that we were asking. It's a small police force around here; word would quickly spread. Then Mister Yamasuka would be told, and hide whatever is in the pond someplace else." He paused, thinking about our options. "There is, I think, one small ray of hope. Maybe."

"Maybe?" I asked, my heart still pounding from all the recent activities that had befallen us.

"Maybe," he repeated. "If he's willing to help."

"Ah," I ahed, somehow guessing what he was getting at. "That's a big maybe, though."

"Better a big maybe than nothing at all," said he, just as the ambulances and police cars arrived, there lights filling the dark void at the bottom of the hill.

✳✳✳

Now's where things got tricky—yeah, I know, as if things hadn't already been tricky enough, right? See, legally, we should've stayed and given the police some sort of report, Will especially, but four murders would've meant our being down at the station for hours and hours trying to explain why we were at the scene of the gruesome crime. Plus, we knew that not all the police were on our side. In other words, if this damn investigation was ever to end, Will would have to take it upon himself, with our support, to go commando—and not the fun underwearless type of commando, either. And, really, we had little choice now. With so many people turning up dead, and the trial a scant few days away, it was either that or see all those deaths, especially Lenny's, go unpunished.

So, after we wiped the place clean of our fingerprints as best we could, we skedaddled. We tucked our tails between our legs and took off down the other side of the hill before reaching the road a short while later. We'd already arranged for our cab to pick us up an hour after we were dropped off. He arrived just in time, taking us back to our hotel and away from that gigantic mess we illegally left behind.

We quickly changed out of our stolen clothes, tossing them in the hotel's dumpster, and planned to begin our search, early the next morning, for the one person left who could still lend some support.

***

And so, another day in fucking paradise began.

"He's never going to help us," Briana said with a low, deep sigh as we searched the food court, our initial point of contact.

We split up, Briana with Brandon, Will with me. I looked to my partner, and said, "You look glum. We'll find him and he'll help, I'm sure."

"It's not that," Will replied, his head turning from side to side, looking for Koni, who sadly wasn't anywhere in sight. "It's just, I hate that we left the ranger house like we did. I could lose my job if they ever find that out. Not to mention, it's a blatant crime."

I paused and gripped his hand in mine. "They were already dead. There was nothing more we could do to help. Now, searching for Koni, that's how we can help them, to find their killers. Telling the police everything we know might've had the opposite effect, causing the bad guys to cover their tracks even more."

He nodded, forcing a smile on his handsome face. "I know. Still, it goes against everything I've been taught. But you're right; this is the only way."

And it was. There were at least two rogue cops and an evidently dangerous Japanese business man to contend with, and none of them knew for certain that we were hopefully hot on their trail. Then again, without Koni's assistance, there was no longer a trail to follow, hot or otherwise.

We regrouped, the four of us shaking our heads back and forth. Our lithe little friend was nowhere inside the

International Marketplace, so we walked the couple of blocks to his sleeping quarters. The mattress was gone, as were his meager belongings. We looked at each other, our faces all frowning.

"Not good," said Brandon.

"Nope," agreed Briana.

"Any other ideas?" asked Will.

We paused, each of us deep in thought.

"Drinks?" suggested Brandon. Seems some of us were deeper in thought than others.

"Later," I responded. "After one more stop." I started walking back to the main strip, the others following in my wake. "I think I may know where he is," I hollered over my shoulder. At least I prayed as much.

We hailed a cab and, somehow, I remembered the address.

"Ah," ahed my friends, picking up on my thinking. "Makes sense," added Briana. "As good a place as any to go."

"Yep," I told her. "A spare bed and a mother desperately in need of someone to take care of." I suppose, had it been me, it's the one place I too would've gone.

We drove the rest of the way in silence, hoping my hunch proved correct as we admired the passing scenery, the lush vegetation that sprouted up on all sides of us, made all the more brilliant by the pounding sun. We arrived and were greeted by a surprised Koni, who was sitting on the porch, his feet propped up on a rickety railing, a stunned look on his adorable face.

"How?" he asked, his face scrunched up, trying and failing to squelch a smile.

We walked from the waiting cab and stood on the grass, staring nervously up at him. "We looked everywhere else," I told him. "This seemed the only other place you could go."

He sighed, his eyes shutting tight for the briefest of moments. "Funny," he eventually said. "I went looking for the people who took Lenny's life, and found the ones that gave him life instead. Bitter irony, I think they call it."

I smiled, as did my friends, as did Koni, despite the awfulness that had brought us all to that location, to that spot in time. "They took you in, huh?"

He nodded. "Gladly. With open arms. No questions asked. Even gave me a job at their store. I was just about to go there. Hard work, but better than…well, you know." He slumped his head to his chest, probably not so much in shame as regret. "Weird to sleep in his bed, though. Still, they seem happy to have me here." His head rose, the smile fast returning. "Is that why you stopped by, came looking for me? To make sure we're all happy as clams now?"

He was being ironic. And bitter, again, to boot. "Yes and no," Brandon replied.

"More of which?" he asked, clearly on to our usual games.

Brandon laughed. "What do you think, kid? The latter, of course. Still, really, honestly, we couldn't be happier that you found a home. Indoors."

Our young friend nodded. "Okay, I get it, dude. You need me for something, right? Need the little island boy to help you out of a jam?"

"We always needed you," I said, sensing his growing hostility. "And we're sorry we deceived you, however much we did so because we cared about you." The four of us nodded in unison. And then I added, "And now we need you even more. Liko and Jed are dead, and we may be the only ones able to get the bad guys now. Except, we can't do it without your help."

He paused, the grin growing as bright as the sun high overhead. "Well," he said. "I guess wonders never cease."

"Dude," Brandon interjected. "Wonders ceased about three murders ago. So, get the hell off the cross, we need the fucking wood."

He laughed. It was a good sign, considering Brandon's sacrilege. "Fine," he eventually replied, pretending to think it over. "So long as we're all equal partners this time."

Brandon shrugged. "Fuck if I care. You can take over the whole damn thing if you want. Just get off that cute little ass of yours and help already."

Again, he laughed. "Gee, you think my ass is cute?" We

turned and walked back the way we came. Exit, stage right. "Wait," he shouted after us.

We stopped and turned. "Are you coming or not?" Brandon yelled.

"Coming. I mean, yes," he hollered back, his head bobbing up and down. "Just give me five minutes to tell Mrs. Hallanah what's going on, abstractly as possible. I'll meet you in the cab."

We nodded, smiling as he ran inside. "Thank goodness," I said as we piled in.

"Oh, hell no," Brandon said, getting into the front side. "Goodness had nothing to do with it." As if it ever did.

As promised, five minutes later, he came running out. Fortunately for us, he really did have a little ass. I mean, four in the back seat was a snug fit.

We drove back in silence, choosing to explain the situation to him in the privacy of our hotel room. Lord only knew how far Mister Yamasuka's tentacles spread. If the cops were reporting back to him, we could only imagine that the cabbies were as well.

"Home sweet home," the prodigal son commented upon his return, soon after the cab dropped us off out front.

I put my arm around him, and said, "And not a moment too soon."

We made it back to our room, surprisingly in one collective piece. It was dinner time. We ordered room service—and ample quantities of fluids—and filled him in on everything he'd missed thus far.

"Geez," he groaned. "I've barley been gone, and just look at the miss you're in."

We echoed his groan with our own. "We know," I said. "But can you help? I mean, can you find out where Mister Yamasuka lives? And then, somehow, get us in there?"

He flopped on the bed, his face buried in the soft down. "Mrbx," we heard some minutes later.

"Huh?" I huhed.

He turned his head sideways. "I said, maybe. I mean, this

Yamasuka dude was obviously a regular of Liko's. Stands to reason, there were others that had been up to his estate before. Other locals who'd know how to get back up there. I mean, if the price was right."

"Meaning, we pay for the information?" Briana said.

"More than likely," came the response from the bed.

"But how do we find the person with the information?" she asked. "Do you know how to find everyone that worked for Liko?"

He chuckled. "Not everyone, but enough. Besides, once word gets out that Liko and Jed are no more, there will be plenty of loose eager lips."

"But," I said, "word won't get out. Not while the police are investigating their murders. At least not in the short term. Which is all we have, right now."

He sighed as he whipped out his cell phone from his back pocket. "Guess that's why I call you cute dude and not smart dude."

"Ouch," Brandon said, wincing and chuckling to himself.

Two against one; no fair. "Hey," I grumbled, then realized that I should just settle for being called cute. In any case, Koni was already putting his plan into action, whatever plan that was.

Ten minutes later, we were set—though, still, we hadn't a clue what he'd done. Much of the conversations were one-sided and in street lingo. And, apart from our excessive use of the word dude, we had little knowledge of his lexicon.

"Well?" I asked when he turned over, apparently done with his phone calls.

"Well," he replied. "The maybe has grown to a distinct possibly."

"Oh joy," I groused. "I revel in the possible."

He laughed. "Stop being so bitter, cute dude. You'll get frown lines."

That indeed got my attention. I turned my frown upside down, and asked, "So, what now?"

"Now?" he replied, hopping back up to stand before us with

a worrying shrug. "Now, we wait."

"But time is not on our side," I tried.

His smile widened. "I didn't say we wait for very long."

He pushed past us and out the hotel room door. With little option, we followed close behind. He got on the elevator, and then so did we. Seconds later, we were outside, behind the hotel. He marched to the bar and ordered five drinks, four alcoholic and one not. "To keep you guys quiet," he informed.

"Just one?" Brandon whined. "We won't be quiet for long."

He nodded and doubled the order. And then, with our hands full of booze, we marched to the beach and waited off to the side of the hotel.

One drink down, and his phone calls began to pay off. One girl and one guy emerged, young, like Koni, world-weary looks on their too-young-to-be-troubled faces. They high-fived him and gave him air hugs, their chests just barely bumping. He handed them both of his Cokes and bade them to wait a few more minutes. They hunkered down in the sand, as did we, forming a protective ring around them. Minutes later, more like them arrived, all young, all with smiles on their faces.

"What gives?" I whispered into Brandon's ear.

"Beats me," he whispered back. "It's like some sort of odd reunion."

"Is that why they all look so happy?"

He shrugged as we watched and waited for an answer.

Thankfully, it was soon forthcoming.

A half hour had transpired since we'd left the room and found ourselves on the beach. By then, a dozen of Koni's friends appeared, seemingly out of nowhere. They sat bunched together, all smiles, gabbing away in the foreign language of youth. And then Koni stood up, casting a hush across the crowd that had gathered.

"Thanks, everyone, for coming," he announced, a mischievous grin on his lovable face, the pied-piper of the down and out. They nodded, matching him grin for grin. "As I told you all already on the phone, Liko and Jed are dead."

Strangely, or maybe not so much, they all started to clap. It was then I realized what was happening. It was like that scene in the Wizard of Oz when the wicked witch gets the bucket of water thrown over her; only, it was two wicked pimps that got melted this time around, freeing the group from the invisible chains that bound them.

Koni continued. "The four people sitting around you are responsible for this." They all turned and stared. We smiled and shrugged in an aw shucks, tweren't nothin' look. "The thing is," he added, "now they need your help."

"Name it," one of them hollered.

"To find their killers," added Koni.

"Oh, fuck it then," the same one quickly rescinded with.

Koni laughed. The four of us squirmed in our sandy seats. "Yeah, I would've said the same thing. Only, there were more needless deaths than theirs, and they'll be more tragedy down the line. And others will come to take Jed and Liko's places, others who will gladly steal our very souls for a quick buck. Maybe we can prevent this. Not forever, no. I mean, none of us are that naïve. But at least for a while, anyway, we can put an end to this, to stand up for ourselves, to take our lives back."

I was shocked at his eloquence, but not surprised. Nothing Koni said or did surprised me anymore. Still, a lone tear managed its way from my eye and down my cheek. The sniffling around me meant I wasn't alone. And then, to our great relief, fists went up in solidarity. Koni smiled, big and bright. I was sure that he knew he'd get his way, even before he gave his impassioned speech. And I smiled as well. Proudly.

"But what can we do?" asked one of them. "Not like the cops are gonna listen to anything we have to say."

"Nope," Koni agreed. "But you can still help." He paused and glanced around at the motley crew that circled around him. "There's a john of Liko's, a Mister Yamasuka, digs pain, rich Japanese guy, has a koi pond inside his house. Any of you trick with this dude?"

Nothing. No reply. My heart leapt to my throat. We were

fucked.

And then one lone, small hand resting above a bony wrist rose about the crowd. A girl. Waifish, slight, timid at first, and then all smiles, glad to be the one with the knowledge that we needed. "Easy money," she whispered. "Small balls and a butt-plug, right?"

I jumped from my seated position. "That's him!" I shouted.

The others turned, smiled, nodded. "Right on," one of them said, high-fiving me.

"Exactly," Koni said, wiping the sweat that had formed on his brow. "Now, where does this teeny-balled dude live?"

She paused and scratched her head. I sucked in my breath and waited, prayed, hoping beyond hope that she'd remember. She snapped her fingers, the slightest of grins spreading from east to west across her narrow face. She pulled her cellphone from her back pocket, hit some numbers, and proclaimed, "Got it. Liko texted me the address a while back. Here it is." She handed Koni the phone. He smiled, putting the address to memory, and handed it back to her.

"Thank you," he said, bowing his head. "And now that you're all free again, please try to stay that way." He grinned and nodded to them.

They, in turn, nodded back up at him. Easier said than done, I figured. Still, at least for the time being, they were, as he said, free. Perhaps, I hoped, they'd stay that way. With my eyes shut tight, I willed the same thing for my young, little friend. He was, thank goodness, off to a good start.

But were we?

The crowd dispersed, leaving the five of us alone on the beach yet again. "Now what?" I asked. "We have the address, but what good will it do us? We can't break in. The place must be totally wired. Plus, if past experiences are any indication, he knows that someone is on to him. Meaning, I think we can all assume, he's playing it extra safe, at least until the trial is over. And with Liko very much out of the picture, Yamasuka will beat the wrap."

Strangely, though my speech was most certainly impassioned, if not a tad overwrought and overdramatic, Koni was giggling by the end of it.

"Why the guffaws?" Briana asked.

He broke out into full-on laughter. "Because," he managed. "The cute dude just gave me a great idea."

"I did?" I asked, surprised.

"Yeah, he did?" Brandon asked. "Chase did?"

"Yep, he did," Koni replied, nodding his head. "He said the wrap."

"I don't get it," I admitted for the umpteenth time that week.

"That makes two of us," Will said.

"Three," Briana said, raising her hand.

"It's unanimous," fourthed Brandon.

And still Koni remained smiling. "Surprise, surprise," he said, shaking his head, well-accustomed to our dimwittedness. "Anyway, admittedly, this Yamasuka dude will be playing it safe, for now. But if there's one thing I know about men, and, trust me, I know plenty, it's that, when sex is on the menu, safety gets thrown out the window."

"In English, please," Brandon admonished.

He sighed. "How did Chase get into his house the last time?" he asked, slowly and evenly, for even us imbeciles to understand.

"Ah," I ahed. "The wrap. Now I get it. I got dressed as Judy. And a horny old man will let his guard down for a sexy young woman."

"Sexy and young?" asked Brandon. "Who are you trying to kid?"

"Fine," I allowed. "In any case, he is a horny old man. And a horny old man will fling his proverbial window open for an able and willing female."

"Two," corrected our young friend.

"Two?" Briana asked. "Who, me?"

His mop of a head swung from left to right. "Try again," he said.

We looked around, our eyes landing on the only other person he could be talking about. "Me?" asked Brandon.

"Bingo," said Koni. "There's safety in numbers."

"Yeah," Brandon replied. "And there's safety staying put, too. I say we sacrifice the homelier one."

"Gee, thanks," I groaned. "With friends like you, who needs enemas?"

"Stop," Briana shouted, hand held up high. "Before this escalates into the usual bitch fight, I say we take a vote. Those in favor of both Judy and Liza going to Mister Yamasuka's, say aye."

Naturally, the vote was three to one. I abstained, on the grounds that I didn't want to go, either.

And then a new and terrifying thought popped into my head. "Um, but with Liko dead, and Mister Yamasuka responsible, how do we arrange all this? We don't even have his phone number." And then there was that great, big smile of Koni's again. It, too, was terrifying. "Let me guess," I guessed, "you have his number, right?"

He nodded. "It was below his address on that girl's cellphone. Needless to say, in my line of work, it helps to have a photographic memory."

I groaned. "Couldn't you just take photographic memories of scantily clad surfers, like Brandon does?"

"Hey," Brandon protested. "Don't knock it. Anyway, kid, even with the guy's phone number, how do you intend on arranging all this? This Yamasuka dude had a working relationship with Liko. May I remind you, we don't."

He scrunched up his adorable face and pulled at his meager chin whiskers, a sure sign that we were in trouble. I know, as if all those bodies piling up weren't indication enough, right? "Just leave that up to me. All you two need to do is look pretty." He paused and stared at us. "Well, pretty enough." I started to protest, when he interjected with, "And you'll need new sarongs, which seem to have worked for Yamasuka before. He's already seen you in the one you own, Chase."

That, of course, shut us up. However temporarily. I reached out my hand to Brandon. "Shall we, Liza?"

"Let's, Judy."

And we were off, the joy of shopping replacing our abject fear of, gulp, imminent death.

It was late by then, the store just about to close, but with Brandon's Prada wallet waving the salesclerk down, we had no problem getting in. Thirty minutes later, our shopping bags were full. After all, what's a sarong without the appropriate accessories to go along with it?

Unbelievably, that half an hour was all it took for our bright, young schemer to arrange everything.

"Done," he proclaimed, upon our return, all three of them lounging around our room, celebratory champagne and Coke already flowing.

"Done?" I asked, instantly panic-stricken at the thought. "But how?" I reached for the nearest bottle of booze, beating Brandon to the punch by a mere two seconds.

"Kid's a genius," Will informed, lifting his glass in a toast.

"But how?" I repeated, collapsing on the bed and downing my glass in one giant gulp.

"It was easy, really," Koni admitted, a look of pride stretching from ear-to-ear. "I told Yamasuka that I was Liko's cousin, just starting a new enterprise on the island. I mean, I figured he knew that Liko was, well, dead, so he'd be looking for a new pimp, right? Guy like Yamasuka ain't going to no bars to pick up bimbos to beat his ass, right?"

"I'm, um, not a bimbo, thank you kindly," I protested.

"Oh, right," he said. "I meant ladies. Ladies to beat him." I nodded for him to continue, which he did. "Anyway, I said that, being Liko's cousin, I had access to his, well, stable of ladies. And then, adding the cherry to the sundae, I told him I was running a two for one sale. And then I asked him if he had any, um, ladies in mind."

"Gee," I interrupted. "And he asked for me, right? What a compliment."

"Well, in any case, he did ask for you, which was what we were hoping for, right?"

I moaned. "Guess that old saying was once again proven correct. You should be careful what you wish for, because it might just come true."

Koni giggled, and then finished with, "Anyway, I told him you were available, and said you had a partner you usually work with, namely Liza. Needless to say, he was delighted."

"At least one of us is," I managed.

"Oh, come on now," Briana piped in with. "This is what we were hoping for. The guy seems harmless enough." She paused, realizing immediately the error in her assessment. "I mean sexually, of course. You go in, tie him up, beat him up, and search the koi pond. Easy as pie."

"Too bad I'm a cake person," I sighed, head in hand.

"I like pie," Brandon said, downing his second glass of champagne.

"You're not helping any, asshole," I told him.

He paused. "Oh yeah, sorry. I mean, I hate pie, too. Well, not apple. Or cherry. Key lime, now that I hate. And rhubarb. Who came up with that one anyway?"

I threw a pillow at him. "Please, Brandon, shut up."

He shut up, adding a quick and whispered, "And mincemeat. Gross." The second pillow found its mark, as did a third.

In any case, as Koni had said, done. We were all set to go. Ready, though not raring.

We arranged to meet the next morning, Yamasuka in his black Cadillac just outside the food court, same as last time. He nodded his greeting to the two of us, but otherwise remained silent, just like our first outing. Needless to say, we kept quiet as well. The less said to this guy, the better. Still, we did have something up our sleeves, however short they were in our form-hugging sarongs.

He drove the same way as before, thankfully. Meaning, we were headed to where we wanted to go. And then, soon enough, we arrived.

He led us in; we followed close behind. He closed the door, slamming it shut behind us with a bang. My breath got stuck in my throat. And then, there at last was the koi pond. My heart began to pound even faster at the sight of it.

And that's where things got tricky. Well, tricky-er, that is. Brandon and I had never had sex with each other before. Oh sure, when we first met, there was, well, some chemistry. Heck, you just have to look at Brandon, and you're already on your way to a Masters in Chemistry. Still, where sex was concerned, we'd managed to keep that part of our lives separate. Now, we were hookers in drag, getting paid to have sex with a shrimp-dicked Japanese business man. And a killer at that.

That's where the sleeves came into play.

He stood in front of us and bowed. We bowed, and then I slapped his cheek. A glimmer of a grin appeared. Liza echoed the gesture. The grin grew wide, wider still, as did the tenting in his slacks.

I nodded toward Liza. The signal was received, her/his sarong sleeve lifting up. A blindfold was seductively pulled out and placed over Yamasuka's eyes. He moaned when warm leather touched hot flesh, a visual shiver running down his body once he realized who was in control.

I grabbed him by his shirt and led him to the bedroom. Luckily, it was easy to find. He whimpered when I tossed him to the bed, and groaned when I held him down, then groaned louder when I applied the wrist restraints, plastic and unbreakable, a gift from Will; proving that it does indeed pay to have friends in high places.

Now we were safe, relatively speaking. As far as we could see, all the cameras were outside, as were the guards, Yamasuka obviously liking his privacy. Still, we had to keep him occupied so that he wouldn't get suspicious.

Liza unbuttoned his shirt, revealing that pale torso of his, fingernail trails still visible from whatever last encounter he had. My friend shuddered and moved to his pants before unbuttoning them, unbelting them, and tugging them down with a long, hard tug. His prick sprang up, short and thin, hooded and dripping copious amounts of precome. Liza looked over to me and mouthed, "teeny".

I nodded and removed our final up-the-sleeve trick; only this one was hidden in my purse, an item I'd brought with me on vacation. Just in case. I mean, a battery powered cock sheath with jacking action comes in handy—no pun intended. It was quickly placed over Yamasuka's prick and flicked on, the setting set to slow and steady, to keep him on the edge without bringing him over.

And that was my cue to get going.

Liza sat on a nearby chair, whacking him from time to time, to keep him occupied while I started the search. Within seconds, I was at the koi pond, which, by indoor standards, was quite large. Meaning, this wasn't going to be easy. And we didn't have all the time in the world. Eventually, the guy was gonna spew like, well, Diamond Head once had.

At first, I scanned the round pool with my eyes, looking for any obvious inconsistencies, places a dastardly murderer would hide vital information. Needless to say, the koi pond looked just like a koi pond, with koi swimming to and fro. If there was a hidden compartment somewhere, it wasn't noticeably visible.

In other words, I had to get in. The fish, of course were none too happy with my intrusion. They moved to the opposite side of the pond, whacking the water with their thick, opalescent bodies.

"Fine," I said to them. "See if I care. Just be glad I'm a meat and potatoes kind of guy. Sushi ain't my cup of tea." Talking to fish. I know, what next?

I bent down and tapped the tiled walls, hoping to hear some kind of hollow pinging sound, like you do in the movies. Only, with the water and everything, I just kept hearing dull thuds. I walked in a circle, tap, tap, tapping, the fish clearly pissed at all the hubbub. Still nothing. I tried the flooring, butting it with my heels. It was cement. No trap doors, no secret boxes springing out at me.

"Hmm," I hummed. "If I was something important in a koi pond, where would I hide?"

Naturally, my eyes landed on the koi themselves. Maybe the sushi idea wasn't half bad. Then again, without a fairly sharp knife handy, it wasn't much of an option. Plus, there were at least thirty of them. It would've taken far too long to gut each and every one. Besides, it seemed unlikely, not to mention difficult to achieve, that Yamasuka was hiding whatever he was hiding in his precious fish.

And then I spotted it. Oh sure, it seemed blatantly obvious, but aren't the best places to hide things the ones that are the most obvious, thereby making them the last place you'd look? Despite my logic, or lack thereof, it seemed reasonable enough. Anyway, Yamasuka probably didn't even realize that X marks the spot, not seeming like much of the pirate aficionado to me. Not unless the pirate wore a butt-plug instead of a peg-leg. Yo, ho, ho and a bucket of Crisco.

But there was indeed an X laid out within the tiles, dead center. I sloshed over to it, pounding on it with my heel. Again, I was greeted to a thud and nothing else. I reached down, my hands beneath the water, and tried to pry a tile free or to see if there were any gaps. Once more, nothing. Zip, zilch, nada. Just a bunch of angry fish shitting all around me.

"Fuck," I sighed, hearing my friend slap our, yuck, john in the other room. I knelt and stared at the koi as they grew accustomed to my presence, gliding past me as they circled around and around and around. Naturally, watching them made me dizzy. And, naturally, I then slipped and fell, landing, thwack, on my butt. "Fuck," I repeated with a groan.

Only, my butt kept sinking. I jumped up, turned around, and glanced back down. "Ah," I ahed, realizing what I had done. Apparently, you didn't have to press just one tile to get the secret chamber to open; you had to press at least several of them. Fortunately, my ass did the trick, tiny and petite though it might be.

The X was now several inches further down and, lo and

fucking behold, several drawers lined the now-visible interior. Jackpot. "Thanks, Liko," I whispered, pulling each of the hidden containers out. "Empty." Groan. "Empty." Groan. "Empty." Deep, pitiful groan. "Full." Finally, there was a big, joyful, relieved sigh.

I pulled the plastic interior out and retrieved a pouch, which was sealed from the water. I shoved the contents, a piece of paper, inside my sarong, stuffed the drawers back, figured out how to bring the X back to its spot, and tiptoed back to the bedroom.

"Ta da!" I silently shouted, arms raised up high.

He glanced my way, his palm red from slapping, a look of disgust spread across his face. He twirled his fingers in the air, silently replying, "About fucking time."

I shrugged and walked over to the bed, setting the cock sheath on high. Yamasuka's grin widened, his skin tone going from pale white to off-pink. His body quaked. His back arched. And he erupted a split second later, dousing himself in a spray of pungent come. Amazingly, it didn't even make our top-ten most nauseating events list. Sad but true.

We removed the sheath and the blindfold. He smiled and nodded at us. "You clean now," he told us.

We forced smiles on our faces and went searching for the bathroom. Across the wide expanse of his bedroom, we spotted a door, and went inside. The bathroom was huge, stark, and blindingly white. We found a towel and wet it. In cold water. Let the fucker freeze for all we cared. Then we returned.

We stopped, dead, as it were, in our tracks.

"Wh…what's that for?" I stammered, staring down the barrel of a jet-black gun.

"Wr…wrong towel?" Brandon managed.

He laughed. Guy had a sense of humor, after all. Too little, too late, I figured. Too late for us, that is. The point was driven home when the bedroom door open and in stepped the one man we never expected to see.

Again.

Alive, that is.

"Jed?" I squeaked out.

He nodded, a sinister smile spreading across his nasty face. "Resourceful little bitches, ain't you?"

And that we were. But not this time. Maybe not ever again.

🌴 Justice Served 🌴

"But how?" I managed. Given that he was theoretically dead, and all, it was amazing that I got that much out.

He smiled, a wicked, crooked grin, as he waved the gun at me and Brandon and Yamasuka. I stared at the hole in his shirt, at the massive circle of blood that had dyed it a deep, dark red, and I began to wonder if perhaps those stories of zombies weren't only stories. "Come on now, give me some credit," he replied. "Powerful people are after me. Do you think I'd go unprotected?" And then, lifting his shirt up, he revealed the protection he was referring to: namely, a bullet-proof vest.

"But we saw you dead on the floor back at the ranger cabin," Brandon said. "And you're covered in blood."

Jed shook his head. "Oh, I was on the floor, alright. That's because I needed them to think I was shot and killed. And the blood? Just red dye packs. Boom, boom, and then splat, squish. Worked like a charm." He paused and stared at us. "Still, there's something I don't get. After you left, I followed you and waited to see what you'd do next, to make sure what you told me was true, that you were just after Lenny's killer. So, I ask you, why the fuck are you here? Yamasuka had nothing to do with Lenny's death. Oh, I'm sure he's responsible for Liko's, since Liko was about to spill the man's proverbial beans, so that makes sense. And my supposed death, well I was just a not-so-innocent bystander, which this gentleman and I will discuss, after I dispose of the two of you. But not Lenny. Meaning, you bitches are lying something fierce."

The gun was raised and pointed our way, his finger twitching on the trigger.

"You're wrong," I hollered.

"Nice try," he said. "Now, bye-bye."

"Lenny worked for Yamasuka," Brandon hollered.

Now, that caught his attention, causing Jed to lower the gun by an inch or so. "You've got one minute. Explain."

I gulped, trying my darndest to prevent myself from hyperventilating. "Okay, first, did Lenny ever trick with Yamasuka, through you, before, um, before you two started dating?"

The gun went another inch downward. "As a matter of fact, yes. But how did you know that?"

Good guess on my part. Still, it made sense. "Doesn't matter. What matters is that Yamasuka needed to find out what Liko knew about him. Yamasuka knew that you were dating Lenny, and hired Lenny to get information out of Liko, figuring Lenny's connection to you would be good bait. That's why Lenny started dating Liko in the first place. In the end, Lenny probably knew too much, and, well…"

Jed sighed and lowered the gun. "Fuckin-A. Stupid Lenny. Got in way over his head on that one. I always gave him enough money. He didn't need to get any more from this creep." He nodded over to Yamasuka, who had remained quiet and still throughout the whole encounter. Strangely, Jed then began to laugh.

"What's so funny?" I asked.

"This mess," he replied. "And the irony of it all."

It was then I got it, understood why he was suddenly chuckling—the sound like nails raked across a chalkboard. "Yamasuka hires Lenny to get information out of Liko," I began, my breathing growing stable again. I prayed I had a few more breaths remaining, all things considered. "Lenny gets the information and a second boyfriend to boot. You're none too happy about that, and set up Lenny to take the fall for Makani, who works for Edward Beles, who, in turn, is out to kill you because he thinks you set him up, even though it was Liko that set you up." I paused, staring at our captor, who wasn't saying I wrong about anything. Then I added the final piece to that puzzle of ours. "And the reason you're laughing, I can only guess now, is because the reason you were setting up Lenny to take the fall for Makani is because Yamasuka asked you to. Because Beles's boss is Yamasuka. Right?"

The laughter abruptly stopped. "Like I said," he said. "Smart bitches." He nodded and again raised the gun. "Seems like all roads lead back here, after all. Un-fucking-believable."

And then bang, bang, bang. Three ear-splitting shots fired in our direction. My eyes shut tight as I fell to the floor, hearing Brandon do the same. We were dead meat for sure. I screamed, my hand roaming my body, searching for wounds. Strangely, I couldn't find any. I popped my eyes open and looked around. Brandon was by my side, apparently alive and well.

Yamasuka, of course, was a big dead mess.

"Now, what do I do with the two of you?" Jed asked, the gun still out, still smoking.

"Buy us a drink," tried Brandon. Inappropriate, yes, but when staring into the face of death, perhaps it's better to snicker than to sob.

Again, Jed laughed. "You really were just trying to find Lenny's killer, weren't you?"

"Just like we said," I said. "And it was Yamasuka, through some hired thugs, who killed your boyfriend." I left the police thing out it. No need for him to know everything we knew. At least not yet.

He shook his head. "Poor Lenny. I did love him, you know. In my own way. Still, why come here? You obviously don't have guns on you, so you weren't planning on killing Yamasuka. Were you working for him, too?" He paused, staring intently at us. "I mean, seems like everyone else was." Again, the gun went up, pointed once more at us two poor defenseless hooker drag queens.

"We were looking for information, that's all," I blurted out. "We knew that Yamasuka was standing trial in a couple of days. With Liko dead, there would be no one to testify against him.

Lenny's killer would go free. All our work would be for nothing."

He aimed, his finger again on the trigger. "And what did you find out?"

"Oh, um, nothing," Brandon lied.

Jed took three fast strides our way, the gun now pointing to the side of Brandon's wig. "You've been smart until now, bitch. Why not stay that way?"

"Fine," I shouted, reaching into my sarong. "Here." I handed him the paper I'd found in the koi pond.

He grabbed it and backed away, quickly unfolding it as he once more pointed the gun at us.

"What's it say?" I couldn't help but ask.

"It's in Japanese," he replied. "Give me a minute, my interpretation skills are rusty."

"Take your time," my friend coughed out. "Hell, take a year or two, or ten."

Jed chuckled at the apparent joke, then shot a hole in the floor by our feet. "Shut the fuck up!" he bellowed. Naturally, we did, after we first let go with two girly screams. And perhaps just a little bit of tinkle in my panties. "Now, let's see." He squinted and slowly scanned the paper before looking back down at us. "Not it," he said.

"What?" I asked. "Are we playing tag now?"

He kicked me, eliciting a painful groan. "No. The paper. It's not what you two were looking for. It's got nothing to do with the trial. Yamasuka is up on charges for a land development scam. The Japanese have been buying up Hawaii for years, Yamasuka especially. Only, he's been selling back some of the land using overvalued appraisals. He is, or he was, I mean, making a fortune on crap land that's nothing more than old lava beds. Still, with just about everyone in his pocket, and no evidence to tie him directly to the sales, because he uses intermediaries, and with Liko dead, he would've gotten off without a hitch."

"So, what's on that paper?" I asked.

"Everyone in his pocket. Me, Liko, the cops, city officials. It's a long list. And all with payouts. Illegal stuff, to be sure, but nothing directly associated with the trial. No mention of his holding companies or the land purchases and subsequent sales. It's a dead end, ladies. Literally."

"Wait," I shouted, hand over head, offering no real protection. "What good would it do to kill us? Like we said, we're not after you."

Again, he laughed. "Nah," he nahed. "I ain't gonna kill you two. I meant Yamasuka was a dead end. If he set up Lenny, and I'm sure he did, and he had Lenny and Liko killed, then I'm certain I was somewhere on his hit list. I mean, Beles wants me dead, so who does he ask to have that taken care of?"

"Yamasuka." I said. "His boss."

"Yep. Besides, I got too much dirt on Yamasuka myself. I'm sure he would've taken care of me, eventually. This way, it's him instead of me. Fair enough, don't you think?"

"Um, sure," I said. "So, we can just, um, go? Go free, I mean?"

He stuck the gun inside his pants and folded the paper inside his wallet. "Go, yes. Free, no."

Always a catch, right? "Um, what's that supposed to mean?" I asked.

"You were working for Liko, right? I mean, before his untimely death," he asked.

"Let me guess," I guessed. "We're working for you now?"

"See, smart girl. Just like I said. And I need smart girls working for me. Besides, I think it's best if I keep an eye out on the two of you, seeing as you both stir up a heap of shit. Plus, if you ever try and report any of this to the cops, I'll know where to find you. Get it?"

"Got it," we replied.

"Good," he said, leading us outside, where we found Yamasuka's guards, two gaping wounds in each of their chests. "See, ladies, it's not good to get in my way."

We cringed and looked away from the gruesome spectacle,

the sight of death never getting any easier to take in. I suppose that's a good thing. "No problem," I said. "You're the boss."

"Exactly. Now give me your cell phone numbers. I'll call you in a day or two, give you some work," he told us.

Oh fuck, not what we wanted to hear. Cellphone numbers are probably traceable, if you have the means. And Jed clearly had lots of means. But what choice did I have? So, I pulled out a pen and a piece of paper from my purse and wrote them down. Sort of. "Here you go," I said. "Just one more question, though."

He scowled, but nodded. "What is it?"

"The reason you couldn't pick up Liko on your own," I said. "The reason you needed us to bring him to you. Was that because you knew Yamasuka would be after him and would want to get to him first?"

He grinned. "Smart bitches. Damn smart. Yep, I knew Liko was giving evidence against Yamasuka. See, that Lenny thing worked both ways. I knew what Liko was up to and he knew what I was up too. Lenny was cute, but he had a big fucking mouth. Still, for both Liko and myself, it seemed smart to keep Lenny around. We both knew what the other was up to, but kept out of the other one's business. All in all, it was a good working relationship."

I nodded. "But if he should turn up at your door, looking for trouble…"

"Then what choice would I have, right? Yamasuka couldn't hold that against me, could he?" He laughed, one final awful time, and then was off, yelling over his shoulder, "Have a nice day, ladies. Talk to you bitches soon enough."

And then he was gone, running around the side of the house, quickly disappearing from sight. Good riddance to bad rubbish. We turned the opposite corner, away from all the corpses.

"Fuck," I groaned, plopping my ass down on a garden chair.

"You can say that again," Brandon agreed, sitting down on a chair facing me.

"Fuck," I echoed. Clearly, it warranted repeating. This was

soon followed, of course, by the oft-repeated, "now what?"

And then, as if on cue, "Oh, thank God." It was Will, followed close behind by Briana and Koni, turning the same corner we'd just come around from.

"Yeah, we can try to thank him," I quipped, "but it doesn't seem like he's listening much anymore."

They ran over, and Briana offered, "Well, you are both still alive."

I giggled—a nervous giggle, of course, bordering on hysteria. "I said, much."

"Man, I'm so sorry we couldn't get here sooner to help," Will apologized, the look of concern still evident on his handsome face. "We were following you, but the cab blew a tire. And no spare. We had to wait for another cab to come get us. We heard some gunshots echoing way down the road. When we got here, we found…"

"Yeah," I interrupted. "We know what you found. Don't worry, though; we're fine. And, wonder of all wonders, still gainfully employed."

They looked at me quizzically before Brandon and I filled them in. "Fuck," Briana said.

"Yeah," Brandon told her. "Been there, done that."

"And, once again, now what?" asked I. "Yamasuka is dead. The trial will be cancelled. No one to bring to justice. And still no evidence, even if we could present any."

"Wrong koi pond," added Brandon miserably.

"Maybe," Will said, standing behind me and offering up a much-needed back rub.

Brandon frowned. "I don't like the sound of that maybe."

And neither did I, but here's how it went down anyway.

***

We discussed what we needed to do as we quickly moved away from the house. If our friends heard the gunshots from far down the road, the police would soon be on their way. Needless to say, we weren't ready for their involvement just yet.

And it was at that very moment, with my brain simply concentrating on getting us to safety, that my subconscious sent out a delayed message: This just in, it said. There's another koi pond you guys know about.

"Wait!" I shouted, causing our group to come to a screeching halt. "There's another koi pond we know about!"

"Oh, God," moaned Brandon. "Not another one."

I kept moving, the others following me. "Tell me," I said to Brandon as we rapidly walked down the hill. "Where did we always meet Liko?"

He thought about it, then snapped his fingers, and replied, "The International Marketplace."

"And what's right out in front of there?" asked I, just as we reached the road behind Yamasuka's house, Will's cab thankfully waiting for us.

"A fucking koi pond," replied Brandon as we all piled in.

"Pray it's the right one this time," I said, the cab speeding away, passing three sets of cop cars a mile down the road. "Pray for a whole lot of things while you're at it," I added. "Better to hedge our bets."

***

We made it back to the hotel, thankfully and miraculously, in one piece. All things considered, maybe God really was watching out for us, seeing as we were the only ones still alive.

Well, us and Jed, at any rate.

But one problem at a time.

Back in our rooms, we got out of our girl drag and back into our boy stuff. Then we picked up dinner at the hotel pool bar and camped ourselves out on the beach. The hornet's nest was already riled up and now emptied; we could, it seemed, work at our own pace, finally.

So, we ate and formulated our plan, watching the tourists stroll by, blissfully unaware of the turmoil all around them—

well, around us, anyway. Soon enough, the sun started getting ready for bed, turning the sky a glorious red and the ocean a sparkling orange. "Forget that retiring here crap," I announced. "Oahu's a nice place to visit, but no fucking way am I moving here."

"Hell," added Brandon, "it's not even all that nice. I mean, we have the same sun and the same ocean back home. And there, no one's trying to kill us or hire us as hookers."

We raised our glasses to the setting sun. "To no more tricking," I toasted.

"At least not for money," amended Brandon.

"Here, here," Briana seconded, our group readily repeating my toast. And then we were off and running again, out of the hotel, across the street, and down the block.

The Marketplace was jammed with tourists, hundreds of them sauntering this way and that, all in search of crap to buy for their friends and family. We, however, were not there to shop. Not this time. And yes, I know, it was killing me, too.

Luckily, the area was well-lit. The five of us crouched down, ringing the fish-laden pond, pretending to admire them as they swam around. In reality, we were nonchalantly as possible running our fingers along the inner wall and thankfully shallow bottom. With the pond being relatively small, our search was over almost soon after it had begun.

"Bingo," I whispered to my comrades, yanking up a loose stone, clearly one that didn't look like the others. They smiled, stood, and we quickly vacated the premises, opting for a more discrete location, namely our hotel room.

We all jumped on the bed and threw the rock in the center. It bounced, as did my heart. Will lifted it up and gave it a shake. "Hollow," he informed. "And something's rattling around inside." He turned it over in his hand, finding the well-concealed latch in just a few seconds. Holding our collective breath, we watched as he pried it open. The rock wasn't waterproofed; it didn't need to be, though, as the singular container inside clearly was.

"It's a CD case," Koni said. "Taped up to keep the CD dry."

Will removed the protective tape and then the CD from inside. It was all silver, no writing on the outside. He hopped up and walked to the player beneath the TV. He turned both on, and we listened as the whir of the spinning disc filled our ears.

A menu popped up on the screen. There was a long roster of names. Yamasuka was listed three times. "Is this what I think it is?" I asked expectantly.

Will scrolled down and played one of Yamasuka's listings. We waited while the recording played, and then laughed good and hard. "Yep," replied Will. "Guess Liko was smart enough to not only listen to the conversations in his limo, but also to record them. This would've been ideal at the trial. Even if it was somehow inadmissible, the evidence on this would give the authorities plenty of leads to go on."

"Except, there won't be a trial," I reminded him. "No more Mister Yamasuka."

"True," Will agreed. "But it doesn't much matter. I'm sure enough people are implicated on this CD for dozens of trials yet to come. Besides, for all intents and purposes, we're only after three people now. Three people who won't know what hit them."

"Or whom," Briana reminded him.

"Or whom," he echoed. "Thank goodness for that."

***

Now, all we had to do was wait for the inevitable call. That, of course, was why it was so good to have a federal agent on our side. I mean, really, I couldn't give Jed our own cellphone numbers. He'd have found us for sure, then. And by us, I don't mean Judy and Liza; I mean, Brandon and Chase. And that was a definite no-no. So, what did I give Jed if not our real phone numbers?

Ah, bravo for my quick thinking. You see, when I'd lost my job and our office was closed—you'll remember that severance package I mentioned at the very start of all this—the lines were shut down, mine and the main number, plus a whole bunch of others. In other words, I knew of at least two numbers that were recently disconnected. All Will had to do was make a quick call to his office, and those lines were switched back on and transferred to our cells. Even if the numbers were now traceable, they weren't, thankfully, traceable to us.

Like I said, quick thinking on my part—but, please, don't get accustomed to it; just dumb luck. Literally.

In any case, Jed wasted no time in finding us work, which we were now counting on. No work, after all, meant no plan to put into action. Luckily for us, he called first thing the next morning.

"Judy," he said, smooth as silk, having tried me first. "It's Jed. I have a job for you and Liza. Bachelor party up north. Big bucks."

"That's great," I told him, trying to keep my rattled nerves in check. "Only, we don't drive. Liko usually drove us to our gigs."

He laughed, that same sinister laugh I'd grown to detest. "Well, I ain't Liko. But I do make exceptions for bachelor parties. I bring the girls to those. Let the customers know they need to treat my ladies with respect. Plus, for the really big money, I go up and get it in advance. No offense, just good business."

"None taken. When can we expect you?" I asked.

"Tonight at seven," he informed, arranging to pick us up just up the street from our hotel.

"Seven it is," I told him. "See you then." I hung up and smiled at my team. "Perfect," I said. "Now, Will has to get everything set up before tonight's rendezvous."

Will, of course, was already working on it.

And so was Brandon, fixing us all large, strong cocktails— that is to say, well-deserved, much-needed, large, strong cocktails.

Ten minutes later, Will snapped his phone shut and looked over at us with a grin and a thumbs-up. "All in place. Few questions asked. When the feds demand an unmarked car, it's given to them. Cool job perk, huh?"

And that meant, at long, long, long last, we had a day to, pardon the expression, kill. No scheming, no hiding out, no getting dragged up—at least not yet—and no rescues. Just the five of us on the beach, the sun baking are group to a golden brown while we sipped our tropical drinks and relaxed. Well, tried to relax, anyway. We still had the evening to contend with. But, if the plan went as, well, planned, everything would unfold without directly implicating us or putting us in harm's way. Because, whatever we did from here on out, none of us could be tied to it. Protecting Koni, who could easily be traced back to us, just as Buck had been, was now paramount.

So, we ate, we drank—duh—we cruised guys—also, duh—and tried to forget what lay ahead—oh, which also meant we popped a good number of pretty blue pills—one final duh.

Then, before we knew it, we were gussied up in our trampiest, yet surprisingly expensive, outfits, waiting patiently on a street corner for our pimp. I know, I know. Even to me that sounded God-awful. What on earth would I tell my mother when she asked what we did on our vacation? Then again, I prayed we'd get back from our vacation in one piece so we could tell her whatever lies we dreamed up. Not to mention, we had a suitcase full of crap we now had to distribute.

Jed pulled up as promised, honked the horn, and waved for us to get in. And no, he didn't run around the car to open the door for us ladies. I know, shock, right? In any case, we hopped in back. Brief hellos were offered, but, beyond that, no idle chatter, no small-talk except how much he was charging, what we'd be making—and, damn, if it wasn't a bundle that we'd never see—and what time he'd be picking us back up.

For our part, we simply nodded and held hands for support.

Ten minutes later, we heard the siren and saw the red and blue lights reflecting off the windows.

"Fuck," Jed cursed before slamming his fist on the steering wheel.

"Yeah, fuck," we agreed, for effect.

We waited, and then Will appeared, wearing our blond wig, now cut for a man. He also had on a hat and a pair of sunglasses, despite the fact that it was nighttime. He flashed his badge, but only for a second or two. It didn't really matter, though, as Jed was pissed off and just wanted to get the hell out of there.

"What's wrong, officer? I wasn't speeding," Jed told him.

"License and registration," came the standard response.

Jed sighed and reached into the glove compartment and handed over the requisite paperwork. Then he took the wallet out of his back pocket. We sucked in our breaths, knowing that this would be the only tricky part. "I'll take the whole wallet, sir," Will informed him.

"Why's that, officer?" Jed asked, staring up directly into the beam of a flashlight that Will had wisely purchased at the nearest ABC store.

"New protocol, sir."

Again, Jed sighed, but did as he was told. Not too wise, I guess he figured, for a pimp/murderer to argue with a cop.

Will took the wallet and returned to his car with it. Five minutes later, also for effect, he gave it back to Jed. Now, we had the folded list back in out possession, the one no longer in Jed's wallet. "Thank you, sir. Just a random check. All clear. Have a good evening." He didn't wait for a response; he just walked back to his car, flashing us a discreet nod as he went by.

I squeezed Brandon's hand and he squeezed mine back. All systems go. We could now continue as planned.

The car pulled away. Will, we knew, was following a few car lengths behind. A short while later, we arrived. Now, I'd never been to a bachelor party before, though I had seen the movie with Tom Hanks. Did this prepare me for what we were about to witness?

Oh, hell no. Not even remotely close.

We pulled up to a condo complex. All seemed quiet on the western front—mainly due to the fact that the party was in full swing on the eastern one. Jed got out first and told us to sit tight. In truth, we were already frozen to the spot. Hooking with a middle-aged Japanese business man was one thing, albeit one big thing, but what about dancing for an entire room of straight men, while in drag, no less? Even for Brandon, this was a new experience. And, trust me, that's really saying something.

Minutes later, Jed returned, and we got out of the car. "Big fucking party," he told us, offering no more than that.

"How big?" I asked, forcing down a gulp.

"Big-big. But I told the boys to behave. Or else." He flashed a concealed gun, which, of course, would do us little to no good, seeing as Jed would be driving off in a minute or so. "Just stay in a corner. Flirt. Dance. Strip. I'll be back to pick you up in exactly two hours. Here's my emergency cell number, in case there's any trouble." He handed us a card and quickly got in the car.

"Um," I umed. "What kind of trouble are we talking about here?"

He shrugged. "Usual stuff. Boys will be boys." He didn't elucidate any further; instead, he drove off.

"Boys will be boys," I said to Brandon/Liza.

"Except when they're dressed like girls," he needlessly reminded me.

We started walking, hearing the party long before we witnessed it. "Will better get here just after flirt and dance," Brandon groaned.

"Yeah," I agreed, trudging up the stairs. "Beaten to a pulp doesn't flow to well on our monosyllabic list."

We didn't knock; there would've been little point. We simply walked in, our ears immediately assaulted by the sound of heavy metal music, our sensitive noses drowning in the stink of sweat and beer and nacho cheese dip, and then two seconds of crowd silence as fifty heads turned our way. This was followed immediately thereafter by, "Whores!" And then, of course, the usual chanting and fists pounding the air. "Whores! Whores! Whores!"

I suppose they meant this in a complimentary way. You know, just glad to see us. They did look like fine, decent young men, after all. Well, at least the two who weren't bleary eyed and/or chugging from a bear funnel. Just the same, it was hard to smile and nod. Harder, still, to find a protective corner to stand in. Jed neglected to tell us that one corner was used for the kegs, plural, and that all the furniture was piled in the other three. Meaning, we were front and center.

"Flirt, dance," I managed out of the corner of my mouth, moving my arms and legs as best I could to the barely-there rhythm.

"Flirt, dance," Brandon repeated, nodding and winking to the throng.

Sadly—for us, I mean—the throng in question was yelling "Strip!" within seconds.

"Not good!" I shouted into Brandon's ear.

"No!" he shouted back, shaking his head. "But I have an idea!"

"Hurry!" I hollered, though the sound of my voice could scarcely be heard above the din.

He held up his hand. I did the same. There was a brief lapse in the clamoring for our clothes. "Were. Is. The. Bathroom?" Brandon yelled, slowly and distinctly. "We. Need. To. Change!"

The bathroom was pointed to, and the crowd parted just enough to let us go by—with only a modicum of groping. Three minutes later, we were in the bathroom, the door shut behind us and instantaneously locked.

"Now what do we do?" I asked. "I didn't bring a change of clothes."

He punched me in the arm. "Idiot. Now we wait for Will to come and rescue us."

"Oh, yeah. Sorry, I forgot. Temporary insanity. Must be all the friggin' testosterone in this place."

And the purveyors of said testosterone were none too happy with our sudden and prolonged disappearance. Between the pounding on the door and the pounding of my heart, it was a wonder I didn't go deaf. I tried calling Will, but couldn't get a signal. If the door didn't hold, I was sure we'd be torn to pieces. Sad, because we were wearing designer threads.

"Wait!" I shouted to the masses on the other side. "We'll be right out."

Strangely, the noise ebbed. Briefly. Replaced, suddenly, by a new and even more terrifying sound: a megaphone. "This is the police! Party's over!" it was shouted over said megaphone to deleterious effect. And no, this was not part of our plan.

It was a gross understatement to say that the revelers were disappointed that their party was, as was notified, over. In fact, they didn't take it lightly. Or quietly. Or peacefully. In other words, all hell quickly, loudly, and agitatedly broke loose. And mob violence in a small, cramped condo is not something you want to witness firsthand. Fortunately, we were still in the bathroom, but even secondhand was no fun.

It was like a Batman comic strip come to life. Pow! Bam! Crash! Ouch! And then Knock! Knock! Knock! And then "This is the police! Open up!"

I looked to Brandon. He looked to me. "We're fucked," I said.

"Boo-yeah," he agreed with a nod before unlocking the door and slowly opening it up.

Four policemen were there to great us. "You the whores?"

"Strippers," we corrected him with.

Which didn't make the handcuffs feel any better as they were clamped behind our backs. We glanced around upon our exit from the john. The place was in a shamble, the partiers either leaving on their own accord or handcuffed, much like ourselves. We were then summarily shoved to the front door, just as Will made it up the stairs. After all, it was supposed to have been him bringing us in.

He looked at us with his mouth hanging open, trying, I could tell, to suppress a wry grin. "Don't worry," he mouthed.

"Easy for you to say," Brandon yelled back as we were taken away.

***

They threw us into the back of one of the squad cars and read us our rights through the dividing sheet of meshed wire.

"Well, Lucy," I said, soon thereafter, "out of the frying pan..."

He finished my train of thought with, "And into the jail cell, Ethel."

And that is, indeed, where we ended up. After, of course, the booking, fingerprinting, and picture taking. Oh, and that one phone call we were allowed. Jed, needless to say, was none too thrilled at hearing from us so soon. "Bail is coming out of your share," he informed, then hung up on us.

He arrived an hour later, handing over his I.D. upon arrival.

He saw us from across the station, but didn't even bother to nod or wave. Instead, he grimaced and looked the other way.

"Fucker," I said, watching and waiting for his inevitable comeuppance.

That, of course, came a split second later. And then that grimace of his was really and truly well-deserved.

See, it's never good to hand over your identification to the police, in a police station, when there's been an A.P.B. issued for your arrest for kidnapping, murder, and blackmail, just to name a few. And, trust me, the list went way beyond those few. Those were merely the highlights.

And he didn't go quietly into the night. No, sir.

"Hey, let me go," he shouted, kicking and screaming as several cops surrounded him and took him down, smashing his face to the cement floor. "Do you know who I am? I'll have your badges for this!" And then he ran off a list of names of all the people he'd call to get those badges.

Now then, wouldn't you know it, those exact same people all had A.P.B.s out for them as well. They were, after all, the same names that were on Yamasuka's list. The same list that was now in the hands of the F.B.I., provided, as planned, by Will.

Not that anything could be proven right of the bat, mind you, but the ball was rolling. Fortunately, the feds also had Liko's CD. Meaning, the ball was amply greased, to boot. And it wasn't only Jed that was arrested that evening. The night officer, Sergeant Sloan, was also taken in, right on the spot. As was a certain other officer. Yep, their names were also on the same list. Not that it took Will all that long to figure out that Sloan had to be one of the two policemen we'd heard from the other side of the surfboards. The same one Sergeant Beles had spoken to the night Will was abducted. The one who, we figured, must've killed Beles and hid the fact that Will had been captured, thereby preventing Will's superiors from sending reinforcements.

In fact, a good dozen people were arrested that night, booked under suspicion of numerous crimes, and all tied to the late, not-so-great Yamasuka. Most were quickly released on bail, pending further investigation. None were allowed to leave Oahu. Fortunately, as has often been stated, the island was small. No place to run to, no place to hide. And now, no more strings to pull.

Jed, thank goodness, was stupid enough to show up with that gun of his still in his pants. Not that he left any clues after he killed Yamasuka, but, I mean, it was from that same gun that he sent a minimum of three people to their early graves. In other words, Jed wasn't going anywhere anytime soon.

As for me and Brandon, Will arranged for our release a short while later, no one being the wiser that any of the three of us were involved in what had just transpired.

In other words, Koni was safe.

In more ways than one.

***

Will drove us back to our hotel just after that. We'd already phoned ahead. Our friends and our drinks were waiting for us, as were three rocking chairs on the front porch of the Moana.

"What's new?" Briana asked, all smiles, handing us our hurricane glasses, filled, thank goodness, to the brim.

"Not much," I replied, collapsing in my proffered chair. "What's up with you two?"

The five of us rocked and stared out at the street, the moon casting a lovely glow over the peaceful scene in front of us.

"Not much on our end," Koni eventually replied. "I did get an interesting phone call, though."

I turned to look at him. He was smiling big and wide and bright. "Really? From whom?"

We all turned to look his way, Brandon and I from his right side, Briana and Will from his left. "Mrs. Hallanah. Seems she just got a call from the police. Lenny has been cleared of all the charges against him."

I grinned, the smile bittersweet, looking to Will for information. "It was on the CD, too," he informed. "Lenny was set up. What a shock."

I laughed and closed my eyes, saying a silent prayer for him.

"Um, but that's not all," Briana soon added.

I pried my eyes open and looked her way. "Really, there's more than that?"

She nodded, her rocker suddenly going still. "Once they cleared him, they also unfroze his bank account."

And then five rockers were no longer rocking. "How much" I asked, my breathing instantly growing shallow.

To which Koni replied, rather cryptically, "Well now, that depends."

"On what, kid?" Brandon asked, downing his drink in one anxious gulp.

"On when Liko's insurance policy gets cashed in," he replied. "The settlement would then be added to the hundred thousand that's already going to go to Lenny's next of kin."

"How much," I asked, yet again, a trickle of sweat cascading down my forehead.

"Five million," he told us, the chair again rocking as he started to laugh. "And not in fucking yen, cute dude. No way, no fucking how."

***

Three months went by in the blink of an eye.

Time, you see, really does go by fast when you're having fun.

And, man, was I having fun.

Oh, and no, I still didn't have a job. For that matter, I still didn't need one. Not just yet, anyway.

I mean, I still had a large chunk of that severance cash of mine. Okay, that and the additional fifty thousand. Yep, remember that rhinestone necklace Yamasuka gave me for, well, oh come on now, you remember; please don't make me go through all that again. In any case, turns out, those weren't rhinestones.

Guess I made a convincing woman after all.

Plus, I was only paying half my rent now. See, wouldn't you know it, but there's an FBI office in San Francisco, too. And a star agent such as Will had no problems getting a transfer, especially after all those lovely arrests in Oahu, all credited to him.

He came up from behind me, his hands on my shoulders, a tender kiss on my neck. Both of us stared down at my laptop at the email attachment, at the photo of a group of young people, all of them with smiles stretched wide across their faces, Koni's the widest and the brightest of them all. They were standing in front of a cement building that was well under construction, the ocean stretching out below as far as the eye could see. And over the doorway to the building, a newly added sign read: The Lenny Hallanah Center for Runaways. All are Welcome.

Aloha, cute dude, the email read. Great place, huh? And there's really good shopping just down the street.

"Aloha, Koni," I said, touching my finger to the screen, my own smile now matching his as I flicked off the computer, my head leaning back into Will's tight abs. "Alo-ha."

If you enjoyed *Hot Lava*, please check out my other novels:

Sparkle: The Queerest Book You'll Ever Love
Divas Las Vegas
Hot Lava
Southern Fried
Queerwolf
Vamp
Queens of the Apocalypse
Creature Comfort
Fate
Midlife Crisis
And my erotica collection, *Good & Hot*

I am also the editor of the following anthologies:
Lust in Time: Erotic Romance Through the Ages
Men of the Manor: Erotic Encounters between Upstairs Lords and Downstairs Lads
Best Gay Erotica 2015
Best Gay Erotica of the Year, Volume 1
Best Gay Erotica of the Year, Volume 2: Warlords & Warriors

And feel free to visit my website for more on me, my work and my life: www.therobrosen.com

Or drop me an email at: robrosen@therobrosen.com

Much Love,

Rob

PRAISE FOR ROB ROSEN'S PREVIOUS NOVELS

Fate
"If you like Rob Rosen's sense of humor, if you're ready to forget everything you ever learned about the "rules of gay romance", and if you're looking for a read that is as hilariously funny as it is totally over the top, then you will probably enjoy this novel." – Rainbow Book Reviews

Creature Comfort
"If you have an appreciation for gay camp culture, from Lifetime movies to feather boas, you'll love this book." – Inked Rainbow Reads

Queens of the Apocalypse
"One part tongue-in-cheek humor, one part sweet romance, and one part paranormal free for all." – Joyfully Jay

Vamp
"This is a highly original twist on the whole vampire/werewolf genre. Snarky, saucy, witty. It will keep you howling." – The San Francisco Examiner

Queerwolf
"You have to read this book. It is by far the funniest, best crafted novel I've read in a long time!" – Reviews by Jessewave

Southern Fried
"Hands down, this is one of the funniest and oddest books I've ever read, and I mean that in a really good way!" – Rainbow Book Reviews

Hot Lava
"Hot Lava by Rob Rosen is, for this reader, another vastly entertaining and winning book. Actually, I'd go so far as to say that it is a winner for anyone who loves humor, mystery, adventure and, oh yes, men." – Dark Divas

Divas Las Vegas
"A rollicking, roller coaster of a read, sure to keep you smiling. Five stars out of five on your fun reading slot machine!" – Echo Magazine

Sparkle: The Queerest Book You'll Ever Love
"A gloriously, uproariously funny and immensely touching novel that's impossible to pigeonhole into a single genre. Part who-dunnit, part satire, part memoir, with a perfectly portioned serving of poignancy on the side."
– Top 2 Bottom Reviews